THE KIELBASA KILLER

THE KIELBASA KILLER

Geri Krotow

**SEVERN
HOUSE**

First world edition published in Great Britain and the USA in 2023
by Severn House, an imprint of Canongate Books Ltd,
14 High Street, Edinburgh EH1 1TE.

severnhouse.com

British Library Cataloguing-in-Publication Data
A CIP catalogue record for this title is available from the British Library.

ISBN-13: 978-1-4483-1118-7 (cased)
ISBN-13: 978-1-4483-1119-4 (e-book)

This is a work of fiction. Names, characters, places and incidents
are either the product of the author's imagination or are used fictitiously.
Except where actual historical events and characters are being described
for the storyline of this novel, all situations in this publication are
fictitious and any resemblance to actual persons, living or dead,
business establishments, events or locales is purely coincidental.

All Severn House titles are printed on acid-free paper.

Typeset by Palimpsest Book Production Ltd.,
Falkirk, Stirlingshire, Scotland.
Printed and bound in Great Britain by
TJ Books, Padstow, Cornwall.

To Stephen–
It's time to polka, my love

About the author

Geri Krotow is an award-winning author of over thirty novels, including the Whidbey Island contemporary romance series and the Silver Valley, PD romantic suspense series. A US Naval Academy graduate and former Naval Intelligence Officer, Geri left her Navy career after nine years to follow her heart and focus on her dream of becoming an author. When not writing or reading, Geri loves to knit and go on long walks with her beloved dogs. A native of Buffalo, New York, she relishes frequent return visits.

www.gerikrotow.com

ACKNOWLEDGEMENTS

This book and series is a love letter to my native city of Buffalo, NY, and the town I was raised in, Cheektowaga, NY. I am indebted to so many, as listed here and more. This is a work of fiction, of course, and all the characters products of my imagination, but I hope you can sense the love I have for Buffalo. You can take the girl out of Buffalo but you'll never take my hometown out of my heart. A story becomes an enjoyable read thanks to an entire community of professionals, and if you're as lucky as I've been, they become your friends, too.

For particulars with this book and the Kielbasa Queen series, thanks to Michael Graczyk and Lori Petruno Gorski (no relation to Stanley).

I am blessed with the world's best agent, Emily Sylvan Kim, who forever has my deepest gratitude for always demanding my utmost effort, and never shying away from pushing me to dig deeper until I discover the whole story. Emily, you are a trusted anchor in this often choppy business. To Sara Porter at Severn House, whose support of the Kielbasa Queen Mystery Series has never been anything but total and enthusiastic. It's a dream to work with you and the entire SH team! To Michelle Haring, owner of Cupboard Maker Books in Pennsylvania, thank you for expertly handselling all of my novels to the most excellent readers. To Cathy M., for the faithful accountability. For my writing support group of Heidi, Hope and Cathy; may all of our writing dreams come true. To Mary K. who saw me through one of the most painful yet joyful transitions of my life. For Mary F. B. and Patti M., your steadfast love and support got me here. Aunt Margie, my forever champion, I love you. For my brother Paul, who survived the Blizzard of '77 with me, and helped with the 1982 playlist. For Dad; you inspire me to get it done each and every day. To Alexander and Ellen, my life's most precious gifts. And to my soulmate Stephen—your support is everything.

ONE

April, 1982
Good Friday

The clang of her Baby Ben alarm clock woke Lydia Wienewski from deep layers of precious slumber. She reached her hand through the garage apartment's chilly air and switched it off, forcing herself to sit up. It was too tempting to curl back under her blankets for a few more minutes. She'd slept like the dead for the short time she'd been able to, and it had to be enough this morning. Besides, her exhaustion was nothing a couple of mugs of hot coffee couldn't handle. The mere thought of fresh brew once she was in the shop kept her up and moving.

Tiptoeing so as to not wake Grandma Mary, she went to the opposite end of their flat and entered the bathroom, softly closing the door behind her. She paused to stare out the top half of the window, the part that wasn't covered with opaque, sticky, diamond-patterned window film. At four-thirty in the morning the stars glittered across the indigo sky, visible through the bare branches of the humongous maple tree between her parents' house and the garage. Lydia saw more than the predawn sky. She saw hope, a promise that her stint as the family butcher would end soon, that Lydia's Lakeside Café and Bakery would be her full-time gig. For as long as she'd lived at 10 Pulaski Place in Cheektowaga, New York, Lydia had wanted to own both a restaurant and bakery. This equated to twenty-five of her twenty-nine years, as she'd been four years old when Pop found the house only two blocks from the family store. Her dream was about to come true, as she owned the building for her business and was in the final preparations before its grand opening at the end of May.

Of course, Pop had to be back on his feet by then, which her mother prayed about nightly to the Blessed Mother. Lydia tried to keep her angst hidden, but the thought of having to manage Pop's job while working at her new full-time gig overwhelmed her.

Shouldering two businesses was going mean she'd be working 'round the clock' for a bit. She could do it. Anything for her Pop. He'd been knocked down by a stroke on Christmas, right when they were getting ready to go to Midnight Mass. Never had Lydia seen her mother look so helpless, so frightened, as when Pop was loaded into the ambulance. She blinked back tears.

It's OK. Pop was getting stronger, and the shop was going to make it. Her emotions were on the surface today, and she blamed it on the anticipation of this weekend's sales. It was Good Friday, only two days before the Polish Easter holiday celebrated with smoked ham, kielbasa, and *placek*, the rich yeast coffee cake that Madame Delphine would lift her nose at.

Ugh. She shoved the memory of her time at Madame Delphine's pastry school in Ottawa last year back where it belonged, in her distant past. She'd been mistaken to believe that she needed a diploma to be able to call herself a baker or cook, especially the Polish-American baked goods and savory meals she excelled at. A spark of pride warmed her heart in the cold room. Last night, while waiting for her extra batch of kielbasa to smoke, she'd made several dozen *chrusciki*, or angel wings, as the locals referred to them. Mounds of thin cookies doused with powdered sugar awaited wrapping and stacking for sale in the shop. Customers were in buying mood as they prepared for Easter and, being the businesswoman she was, Lydia relished the opportunity to increase their bottom line.

Lucky for her, Lydia had discovered a better dream than becoming Western New York's best pastry chef. From authentic Polish-American baked goods, to *pierogi*, to *golabki* – cabbage rolls – she was plowing her own path with the café and bakery, her own career, apart from Wienewski's Wieners & Meats. Lydia's Lakeside Café and Bakery would showcase the best of her skills, managing a business and making everything on the menu. She was a good enough cook, but planned to hire a more seasoned chef so she could focus on the books and baking.

All she needed to do first was to get the family butcher shop out of the red. Toward that singular goal she'd worked long into last night, hanging extra kielbasa in the family's backyard smoker and deep frying chrusciki in a huge cast-iron pan atop a hot plate on her parent's patio until right before midnight. Just in case. Just in case her prayers for a sell-out Easter weekend were answered.

She turned from the window, pulled the string switch for the lightbulb over the sink, and took care of getting ready for work. Her clothes were on the back of the toilet tank where she'd put them, anticipating the early wake-up. Her bed was separated from Grandma's by a beautiful but thin macrame curtain. Grandma liked to stay up late, crocheting or doing macrame, watching her beloved police shows on the TV in the main house or sometimes here in front of their tiny television. Lydia was usually asleep by the time Grandma came back to their pad, and woke up a couple of hours earlier. They'd fallen into a routine of sorts since Lydia came back almost five months ago.

Once dressed, she hung her nightgown on the hook and slowly opened the door. A specter emerged from the dark. Lydia sucked in a breath to scream, her hands instinctively crossing over her chest.

'Morning, my Polish princess. How did you sleep?' Mary Romano Wienewski, aka Grandma, greeted her.

'Grandma!' Not a spooky Easter Bunny. She dropped her arms. 'I thought you were asleep.' She flipped the light switch, chasing away the shadows.

'Sleep's for the dead. I'm going in with you.' Grandma Mary's eyes blazed with determination, her cheeks rosy with warmth despite the cold morning. Both features stood out against the wild nest of bleached blonde hair she religiously tamed into a French knot each morning. Grandma held her battered blue jeans, navy wool cardigan, and pale blue turtleneck in her arms. And the denture case she insisted on keeping bedside 'so that I don't clutter up the bathroom sink.'

'No, Grandma. Go back to bed. I'll get more done on my own, at least to start with.'

'But you need the help . . .' Judging from her distracted appearance, Grandma Mary's thoughts were already at the store, wrapping Easter orders. At sixty-five, Grandma was young compared to her friends' grandparents, but her thin frame sagged with the long hours they'd both been putting in. Plus Grandma helped Mom and Pop out a lot, from preparing meals to doing laundry. Getting Pop back at the chopping block was a family affair.

'Please, Grandma. You were up late watching that rerun of *Police Woman*. It won't help any of us if you get sick. If you come in later, it'll give me a chance to take a nap this afternoon.' Lydia had no intention of resting, not today, but Grandma wouldn't budge without incentive. And nothing moved Grandma's heart more than a plea from her granddaughter.

'Well, OK.' Grandma nodded. 'But only if you promise to call me if you need me sooner.' Grandma gestured at their shared phone on the wall of the kitchen nook.

'I promise.' Lydia crossed her fingers behind her back.

'Before I forget, honey, did you hear your sister roar in last night?'

Lydia grinned. 'I did. Maybe around two-thirty?' The sad state of Teri's boyfriend's muffler had broken through a delicious dream she'd been having about Stanley. From the times when she'd never doubted the strength of their bond. Before she'd left for Canada, and before he'd taken a rebound fiancée.

Grandma shook her head. 'I don't want to think of what she was doing until then. Nothing good happens after midnight, not when you're eighteen. That boyfriend of hers needs to fix his car.'

'I'll mention it to her. She's coming in early today, and so is Johnny. I even asked Vi to show up an hour early.' She didn't put any faith in their bookkeeper appearing before the shop opened, but she wanted to get Grandma back under her covers.

'Oh, that reminds me!' Grandma clutched Lydia's upper arm as if she had life-shattering news to report. 'Don't mention getting rid of Vi to your father. Not yet. Yesterday he asked your mother if she'd made sure to include Vi for Easter dinner.'

'Are you kidding me?' Lydia wished she'd fired Vi already. The woman was taking from the shop's bottom line as far as she was concerned, and not doing her share of the workload. 'I specifically told Mom to not invite her.'

'I know, I know. Maybe she won't show up. She's skipped before, right?'

'Only when she's having a hard day, like the anniversary of Uncle Ray's death, or their wedding anniversary.' Vi was widowed when Pop's older brother Ray died unexpectedly almost two decades earlier.

'I hate to say it, because it was my son who died, but Vi needs to move on. Life is for the living, and my Ray wouldn't ever want her to suffer like this.' Grandma never hesitated to express her opinion.

'Vi says she'll never give her heart to another. At least, since her last divorce.' Vi had remarried, and divorced, twice since Uncle Ray died. 'She got her idea that she only had one true love from you, you know. You've never remarried since Grandpa passed.' Lydia didn't want to make Grandma sad, but figured it was unlikely as Grandma had had several beaus over the years, including a recent fiancé, who unfortunately took off to Florida right before their nuptials.

'That's because I don't identify as a widow. Sure, when I first lost your grandfather, I grieved. We all did. But life is for the living. I moved on. Vi needs to stop thinking of herself as Ray's widow – it's why her other marriages didn't work out, if you ask me. Then the men will appear.'

'You'd know, Grandma. The men can't keep away from you.'

'Stop buttering me up, honey bunny.' Grandma giggled. 'Get out of here, then. I'll see you soon.' She waved her away.

'We don't need you until later, Grandma. Go back to bed. Please.' Lydia kissed her cheek, inhaling her grandmother's signature lilac bath powder scent.

Grandma kissed her back. 'Be careful, honey child. It's still dark out.' She dropped her clothes on the tiny kitchen table and padded back to bed.

Lydia shoved into her coat, grabbed a container of raspberry yogurt from the ancient refrigerator to eat later in the morning, placed it in her pocket, and took the milk crate filled with sealed plastic bags of chrusciki she'd carefully stacked last night. She finished bundling herself up for the short but cold walk to work.

It was impossible to keep her snow boots from clomping down the steep stairwell, so she leapt from the third to last step and pushed open the garage side door. Cold air stung her cheeks, sucked at the hairs in her nostrils. She halted in the driveway, wondering if she should check on the kielbasa. Normally she prepared all of the smoked sausage in the commercial smoker adjacent the store's building. Last night she needed more room so she had also used the large, ancient, brick structure her grandfather built decades ago. A quick glance over her shoulder reassured her that there wasn't any smoke coming out of the smoker's tiny chimney. It wasn't predicted to get much above freezing today, meaning the cured meat had no chance of spoiling before noon. She'd come back for it later, after she opened the store and got things going.

Wasting no more time, she left the property and made for the shop, only a couple of blocks away. It was a good chance to sift through her already racing thoughts.

Grandma was right: Pop didn't need to know about her plan to fire Vi. Not until right before she did it, and presented him with her reasons. Since coming back into the business Lydia noticed that the income didn't match up with the payments, as in she was certain they were making decent enough earnings to support the overhead and at least two employees, including Vi. Since Vi did the books, it would be easy for her to do some quick skimming. But Lydia couldn't accuse the once-relative of a crime without proof, and she hadn't had a chance to examine the books herself. To be fair to Vi, it was more probable that the woman had made honest mistakes rather than stolen funds from her family-by-marriage's business. Lydia had to check it out, either way. With Pop still on the mend, managing the entire load of the accounts fell on her shoulders.

You haven't wanted to look at the books.

Lydia had to be honest with herself. If she found out Vi

wasn't cheating the business, then it would be impossible to convince Pop it was OK to let Vi go. Worse, Lydia would have to admit that her gut instinct was kaput. It had certainly proved useless when she'd followed it to Ottawa and her attempt at pastry school, which she'd prematurely left with less than six months until graduation. She refused to think of it as a failure, more a realization that a diploma wasn't always entrée into getting whatever she wanted. It hadn't helped that Madame Delphine had never liked her, and said abhorrence was solidified when she caught Lydia in flagrante delicto with her son, another instructor at the fledgling school. Lydia's departure hadn't been amicable but it had been mutually agreeable. And left Lydia with a personal vow to keep her infrequent drinking to more affordable local beer instead of champagne.

No, firing Vi wasn't going to happen without hard evidence that she'd been cheating them. Like Vi, Pop was forever loyal to the memory of his deceased brother. Ray had been their father's pride and joy, and the chosen one to inherit the butcher shop. But Ray, urged on by Vi – who made it clear that 'making bologna' was beneath Ray – had wanted to make it big in New York City. He was a natural stock trader and left Buffalo to make a go of it. That left Wienewski's Wieners & Meats to Pop. When Ray dropped dead of cardiovascular disease – it plagued the Wienewskis – Vi came running back to Buffalo and begged Pop for a job. Nobody had worked harder than Vi over the years, and Lydia's memories validated that. Lydia had worked for Pop since she was a kid and remembered Vi sitting in that back office, pencil poised over the ledgers.

But Vi hadn't been as nose-to-the-receipts as usual over the past several months, not from what Lydia had surreptitiously – and openly – observed. She was often on the phone talking to who-knew-who while filing her nails and puffing away on the menthol cigarettes she favored. Lydia had forbidden smoking in the shop since her return. What did Vi think this was, 1960s Buffalo?

Enough. Grandma was right. Lydia would worry about Vi next week. After the Easter sales boon and after she took a hard look at the numbers.

Her feet slapped rhythmically upon the slushy sidewalk, soothing her ire. During the day she always took the shortcut through the church cemetery but even her most unsuperstitious self didn't want to pass that way before sunrise. To be fair, she'd been spooked by that awful phone call last night, before she'd locked up shop.

The phone's ringing had broken the after-hours quiet. While it might ring off the hook during the business day, a call after closing always made her fear the worst.

Pop.

She'd raced across the backroom and grabbed the mustard-yellow receiver, its long, coiled cord fighting her attempt to bring it to her ear.

'Mom?' Her heart had pounded. If Dad had had another stroke . . .

'It's not your mother, hon. It's Louie.' The low rasping voice had thrummed with condescension.

Her stomach had knotted. Louie McDaniel, the bane of her life. Well, the bane of the shop's business, at any rate.

'What do you need, Louie?' She'd stopped playing nice with her father's meat supplier a month into her return. He'd sold tainted pork to Pop last Easter, sickening several of their customers, and refused to reimburse the shop for its losses. It had taken Pop the rest of the year to gain back customer trust. Louie was pond scum as far as she was concerned.

'Come on, Lydia. Stop with the nicey-nice. I was at your baptism, for cripe's sake. I told you last week that I need this month's bill paid early. In full. Today.'

'And I told you that thanks to you it's been lean here. Dad's still not back to work, you know. We only owe you for the Easter order, and it's not due until the first of the month. Next month. My family has always paid its debts. You'll have it by Tuesday or Wednesday next week, which is still almost two weeks early.'

'It's tight at my end, too, honey. You think I don't have demands from my creditors? I do. I've got some guys breathing hot and heavy down my neck. I'm asking you, family friend to family friend, for an earlier payment, that's all. You know I'm desperate if I'm begging you like this. Come on, Lydia,

I know you have it. Give your Uncle Louie a break here, sweet cheeks.'

'I'm not your sweet cheeks, Louie.' And he wasn't a blood relative, so he could forget her calling him 'uncle.'

'You've gotten awfully big in your britches for a girl, Lydia. You don't seem to understand how men do business. Listen to me, honey, before you drive your pop's business into the ground.'

'Excuse me? This shop has never been better.' OK, that was a bit of a white lie. She'd know more after she checked the books.

'Word gets out when things aren't going well, Lydia.' The threat in his tone startled her. And stoked her family pride.

'There's no word to get out. If you think our business is so strung out, then why are you asking for an early payment? I'll see you Tuesday, Louie.' She'd slammed the receiver onto its silver hook so hard that it made the bell ring. 'And stop calling me bee shit!'

This morning she was a little taken aback at how she'd screamed at the phone. Certainly not something she'd ever want to do with customers listening, but it would be clutch to do it to the skeevy meat supplier's face. The sooner Louie McDaniel was paid in full and out of her life, the better.

She hurried down the concrete sidewalk she knew as well as the family kielbasa recipe. This was the street she'd hopscotched on, learned to ride a two-wheeler on, and finally, she'd thought, driven away from. Until she drove back less than a year later.

She entered the alley behind the store. A chorus of plaintive 'meows' greeted her. Lydia laughed and stooped down to pet as many of the kittens as she could while she picked up several chipped plates from overturned pallets.

'You didn't miss a single morsel, did you?' She spoke to the momma cat, Luna.

'Meow.' The female matriarch wound her black body around Lydia's feet, her long white-tipped tail curving over her heavy snow boots. Mom had convinced Pop that Luna would be 'good for the rats.' But the single black cat had morphed into eight when Luna's brood was born on New Year's Eve. The kittens, all distinct in their markings, purred like one big motor as they surrounded her.

She hadn't told Pop about the kittens, or that she'd snuck Luna to be spayed last week, paying cash for the procedure. The veterinarian they used for Stashu, their aging terrier-mix, had given her a steep discount and promised to keep her secret.

Entering through the back door, she set the empty plates in the industrial sink, put the crate of chruściki on the work counter, and quickly got the coffee pot brewing. She rubbed her frozen fingers, flicked on the heater.

A full mug of coffee later, she'd packaged and placed the crisp cookies atop the front counter, and begun the trek from the back butchering room and freezer to the refrigerated display case. The fresh kielbasa in the refrigerator room should be more than enough, same for the hams that filled the long shelves. Smoked kielbasa hung in long loops from wooden pegs her grandfather had installed in the 1930s. There was plenty, but she was grateful she'd made the additional batch last night, after all. They might end up with a little extra, but that would sell over the next weeks. It was always better to have too much. At least that's what Grandma always said. So what if she was referring to boyfriends? Besides, it was Pop, and before him Grandpa Wienewski, who had infused the love of kielbasa into Lydia's blood. It came naturally for Lydia to prepare the sausage, from butchering the carefully chosen hog, to grinding the meat, to mixing in the exact proportion of salt, pepper, garlic, a tiny bit of sugar, and the most important herb, marjoram. It wasn't Polish kielbasa, especially the fresh, unsmoked variety, without the tiny, dried leaves. Pop had taught her so much more through the years than how to do his job. He'd shared how his family had expressed love through both food and working hard. Lydia honestly couldn't separate the two, nor did she want to.

She'd focused so intensely on the fresh kielbasa production last week that she'd had a freak out yesterday over not having enough smoked kielbasa. Thus, the extra ropes in the backyard.

Before she'd lived in Canada for her brief stint at Madame Delphine's pastry school, Lydia hadn't realized how unique the neighborhood she'd grown up in was. It was truly a Polish-American enclave that had kept many traditions through the generations, including how Christmas and Easter were celebrated. As with the French Canadians she'd gone to school alongside and studied with at Madame Delphine's school, food played a big part in every holiday. Sure, Lydia considered it her duty to keep the Wienewski's locally famous kielbasa available for the family's livelihood. She also believed, deep down, that it was a sacred privilege to be able to provide such an important part of a family's celebration to their entire community.

As Lydia moved from the case to the backroom, her shoulder brushed up against the shop phone, and the resulting *ding* of its bell jerked her from existential kielbasa thoughts and triggered the memory of Louie's call. Shivers ran down her spine, followed by red-hot anger.

After Tuesday, he's out of the picture.

She shook off the ugly reminder with a gulp of coffee before she went back to prepping the shop. As she straightened the pile of the *Cheektowaga Times* in the wire rack near the shop entrance, her gaze caught on an ad for Dyngus Day at the fire hall. She took one of the papers with her to the back of the building, reading as she walked.

Dyngus Day, the Monday after Easter, was a day of loud polka music and lots of beer to wash down kielbasa, pierogi, and butter-laden sweets. It was a traditional Polish holiday when a boy picked the girl he liked, dumped water on her, and cemented his selection by 'whipping' her with pussy willows. Although Grandma, as an Italian-American who'd married into the Wienewskis, had her own opinion about boys and pussy willows. 'No man is bringing a willow named after my privates near me.'

Lydia giggled at the memory.

The pork chops were running low so she took a side of pork from the refrigerator and hauled it on to the small chopping block Pop kept in the cooler area. Their main butcher block was five times as large and occupied half of the backroom, but she didn't want to have to move aside the kielbasa packaging set up. There were too many orders to fill.

Lydia had butchered several pigs over the past two weeks, using the trimmings for the kielbasa. The fat had been trimmed, as had the pork loin. She liked to save at least half a pig for last-minute cuts like these. Customers knew the difference, Pop had taught her.

With deft moves she used her favorite knife and sliced the length into thick chops, which she arranged on a rectangular stainless steel tray. Once out of the fridge she snipped some lengths of parsley from the bunch Teri had brought from the supermarket yesterday and garnished the meat. Her family had never had pork chops for Easter, but she knew that their Polish traditions weren't common to all Buffalonians. Wienewski's Wieners & Meats aimed to please all. *The customer is always right*. Another lesson from Pop.

She reached for a sip of coffee and heard loud footsteps on the other side of the back door. Lydia stilled. No one was due in just yet. Whoever it was had stopped right outside the door. She swung her gaze to the deadbolt she hadn't turned. There had never been a problem with break-ins before.

Louie. It wouldn't be Louie, though, would it? This early?

If she were a lowlife, though, wouldn't pre-dawn be the perfect time to collect on a debt? He'd sounded so angry yesterday, especially considering she wasn't late on a payment. Louie's behavior had been downright creepy. Had his brittle patience finally cracked?

TWO

Lydia pivoted to make a beeline for her meat cleaver when the door burst open and the man she'd had a crush on since they'd been preschoolers stepped inside the shop. *Not Louie.* Her knees wobbled with relief and she skidded to a halt, foregoing her weapon-grab.

'Hey.' Stanley Gorski was oblivious to her bad scare as he stomped his feet on the entry mat and pulled off his royal blue Buffalo Sabres knit hat, the bedraggled gold pompom limp and gray at its edges. He really should throw it in with his laundry a time or two. 'Lake Effect incoming.' Stanley's grin flashed across his handsome face. He had missed his calling as a TV weatherman.

A smile tugged on her mouth but she fought it, still unable to drop the mask of politeness she wore around him since coming back. The rich, shared history only childhood friends who become sweethearts can enjoy was now a huge chasm between them, something they didn't discuss.

Their families had expected them to make a serious commitment, as in, marriage. In the years after high school, Stanley voiced plans to take over his family's dairy business, hinting at an adjacent bakery for Lydia. But he never came out and proposed, or even said the word 'marry.'

But if he had, would she have been ready to settle down?

Lydia had still been obsessed with becoming Buffalo's premier pastry chef, and was hellbent on getting to Ottawa. Right before she left for a famed pastry school, she and Stanley ended their romantic relationship and agreed to remain good friends, both believing she'd be gone for up to three years. It had been the right decision for each of them at the time. Or so she thought. Fate and time were cruel companions.

She and Stanley weren't meant to be, she'd since figured out. To everyone's surprise, Stanley had applied to law school and found himself a fiancée, all within a month of Lydia's departure. The fiancée had left the scene after a short time, but Stanley remained in law school on a full tuition scholarship. He worked alongside his father to cover his cost of living expenses, which were minimal as he still lived at home. While in Canada, Lydia had missed Stanley more than she could have ever imagined and was crushed when she found out about his engagement. And then more determined than ever to prove herself with her own business. She didn't need a man to move forward.

Except, Pop and her family had needed her, so her momentum had, well, stalled.

She watched her ex while he busied himself with his delivery. Like Lydia, the last year had changed Stanley. Neither were the kids they'd once been, the trusted confidantes who thought nothing of staying up all night to ponder deep questions before, and after, intensely passionate sex. Bittersweet regret clawed at her but she shoved it aside, forced herself to keep it light.

'Hard to believe it's still snowing in April.' Stanley tried to engage her again.

'It's Easter in Buffalo, Stanley. Of course it's going to snow.' She made it a point to always be pleasant to him while never revealing her weeping heart to anyone but herself – and sometimes Grandma – in private.

'Always the pragmatic one, Lydia.' He carried an armload of stacked boxes, his father's dairy logo printed in red letters on the cardboard. 'Dad says these'll be fine out of the fridge as long as you sell them by noon.'

'That shouldn't be a problem.' The hand-molded butter lambs were an Easter table staple. Adorned with red ribbon collars and a toothpick bearing the Polish flag stuck into each and every lamb's flank, the edible figures were as ubiquitous as dyed Easter Eggs. No basket of food brought to church for a special blessing by Father Kroll on Holy Saturday was complete without the butter creatures. Mom had always taken her to church that day for the tradition as a girl while Pop worked in the shop. Nostalgia for holidays when Pop was still healthy wrapped around her already emotionally sore heart.

'You having Easter dinner with your folks?' Stanley stood on the other side of the case. 'On Sunday?'

'I get that part, Stanley. Easter being this Sunday.' She kept her gaze downcast and turned away, hoping he didn't see her blush. No matter that they'd called things off, had been apart for the time she'd been in Ottawa, she still couldn't look at Stanley or be in the same room with him without remembering – and missing – their most intimate times together. Until her stupid hormones got the message that she and Stanley were kaput, it was more comfortable and far safer for her to fall back on their familiar banter. *Sans* any romantic innuendo.

'Nothing gets past you.' His eyes twinkled.

Odd. Stanley hadn't asked her what she was doing for anything, at all, since . . . well, since before she'd gone to Canada. Did this mean that he was having a hard time with his memories, too?

'Um, yes, sure. We're all staying home. My aunt is bringing most of the food.' It was easier for Pops to get around in his own house. That was what he said, but Lydia and her mother were pretty certain he was having the blues over his stroke and loss of work ability.

Stanley nodded. 'We're going to my grandparents, but we'll be back in time for dessert. Your mom invited us for your aunt's cheesecake.'

So that's what this was about. Mom was playing matchmaker again. Lydia had no clue where her mother found time between Pop's rehabilitation routine and arguing with Grandma Mary about changing his diet and overall lifestyle.

'My aunt Dot's cheesecake is the best, no question. And I'm glad there will be more people around. It's good for Pop.' She shut the meat case door and eyed Stanley over the gleaming stainless top, between two sparkling pyramids of bottled horse-radish, Grandma's contribution. She'd ground the creamy roots in the backyard using Mom's blender with Pop's heavy-duty extension cord as the fumes were too strong to prepare indoors.

'Do you need anything else?' She sounded so stern that she didn't recognize herself.

'No.' He shoved the hat back on, covering his thick auburn hair. His hazel eyes contrasted with the yarn's bright hue and she ignored any stirrings in her belly, or worse, her heart. 'See you Sunday night, maybe.'

'Sounds good. Bye.'

She didn't wait to hear the door shut before she went straight to the boxes and unpacked several of the butter lambs, placing the small cellophane window boxes wherever there was a free spot.

'Why are you so mean to him? It's not his fault you failed out of pastry school. And besides, he broke up with that skank. There's nothing for you to be bitter about.' Teri's voice startled her. She'd been so wrapped up in trying to figure out why Stanley was being so chatty she hadn't heard her youngest sibling arrive. Teri – Lydia still thought of her baby sis as 'Teresa' but didn't dare make the mistake of vocalizing her given name – grumbled and stalked about the backroom as if she was being led to the guillotine instead of preparing the Easter pre-orders.

Lydia glanced at the clock on the wall, the one her father swore was a spoil of his uncle's Normandy experience. It was eight-thirty and Teri wasn't due until nine, her usual starting time.

'Morning, dear sister. You're here early.' She noticed the dark circles under Teri's heavy makeup, the smooshed home permanent curls tamed with an herb scented hair mousse Lydia swore smelled stronger than the fresh garlic they'd chopped for kielbasa.

'I thought I may as well come in and get it over with,' Teri grumbled.

'You didn't go to sleep, did you?' It was impossible to keep the 'a-ha' tone out of her voice. 'You do realize that Grandma and I hear everything that happens on the street, right? Like Dave's jalopy?'

Teri paused, her spine stiffening as if weighing how to reply. Her decision to ignore the barb was loud and clear as she ripped a yard-long piece of butcher paper from the giant role. 'I did get some sleep, but I'll need a nap later.' Unlike Lydia, Teri would make sure to get her nap.

Stop being such a jerk of a sister.

'Sorry, sis. What you do for a social life is none of my beeswax. I sure had my late nights when I was your age. It's just that I'm on edge about the shop. I really appreciate you coming in before your classes.' Teri studied at Community College. 'But you really need to talk to Dave about his muffler. How was ladies' night?'

'It was OK. Dave wanted to hang with his friends more than me, though. He doesn't get me anymore.' Petulance laced her tired tone.

'What about *your* friends?' She tried to encourage her sister to rely on her girlfriends more. The group of friends Lydia had relied upon since grade school still meant a lot to her. Even though several were busy with new marriages and young children, they tried to do fun things together as often as possible. She wanted her sister to go after her dreams sooner than she had. Or rather, thought she had. So far, though, at eighteen, Teri's world rose and set on Dave.

'They were doing rum and coke all night. Patty threw up on the dance floor.'

'As long as it was just booze.' The words flew out of her mouth. She knew her sister drank, but never knew her to sample anything else. Motherly instincts she wouldn't usually credit herself with had developed since she'd come back from Ottawa. Mom was too busy with Pop to concern herself with Teri's comings and goings. To be fair, Teri was a legal adult and didn't need her older sister butting into her social life. Lydia wished she could pull her reaction back.

'Coke as in pop, Lydia. *Soda* pop. Not the white stuff.' Contempt dripped from each word. 'I don't know what you were doing in Canada, but I don't touch drugs.'

Booze didn't suit Teri, either, but Lydia thought it best to not mention it while her little sis nursed a hangover. Relief that Teri stayed away from drugs allowed Lydia's shoulders to drop several inches. Even though Grandma told her to stop worrying about her sister, she couldn't turn off her concern.

'I left yesterday's orders in the box out front, next to the phone.' It had rung nonstop with last-minute requests. 'I'll tell Vi, whenever she shows up, that if anyone wants to place an order today, they need to stop in on Saturday morning. If we have leftover, and we just might, they can get it then.'

'OK.' Teri made a point to stare at the clock. 'You know,

Vi should be in here already. Isn't her start time eight during busy holidays?' She sniffed. 'Why don't you fire her?'

'She's family. Pop hired her.' Lydia kept her future plans to herself. She wanted to be the one to tell Pop, and with solid ammunition aka baked books in hand.

'She's not blood. Never has been. And she took Uncle Ray away from the family business, what, twenty years ago?' Teri's voice reflected the love they'd all had for Pop's brother, even Teri, who'd never met him.

'It's not our business. Pop gave her the job out of the goodness of his heart. We can both learn a lot from Pop.'

Lydia said what she needed Teri to hear but really wanted to high-five her sister in agreement. Pop needed to come back to a stress-free environment, whenever that turned out to be. Vi was the antithesis of serene. And without her, her salary would give the business the extra cushion it needed to keep going for at least another year or two. Lydia wasn't a financial whiz, per se, but she'd take over the books for Pop if she had to, until he found someone trustworthy. Vi's days at the shop were numbered. First up, though, was getting rid of Louie. Before one of his shady deals made more problems for the business.

'The shop is my problem, Teri, not yours. Not while you're in school.' Lydia didn't want her younger sis to get worked up over the family's financial straits. Teri's frown said it all, though. She wasn't about to let go of the Vi bone.

'Today's the biggest prep day and Vi knows it. She hates getting her pretty mauve fingernails dirty. We don't need her. That's all I'm saying.' Teri tore another length of paper from the roll.

'Point taken.' Lydia was so not going to continue the debate.

Back out front, Lydia placed perfectly arranged trays of pork chops, pork roasts, and ground pork into the cases.

A tall figure bundled in a drab olive parka approached the front door. For the third time that morning, Lydia froze in place.

Had Louie shown up, after all?

So what if he did? *You're in charge of the store's orders, not Louie.* No matter how much the meat supplier played it the other way around.

As the person neared, she realized the man was too tall to be Louie. Plus this person's parka was fully zipped. Louie always wore his coat open.

It wasn't Louie, but Johnny Bello, their other employee. Lydia shook her head, exasperated with herself. Louie's phone call had shaken her up more than she'd realized. She smiled at Johnny through the window.

Johnny was the shop's single non-family employee. He never used the back entrance because of his 'cat allergies.' Lydia suspected it was more because Johnny didn't want to trudge his sneakers through the pot-holed alley. The guy never wore boots, which was plain ignorant if you asked Lydia. Save the sneakers for jogging. Johnny was in Teri's generation and had different thoughts about dressing for Buffalo weather. As in, they didn't.

She quickly let him in, and locked the door behind him. They still had two hours until opening.

'Man, it's cold out there!' Johnny's bright red nose and droopy lids made her wonder if he'd been dancing the night away at Fast Eddie's nightclub, too. In fact, he looked more tired than Teri, and as far as she knew Johnny didn't wear mascara.

'You OK, Johnny? You look tired.'

'Me?' His gaze went to Teri for a brief moment before he refocused on Lydia. 'I was up late. Reading.'

'Is that so?' Lydia asked.

'Johnny's a big Tolkien fan, plus Stephen King,' Teri offered, before walking to the back to deal with the orders.

Unaware of, or flat-out ignoring the sisterly undercurrents, Johnny shrugged out of his coat. 'The case looks great, Lydia.'

'Thank you.'

'What can I do?' Johnny was all business, the small talk over.

'Why don't you help Teri with the orders, and keep an eye on the coffee pot. Keep it full. It's going to be crazy in here after we open the door.'

'I know. I remember last year.'

When Lydia hadn't been in town, or even the country. When Pop had dealt with Louie's tainted meat order. She blinked, sucked in a breath. Johnny didn't mean to trigger her regrets nor her resentments.

'That's why you're such a great employee, Johnny. One more thing. Keep on top of the ticket dispenser – make sure no one sneaks one from the floor.' She wasn't in the mood to deal with anyone trying to cut in line.

'OK, sure thing. Oh, hey, Lydia. I forgot to mention it to you yesterday, but Louie McDaniel called when you were talking to a customer. Said to tell you to have what you owe ready by today. He wasn't being very nice, if you ask me. Not that he ever is.' Johnny's face tightened into a scowl. 'It's not my business but I'm not sure why you put up with him.'

'You're right on that, Johnny. Louie's anything but nice. Trust me, I don't take anything he says personally.' Heat rushed to her face. If she'd taken the call she knew she would have said something incredibly rude to Louie then, too. No matter how much she dreaded the encounter with Louie next week, getting rid of the loser was going to be a relief. Maybe it'd even give her a boost and make firing Vi easier.

Who was she kidding? Firing Vi would never be easy, if she ever got the courage to do it. Vi was pretty much family, after all.

'You OK, Lydia?' Johnny watched her. How long had she been standing here, staring into space, thinking?

'Yes, yes, I'm fine. I'm still waking up. Thanks for letting me know that Louie called. The bill isn't actually due for two more weeks. I'm going to pay him next week, after we get through Easter.'

'Man, I never want to run my own business. Yous guys put up with a lot.' Johnny's use of the Buffalo vernacular 'yous' punctuated his sincerity. 'Maybe you should give him a call today, anyway. He seemed really upset, Lydia.'

'I actually spoke to him yesterday, after everyone left.' She fought against gritting her teeth. 'Please don't deal with him on your own again. Refer all calls to me. I'll take care of him.'

Johnny nodded. 'OK.' If he found her hot-headedness over Louie unusual, he didn't show it.

Johnny walked behind the counter and through to the back. As soon as he'd hung his coat up he fell into a work routine alongside Teri. The two had a good system, she'd noticed yesterday. One prepped the paper while another weighed the sausage or ham. They enjoyed quiet banter whenever they worked together.

Assured that Teri and Johnny had things under control, Lydia grabbed her coat and shoved her feet back into her snow boots.

'Where are you going?' Teri's query sounded more like a complaint, as if Lydia were leaving her and Johnny with all the work.

'I'm going home to get the rest of the smoked kielbasa out of our backyard. You two don't need me right now. You both know what you're doing. I'll be back before you're through all of the orders, trust me. Besides, my hands aren't going to give me much more today.'

'They look swollen.' Teri had caught a glimpse of her hands before Lydia put her mittens on.

'It's the way of this business.' Her fingers curled inside the thick wool, relishing the warmth against her chapped skin. She didn't admit it to Teri or Johnny, but she was actually proud of her sore hands. Hard work never intimidated Lydia Wienewski.

So why had she allowed one nasty phone call bother her so much? No more letting Louie spook her. Or allowing her worries over Vi encroach on the success she was leading the shop to.

Whatever it took to save the Wienewskis, Lydia was all in.

THREE

Lydia put all thoughts of Louie McDaniel out of her head as she walked home, cutting through the graveyard this time. Her boots crunched on the gravel path that dissected the parish cemetery as her breath clung to the misty air in transparent gray powder puffs. Cold damp air clawed through the soft lilac scarf Grandma crocheted for her last year. Snow fell in heavy, lazy flakes, but its beauty didn't fool her. A spring storm could yield over a foot of snow by the time it stopped. The paper said it wasn't expected to be more than six inches of a slushy mix, and she hoped the prediction proved correct. Buffalonians would drive through just about anything for their Easter sausage, except ice. Slush was OK, though.

Snow surrounded the crocuses that had yet to bloom in Mrs Haas's front yard, and coated the elaborate wrought-iron railings that skirted the majority of concrete stoop porches in their neighborhood. Grateful for her boots, Lydia splashed through a puddle as she turned onto her street. Several cars remained parked along the curb, a fineable offense if the snowplow needed to get through.

Her mother's car, parked on the street, was covered with the slushy mess. Without a second thought, she opened her parents' back door, grabbed the car keys from a rusty hook, and moved Mom's car into the driveway next to her own purple Gremlin. She'd use her car to haul the kielbasa to the shop.

She smiled at the sight of her wheels. She'd paid for the little car with nearly all of the high school graduation money she'd been gifted with by her father's extended family. The Gremlin had seen her through the last ten years in style, including the five-hour drives to and from Ottawa.

Slamming Mom's car door behind her, she pocketed the keys. She'd return them after she'd taken down the sausage. Rounding the back of the house, she unlatched the chain-link fence gate, noting that Stashu, the family's mixed mutt of dubious terrier origins, was nowhere in sight. She stayed as quiet as possible. The five-year-old dog was no doubt under her parents' heavy blankets, and she wanted him to stay there at least until she had the meat safe in its container.

Lydia took the plastic tub from the back concrete patio where she'd left it last night. Trudging across the backyard, she made a diagonal beeline to the twelve-foot by twelve-foot brick structure that dominated the back right-hand corner. As she neared she saw that the thick oak door was ajar. A couple of footprints that looked more from sneakers than from boots led to the muddy mess that decorated its granite threshold. Wild animals weren't a worry but dismay blanketed her enthusiasm, nonetheless. Had Dad come out after she'd so carefully tended the sausages? She hadn't told him about this extra batch, but as he'd taken to going outside on his own, using his four-footed cane for balance, he may have discovered her surreptitious sausage activity.

She shoved the heavy door open with her shoulder, uncaring about the soot that rubbed off on her parka. It was hard to not hold her breath, to anticipate the worst. The last time Pop 'checked' on her smoked kielbasa he'd insisted it wasn't fit for sale and had tossed it.

The waft of marjoram-spiced deliciousness she inhaled confirmed that the kielbasa was still here. *Phew.* Whatever, whoever, had made the prints in the snow hadn't disturbed her kielbasa. The curtains of long brick-red ropes reflected the success of her efforts and she got to work filling the tub. It was dim inside the smoker but she knew every cranny, inching her boots across the floor as she worked.

Halfway to the back wall, her foot hit something. She stopped, a sense of dread washing over her. If a squirrel, or worse, a stray dog, got in here when the fire was still smoking . . .

She bent down, peered into the shadowy depths of the smoker. A foot. She'd bumped into a large, rubber-booted foot. Panic washed over her, tripped her breath into pants.

'No, no, no. Pop!' Somewhere in her brain it registered that it wasn't her father's boot – his were worn brown leather, not black rubber. And he hadn't worn anything but supportive orthopedic shoes since stroke rehab.

It wasn't Pop, but it was for sure a body. A large male body, on its back, wearing an unzipped parka.

'No!' Lydia backed away, knocking into sausage ropes, toward the door. Light. She needed more light. She opened the door as wide as it would go.

There, in the smudgy gray shaft of a Cheektowaga morning, lay Louie McDaniel. His eyes stared upward, unseeing, his heavy winter parka unzipped but covering his large belly nonetheless. It looked like he was wearing his usual dress shirt under his coat, and there was a stain that looked like blood on the shirt, but it was too dark to make out details. Instinct instilled from watching detective shows with Grandma, and from taking the Red Cross first aid course when she was a lifeguard, kicked in. She leaned over, touched the side of Louie's neck with her fingers. It was cool to the touch, with no pulse, no matter how deeply she pressed. Nothing.

Dead. Louie was dead.

Touching his cold skin wasn't the worst thing, though. Neither was seeing Louie's corpse. No, what was making it hard for Lydia to breath, to wrap her mind around this, was the object sticking out of his neck.

The family sausage pricker. The antique tool that her great-grandfather Wienewski had brought over from the old country in the nineteenth century. The wooden handle fit her hand perfectly, smoothed with over a century of use. Three long tines protruded from the handle. Three very sharp points, used to prevent air pockets from forming in the sausages. She'd pricked holes through the sausage casing with it just last night. Mere hours ago.

Lydia's sausages weren't the only thing that had been pricked last night. Someone had killed Louie with the sausage pricker. That same someone had gone to great lengths to put him in the family's private smoker, of all places. Not in the commercial smoker behind the store, where she'd spent weeks making the orders they'd sell today. This was her extra, her just-in-case stash of kielbasa. Kielbasa she'd toss, of course. She'd never heard of a health code about sausages near a corpse but was certain it was a violation.

She shook her head to stop thinking about anything but what lay in front of her.

A murdered Louie that someone wanted her, or her family, to find.

This was personal.

Birdsong erupted from the maple tree and cut through her shock, the persistent feathered creature unaware of the tragedy unfolding beneath its sanctuary. Lydia suddenly realized she was not only alone with Louie, or, um, what remained of him, but alone in the backyard. Was whoever had killed Louie in such a grotesque way still here? Shudders racked her frame as she backed away from the corpse. Where was Stashu's strident barking when she needed it?

She stumbled outside and sucked in halting gasps of cold air. Her thoughts continued to spiral, each one more menacing than the last. One stood out like the glare of the Wienewski's Wieners & Meats neon sign.

Someone was after her family.

The *splat splat* of footsteps on slushy snow sounded. She whirled around.

'Grandma!'

'I know you wanted me to wait, but I thought I'd come in now.' Grandma Mary stopped and stared. 'What's going on, Lydia?' Grandma's eyes were wide and searching in the growing daylight. 'Didn't the kielbasa turn out? You look like you've seen a ghost.' She shucked out of her heavy wool coat and threw it around Lydia's quaking shoulders. A sob escaped Lydia's lips at the loving gesture.

'What happened? You can tell me, child.' Whisps of Grandma's golden hair escaped from under her Buffalo Bills 'Talkin' Proud' knit hat.

'It's . . . it's worse than a ghost, Grandma. It's a dead body.'

Grandma blanched. 'Not my Victor!'

'No, no, not Pop. It's Louie McDaniel. The . . . Pop's . . . our meat supplier.'

Their *former* meat supplier.

FOUR

'I'm going to need you to stand back, Lydia.' Cheektowaga PD Officer Ned Bukowski spoke in an official tone she'd never heard from her cousin before. He stood between her and the smoke shed, Grandma Mary at her side. The scents of garlic and marjoram hung in the air, the bin of kielbasa uncovered and pushed to the side.

Mom and Pop stood at the edge of the concrete patio, Mom fighting to hold Pop back from slushing through the yard, four-pronged cane and all. Lydia had found them at the kitchen table when she'd run into the house at Grandma's urging to 'call the fuzz, now!'

There hadn't been time to explain to Grandma that the current slang for the police was 'cops.' Honestly, Lydia had no problem with social activism but Grandma needed to come into the eighties. The police had a job to do, and who still called the police 'the fuzz,' anyway? The last thing she wanted was for Grandma, or any of them, to offend the police. They needed the police to realize that whatever happened to Louie in the smoke-house, no one in her family had anything to do with it. No. One.

'Ned, you know I didn't do this. This is some kind of gross joke.' Lydia grabbed her cousin's forearm, pressing through his bulky uniform jacket. Ned delicately lifted her hand from his arm with his own cold-chapped hand. Didn't cops have gloves with their uniforms? Belatedly, she saw that he held one large mitten in his other hand, along with the clipboard he'd been writing on.

'I don't know anything except that you've got a dead body in your smoker that you say you found, Lydia. And it's no joke to' – he peered at his notes – 'Louie McDaniel. If that's who he's positively ID'd as.'

Ned's words hit her hard, like a throat punch. He wasn't trusting her identification of Louie? What else was he doubting? Her innocence?

'You should get some Vaseline on that skin of yours. Doesn't the department give you decent gloves, Ned?' Grandma stared at Ned's raw skin. 'Mittens are for kids.'

'He's a grown man, Grandma. And a police officer.' Lydia attempted to whisper but her words came out like a toad croaking.

'Police.' Grandma Mary harrumphed. 'Why, back in 'sixty-five I got tear-gassed right in the bazooka by a pi—'

'Grandma, shhh! Besides, you meant to say "booty."'

'No, I meant "bazooka." The tear gas canister hit my left tit before it blew up!' Ire flashed from Mary's eyes and Lydia knew better than to push her grandma. But too much was at stake.

'You do realize that I found the body, right, Grandma? We need Ned and all of the Cheektowaga Police Department on our side!' This time her whisper was fierce as she uttered 'Cheektowaga Police Department' like an incantation.

'Is there something you need to say to me, Aunt, uh, Mary?' Ned blushed and Lydia took her deepest breath since finding Louie. *Phew.* If Ned was seeing them as family, they'd be OK. Wouldn't they?

'No. I'm taking the fifth.' Grandma invoked her constitutional right. And immediately revoked it. 'But keep it in mind that we're all family here, Ned. Officer Bukowski, that is. I'm the one who cleaned you up after you ate chili as a toddler and had it coming out of both ends.' Grandma nodded as if she was in charge of the investigation and not her nephew-by-marriage. Ned was Lydia's cousin on her father's side, her aunt Dot's son. Dad and Dottie were all that was left of their original seven siblings thanks to bad genetics, too much sausage and maybe much more vodka. The women got cancer of some sort and the men dropped of stroke or heart attack. With a sprinkling of cirrhosis thrown in.

'I'm here on official business.' Ned's stern demeanor, so unlike him, made Lydia itch. He didn't think she or Grandma had killed Louie, did he?

'I'm glad you were the one on duty, Ned,' Lydia piped in. Someone who didn't know her, didn't know what her family was going through, might look at this scene . . . differently. But this was her cousin. 'Who do you think did it?'

Ned's hand paused over a battered notebook, and he didn't meet her gaze. The distinct *ding* of an internal alarm bell sounded in Lydia's mind.

'Ned, what's wrong?' She and Ned were tight. Well, for cousins, they had been, years ago. Hadn't they cried in one another's arms when Uncle Ray died? And she'd set him up with Katie Neal for prom, when his longtime girlfriend had left him high and dry, no thanks to the captain of the football team, that egomaniac macho man. All of that had to reveal to Ned that in no way could Lydia, or her family, ever kill a man. Not on purpose, or premeditatedly.

Ned sighed as he shifted on his feet and scratched the back of his neck, under his jacket collar. She noted the long length of his hair, for a cop, and his five o'clock shadow. More like eight-in-the-morning shadow.

Finally, he looked at her, square on. Lydia wished she could go back to not being able to interpret his expression when his gaze scorched her, made her think he could read her mind.

'Lydia. Aun—' He shook his head. 'Mary. Technically we're family, yes. But I'm here as a CPD officer, and there's a dead man on your property. You are both under suspicion. So are your parents.' He motioned toward Mom and Pop as if they were lawn chairs and not the aunt and uncle who gave him ten dollars in his Easter card each year. To this day. Lydia knew for a fact Mom had sent Ned and his sister a card this year, too, because she'd taken them to the mailbox for Mom.

'I, uh, I know this isn't easy for you either, you know? Even if we weren't family, I don't believe finding a dead body can ever be easy, you know?' Lydia slipped into the local vernacular when she was nervous. As much as Teri's use of 'you know' could drive her nuts, she couldn't help herself from using it, too.

Ned squared his shoulders and shook his head. 'I appreciate your concern, truly, I do. But this isn't about me, or any of us. It's about the dead man in your smoker.'

'And how he got there and who the hell put him there!' Grandma was done with any touchy-feely sharing. 'Let's get to it.' Grandma pulled a Polaroid camera from the large bag she'd retrieved once Ned had acquiesced to a bathroom break. 'I'll help you by getting some photographs of the victim while the morning light's still strong.'

'Grandma!' Lydia cried. She didn't care if she was being overly emotional – was that possible after finding Louie dead? She had to do something about Grandma's playing Sherlock – not to mention her detective show addiction – stat, before they annoyed Ned enough to make him arrest them.

'That won't be necessary, Mary,' Ned said. 'Our forensic team will be here shortly.'

Grandma sniffed. 'It's always Aunt Mary to you, young man. Nobody knows more than I do about solving a crime, especially a murder. I thought you'd want pictures before your colleagues show up and contaminate the scene. I for one am not going to the slammer for a crime I didn't commit. How do I know that there isn't a bad copper on your team? You saw *Serpico*, right?'

'Grandma!' Lydia hissed her admonition this time.

Ned sucked in a breath and Lydia held hers. This was it. He was going to arrest them, after all. Instead, he let out a muffled laugh, then put his game face back on.

'Aunt Mary, I really, really appreciate your concern. But please, let me get my job done. I promise that no one here has anything to be concerned about as long as you fully cooperate.'

Lydia walked back to her parents, concerned they weren't able to hear the entire conversation. Mom was wrapped up in her parka and Pop wore his battered plaid work jacket. Both had mugs of coffee in hand as if birdwatching and not viewing a death scene.

'Did you catch any of that?' She filled them in on what Ned said.

'My speech might slur but my hearing's perfect, Lydia,' Pop said slowly.

'Stop worrying about us and stay with Ned and your grandmother.' Mom appeared her usual unflappable self. Through Pop's stroke, his rehab, and now a dead body in their smoker, did anything faze her mother? When Mom took a sip of her coffee, Lydia noticed her hands were shaking, ever so slightly. Anger surged, a necessary byproduct of her protectiveness toward her family.

The sound of a car pulling up in front reached the backyard, followed by two doors slamming in quick succession. Lydia walked back to Ned and Grandma and watched a tall, older man dressed in a suit coat walk through the open barbed wire fence gate with a uniformed officer on his heels. The first man's movement appeared energetic and focused, his long strides bringing him to the scene without hesitation of any kind. He didn't miss anything, either. His sharp gaze swept over the scene and Lydia sensed that he'd memorized every last detail of the Wienewski backyard. The bare paver brick patio, where their patio furniture would go by Memorial Day. The garage, with the larger picture window near its apex, revealing the apartment she and Grandma shared. The smoke-house, all of them gathered near. The open oak door, leading to Louie's corpse.

Play it cool. Keep your wits. If Ned had made her knees shake, this man held the power to ruin her world if he was who she figured he was – a homicide detective. She should look away, not risk him seeing her fear, her uncertainty. But his face was too interesting. She couldn't make herself look away if she tried.

The man had probably been a looker in his younger days. Broad shoulders carried a tailored wool overcoat with ease, and Lydia spied the flash of a violet tie under a black – no doubt cashmere from the smooth look of it – scarf. His charcoal fedora reminded her of her Grandpa Wienewski's dress hat, the one he'd wear for Easter Mass. This man's hat was pulled down low and Lydia marveled that his ears weren't as red as Nate's chapped hands. It was frigid out here and the wind still carried the remnants of an Arctic chill.

More like a deadly chill.

A nervous laugh escaped Lydia at the inappropriate thought and she realized her mistake when the man's bright gaze landed on her. His eyes were the color of aquamarine Easter eggs, but unlike the festive food they were edged with the cold steel of knowing.

This man had seen a lot of life, most of it probably a far cry from any kind of holiday joy.

'Detective Nowicki,' Ned greeted.

At the sound of his name, Grandma gasped.

'Officer Bukowski.' Detective Nowicki's gaze swept again over all present: Lydia, Grandma, Ned, and Mom and Pop on the patio.

'Good morning, everyone. I am sorry for the unfortunate event that brings us together.' He turned to Ned. 'Tell me what you know, Officer Bukowski.'

Grandma stood stock-still and Lydia didn't have to guess why. This was one of her beloved detective shows playing out in real life.

'Harry?' Grandma took a step toward Detective Nowicki, imposing on both his and Ned's personal space as they each took a step back.

'Yes?' Detective Nowicki's eyes narrowed as he peered at Grandma, his etched granite expression revealing no sign of recognition.

'Harry Nowicki! What a small world this is. I lived on the West Side for years and never saw you. Then, wouldn't you know, when I move out to the suburbs I start running into all kinds of people I used to know. Harry, don't you recognize me? It's me, Mary. Mary Wienewski. Although, you probably remember me as Maria Romano.' Mary beamed at him and batted her eyelashes.

Lydia silently groaned, her upper teeth cutting into her freezing lower lip. While Grandma's observation was correct in that Buffalo was the biggest metro area in the world that felt very much like a small town, Lydia didn't think this was the right time for her to bring that up. They were dealing with a murder here, not a petty theft, and she wanted to give the detective at least the appearance of her family being sane. Respectful. Definitely not flighty.

At least Grandma hadn't put her false eyelashes on, the ones she said made her look and feel like Angie Dickinson. Since Grandma Mary's legs were short and not at all as slim as Angie's, Lydia didn't think she had to worry about being mistaken for the TV star. The age difference between Grandma and the actress was a factor, too. Though not one she'd ever say aloud to her grandmother.

'Maria Romano? The dancing queen of St Stanislaus Grammar School?' Detective 'Harry' Nowicki's glacial expression shattered into long crevices as he flashed his pearly whites at Grandma Mary.

'Yes, Harry, it's me. Oh, I just knew it had to be you by the cock in your walk!' Mary stood on tiptoe and gave Harry a big smackaroo on his cheek.

Ned's eyes bulged and the coffee in Lydia's stomach rushed to her esophagus. What was Grandma thinking?

'Grandma, Detective Nowicki has a job to do.' Lydia spoke up. But Grandma was in full-on enchantress mode, and Harry seemed to have fallen under her hypnosis.

'I knew you'd made it big with the police but I lost track over these last decades. Oh, Harry. Remember when we won the jitterbug contest? We were the envy of St Stanislaus.'

'Indeed we were.' Nowicki's bemused expression said it all. There was no one Grandma couldn't captivate.

Grandma and Harry were old classmates. Great. Wonderful. But Lydia wondered if anyone remembered the very dead body in the smokehouse? She opened her mouth to help Ned get things back on track when practicality won out. Maybe Grandma's distractions would keep them out of the clink.

The back door of the house creaked open and without warning a sharp yip rent the air. Lydia looked over her shoulder to see Stashu gunning past her parents and going straight for the strangers in his yard, his tiny legs a blur of long caramel-and-white striped fur. Pop's home healthcare worker, Gladys, stood at the back door, her horrified expression accentated by the unsmoked cigarette which somehow remained hanging from her open mouth.

'Stashu!' Lydia swung around to intercept the terrorizing terrier, but only felt the wisps of his coat as he raced past her ankles. She watched as Stashu leapt the last two feet between him and Detective Nowicki.

'Watch out!' Ned warned his boss, but Harry was still starstruck by Grandma Mary's cooing. And perhaps by the way her flannel shirt gaped open at the front, revealing not a little bit of Grandma's ample cleavage. And was that her pink lace bra playing peek-a-boo?

'Grandma!' Lydia shouted, as much to try to get Grandma's help protecting Nowicki from Stashu's ire as to make her back off from her audacious flirting tactics. What she really wanted to do was tell Grandma to button her shirt the hell up, thank you very much, but Lydia had her priorities. Such as keeping Stashu from ticking off law enforcement.

Too late. She watched with sinking despair as Stashu reached his target and sunk his tiny teeth in deep.

'Oof!' Harry grunted and lines appeared between his considerable brows. Gray, but lots to them. He ripped his attention from Mary to the set of tiny but mighty chompers adhered to his trouser cuff. Lydia bet Harry wished he'd worn his snow boots instead of low-slung galoshes over his dress shoes.

'Get over here, Stash.' Lydia grabbed the diminutive terrier by his middle and tugged. Her foot slipped with the effort – darn dog was strong and stubborn – splashing her knees down into the wet mix of snow and mud.

'*Grrr.*' Stashu refused to relinquish his control over Harry Nowicki's ankle. A loud *riiiip* rent the air. To Lydia's horror a large patch of the detective's right trouser leg tore free, exposing pale white skin covered with ample curly hair.

Stashu didn't appear to give a terrier's snout about the damage he'd done as he vigorously shook the fabric as if it was vermin. Without further preamble Lydia reached for the dog's jaw and used her frozen fingers to pry it open, removing the patch of trousers, save for the one thread still wrapped around a fang. Her gaze caught on something bright red. Stashu had actually broken Nowicki's skin. For the second time that morning Lydia saw human blood.

At least this time it was from a live body.

FIVE

'Don't judge me by my slow speech, Detective. I had a stroke. But it didn't affect my memory. If there's anyone to blame for a dead body in my smoker, it's me. I forgot to put the lock on it.' Pop enunciated each word with care, but he'd come so far since his stroke Lydia was certain that Detective Nowicki didn't realize that Victor Wienewski had been barely able to speak only months ago.

'You didn't forget, Pop. I took the lock off.' Lydia never thought that locking the smoker door was necessary. No one stole kielbasa from another neighbor's backyard. Not in Cheektowaga. Not on her street.

But someone had had no compunction about killing Louie and leaving his body in their smoker. Why was Louie in their backyard to begin with? Had he come with someone he knew, trusted, or been surprised by a stranger who then killed him?

'Why did you unlock it?' Pop asked, drawing her out of the spiral of questions she had no answer for.

'What was that, Pop? Oh, why was the smoker unlocked?' Lydia sighed. She couldn't help it. Did Pop really need to know this, right now? 'Because I hung sausage there last night.'

'We've collected the sausage as evidence, for the record,' Detective Nowicki interjected but Pop either didn't hear him, or, more likely, ignored the distraction from his own interrogation.

'Thanks for letting me know. I would have thrown it out, anyway.'

'What were you doing leaving the Easter orders to the last minute like that?' Pop sputtered. 'I thought you were getting the shop out of the red, Lydia.'

'I am. I wanted to make double sure we had more than enough. There's Dyngus Day at the fire hall, you know, Pop.' Lydia wanted to keep the focus on answering the detective's questions but she didn't want Pop's blood pressure going up. His beet red face told her she'd already failed.

'What time was that, Lydia? When you hung the sausage?' Detective Nowicki – she'd best remember he was 'detective' until she was certain neither she nor anyone in her family was a suspect – asked.

'Right around ten o'clock. Then I made some cookies to sell this weekend – I used this kitchen, not the garage apartment's – and I was upstairs in time to watch Johnny Carson at eleven-thirty with my grandmother, Mary.' She gave Detective Nowicki a meaningful glance. As if it could convey 'you remember, the girl whose affections you once coveted.' And maybe he still did, if the way he blushed whenever Grandma looked at him was an indication.

'Don't mind her tone, Harry. She's had a shock, is all.' Grandma spoke from where she knelt on the linoleum floor in front of Detective Nowicki, who sat with his leg out straight on an empty chair, what was left of his right trouser leg dangling, while she cleaned and bandaged his wounds. If the bright red puncture wounds were on his neck instead of his ankle it would be easy to think the detective had been attacked by a vampire. Lydia bit back an inappropriate giggle. It was so not the time to make a *Dracula* reference.

'I'm going to keep asking the questions until I have the answers I need,' Nowicki said.

'Of course you are.' Grandma stood. 'There you go, Harry. Fortunately Stashu's been vaccinated against rabies – I took him myself last month – so you don't need to worry. I'm sure the peroxide I poured on your wounds killed anything else he might have given you. He does like to eat his own crap from time to time – nothing the cold can't kill.'

'We'll still need to see the rabies tag, for our records.' Ned spoke from the other side of Nowicki, nearer the back door.

Lydia watched the action from across the table, ensconced in an avocado upholstered, vinyl swivel chair, resisting the urge to spin herself around as she'd done when she was a kid. Besides, as much as she wished she could ignore this ugly mess, the fact remained that they were all being questioned in a murder investigation.

All six of the worn kitchen chairs were occupied. Pop and Mom sat together at the end, closest the counter, while Ned and Detective Nowicki side by side, across from her and Grandma. Gladys, who'd repeatedly expressed her regret at allowing Stashu out during her smoke break, had disappeared into the basement to 'catch up on laundry' until the interrogation session was over.

Because that's what this was, as far as Lydia was concerned. Nowicki could be as nice as he wanted but she saw past the tailored suit and crisp white dress shirt. The man was looking for a cold-blooded murderer and the Wienewski family was in his sights.

For good or bad, she was as informed as Grandma on police procedure thanks to the hours they spent together watching TV detective shows. If the authorities believed that Lydia and Mary had nothing to do with Louie's death, they would already be back at the station. The evidence, including Louie's body, had been collected and removed almost two hours ago. Now it was closing in on noon, and she wanted to be at the butcher shop. The customers would be packing the place by now.

Instead she was hiding out in her parents' half bathroom, spying on the crime scene. A few police officers had wandered in and out of the yard, and Lydia saw an officer wave off two different men with cameras hanging around their necks. But she also knew, from peering through the powder room's flaking aluminum Venetian blinds, that no less than two news vans were parked on the street in front of the house.

She sent up a silent prayer that the journalists were the only folks who'd been listening to the police scanner this morning. If word got out linking murder with the Wienewski's, it wouldn't be good for their Easter sales.

Which reminded her: she hadn't soaked the golden raisins that she put in her version of placek – Polish coffee cake – yet. She soaked them anywhere from twenty minutes to overnight usually, but liked them to have a little longer. She'd be so busy the rest of today and all of tomorrow she was afraid she'd forget if she didn't tend to her secret ingredient now.

Lydia walked back into the kitchen and headed for the cupboard.

'What are you doing, Lydia?' Her father's authoritarian tone grated on her nerves. Pop got agitated when it came to family appearances. No doubt he wanted their family to give Nowicki the impression that he had their total attention. In truth, he did, but Lydia needed to do this one small baking task. Baking was her respite from the cruelties life cooked up.

'It'll be just a sec. I've got to soak the raisins for the placek.'

'It can wait, honey,' Grandma said.

'Please, Miss Wienewski, this will go faster if you sit down with us.' Nowicki wasn't impressed with her ability to juggle her shock over Louie's death and her secret recipe's needs.

Ignoring him and making haste, Lydia dumped the wrinkly fruits into a glass bowl, then opened the bottle of brandy she'd bought for this very reason. She drowned the raisins with the amber alcohol, where they'd swim until plumped up. 'One more sec, I promise.' She covered the bowl with plastic wrap and shoved it into the refrigerator. Relief eased the tension that had twisted her neck into a ball of agony and she sat back at the table.

Nowicki had moved on, taking his time to review each person's routine last night and this morning. Lydia's thoughts raced as she awaited her turn for more questioning, and she risked a glance at her watch. The shop had opened on this most important day without her.

'Can I make a phone call, please?' Lydia directed her attention to Ned, who sidled his gaze to the man clearly in charge of the investigation.

'Who do you need to call, Lydia?' Detective Nowicki didn't look up from whatever he was scribbling on his notepad. At least his hands appeared as chapped as Ned's. Whatever her personal wariness was toward Nowicki, it was clear that he wasn't a man who hid behind his desk all day.

'Our family business. The butcher shop. We're the "Wienewski" in Wienewski's Wieners and Meats. I'm supposed to be at the store, working. It's one of our busiest days of the year.' She was grateful it wasn't an exaggeration. Surely Harry Nowicki understood the need for kielbasa orders to be filled on Good Friday for Easter Sunday?

'I know who you are.' He looked up and gave a quick smile. 'My mother never shopped anywhere else. If she wasn't going to make her own sausage, it had to be Wienewski's. Go ahead and make a phone call, but do it in here, where I can hear you.'

'Thank you.' Lydia slid out from her seat and reached for the avocado green phone. Her fingers no longer shook but the rotary dial seemed to take forever to spin as she placed the number she knew by heart. One ring, two rings . . . on the tenth ring, it was answered.

'Wienewski's Wieners.' Vi's deep smoker's voice rumbled over the line. Normally the reminder that Vi liked to sneak a smoke inside the shop annoyed Lydia, but at the moment it felt like a warm hug. A reminder that murder hadn't always been a part of her life.

'And Meats.' Lydia couldn't stop herself from adding the rest of the full name, as she was wont to do. Except it came out in a gasped whisper and not in what she considered her shop manager tone. Vi didn't deserve to be treated bad by anyone, and definitely not by her family. Yes, she tested Lydia's patience, but Lydia had no proof that Vi had stolen from the store . . . yet.

Maybe she needed to rethink getting rid of anyone. Had her fervent wish for Louie to go away somehow materialized into his wrongful death?

You're freaked out about Louie. Calm down.

Still, maybe she should reconsider getting rid of Vi, lacka- daisical employee or not. Family being family and all.

'Lydia?' Vi asked. 'Where the heck have you been? No offense, but this isn't the way to run a business on Easter, you know. Please tell me your pop's OK. Oh, dear sweet Jesus, don't let him go like my Ray did—'

'It's not Pop. He's fine.' She spoke louder for Detective Nowicki's sake, noting he kept his gaze on her. Shifting her feet, she wound the long spiral cord around her hand, her wrist. 'I-I've come up against a-a problem. I'll be there, I promise. Soon. I'm running a little late.'

'I'm so glad your pop is good. Phew! And you sure are late, honey. Try three hours late,' Vi observed. 'My Ray would give anything to still be here and have problems, let me tell you. He loved Easter so much.'

Lydia remembered that Uncle Ray enjoyed her father's kielbasa maybe a bit too much, as he'd died of cardiovascular disease. She didn't voice any of this, though. It was absolutely not the time for family nostalgia. Getting off Nowicki's suspect list was the priority. She blew out a prolonged breath. 'I was in the shop earlier, Vi, and came home to check on . . . something.' She had no desire to rehash her story. Not with Nowicki hanging onto her every word like Stashu hung onto ankles. What if, with her nerves and all, she misspoke? Gave away something Nowicki didn't want her to?

'OK, well, maybe a little less checking on things and more help in the store, then. We're really packed to the gills, Lydia!' Vi's propensity for emotional drama was lost on Lydia. She had to get off the phone. Like, yesterday.

'Look, Vi, can you put Teri or Johnny on? I need to talk to one of them.'

'You're out of luck there, Lydia,' Vi huffed over the line and Lydia wondered if she was smoking in the office again. A definite health code violation as well as a Wienewski manners breach. 'Teri left for her class and Johnny's balls to the wall. It's buzzing like bees out front. I can't tear him away from the customers right now.'

'Are you smoking in the store, Vi?' The words slipped out and she silently damned herself to hell. Lydia's mouth could run away on her whenever she was riled up. She hadn't calmed down since finding Louie stone cold dead.

'Aw, Lydia, sweetie, you know my nerves can't take all this commotion. Between the phone ringing off the wall and the cranky customers, I need some way to let off steam,' Vi bemoaned. 'If you really want me to get Johnny, I'll try.'

'No, never mind, please don't bother him. Forget it, Vi. I'm being cranky with all of the holiday stress, is all.'

'I understand. Is there anything else you need from me? I gotta go help Johnny.'

'So we've had a good number of customers so far?' The distraction of the shop's survival was as good as any for Lydia's nerves.

'Are you kidding me? They're standing on the sidewalk waiting to get in!' Vi puffed again and Lydia wanted to reach through the telephone wires and slap the menthol cigarette from Vi's hand. *Oops. Wrong attitude while being looked at for murder.*

The repugnant scent of Vi's cigarettes that would greet her the next time she entered the office was a small price to pay for Easter sales going as she'd hoped. In spite of the macabre, most un-holiday scene in the backyard.

She envisioned Johnny handling the holiday-harried customers, the incessant sound of the register bell, the guttural *riiip* hiss of masking tape as he packaged up meat from the front case.

'That's good to know. Are you taking the call-in orders, then?'

'Yes, I am, just like you asked.' Vi's tone reflected her self-pride. 'I turn the tape recorder on and repeat whatever they ask for. Although I hung up on the pervert who asked me what size milk jugs I have.'

Lydia sighed. At least Vi remembered to use the cassette player. She'd started the practice after seeing Madame Delphine do it in her restaurant. It was better than trusting anyone's handwriting. She'd kept some good habits from Ottawa and brought them back to Buffalo, it seemed.

'OK. Good job, Vi, thank you. We don't want to miss any orders today. I'll be there as soon as I can.'

'Can I ask what's taking up your time that you can't be here today, of all days?' Vi's question drew Lydia up short. It wasn't like Vi to show interest in what she was doing. As long as it didn't interfere with Vi's schedule, Vi didn't say much of anything about the shop.

Stop questioning everything.

'It's . . . it's a personal matter. Please tell Johnny that I'll be right there. Whatever he asks you for, please do it. That's all.'

'It's your call, Lydia.' Vi's subtle yet definite questioning tone indicated that she'd never agreed with Lydia running the store in the first place. But Lydia didn't take it personally, as Vi hadn't wanted Pop to have the shop forever, either. Her aunt had never gotten over Ray dying so young and never getting his shot at the family business, even though technically he'd had the chance but turned it down. Vi believed that Ray meant to return to Buffalo at some point and take over the store. To 'run it just like his father had.' Never mind that Pop had continued the legacy and done a very good job with it. Until the stroke . . .

Lydia sighed. She had to cut Vi some slack. The woman was a traditionalist and had even suggested that Ted, Lydia's older brother, quit his orthopedic residency to come back and run the butcher business. It had to be hard on her to see Lydia in the traditionally male role she'd envisioned for her deceased beloved.

'I'm doing my best here, Vi. And, um, thank you.' The shred of politeness was purely for Nowicki's benefit. She couldn't have the detective who was examining her every action as a murder suspect think that she'd be rude to an employee, much less a family relative.

Frustration writhed in her gut and when she hung up, a silent tear slipped down her cheek. She swiped at it, damning her still-too sensitive emotions straight to purgatory. Ever since quitting pastry school and facing Pop's stroke realities, she'd been overly emotional, and she'd always reacted to her own anger with tears. Normally she brushed it off, but not today.

A day of firsts. First dead body found. First police interrogation. Oh, dear Jesus, it wasn't going to be her first arrest, too, was it?

SIX

An hour after she'd called the shop they were still all at her parents' table. Lydia couldn't stop her foot from jiggling and caught a side-eye from Mom when her toe banged against the pedestal center. She grabbed her coffee, long gone cold, and slugged it back. An immediate wash of stomach acid hit her esophagus, so she plucked a slice of the placek Mom had put out for the un-occasion. Never in her entire three decades of living under the Wienewski roof could Lydia recall indulging in a holiday food before said day. Apparently Mom had caught on that they needed to keep the police on their side if Louie's unfortunate demise was going to remain a tragic but temporary happening for them. What better offering was there than the Polish version of coffee cake, made with almost a pound of butter and brandy-soaked golden raisins?

Lydia made a mental note to whip up another batch of the delicacy so that they'd have enough for Easter dinner. Which meant she'd probably be baking later on Saturday or even Easter morning. Both seemed eons away. How long did murder investigations take, anyway?

Detective Nowicki cleared his throat and she quickly swallowed her bite of the tender cake.

'Sorry! I haven't eaten since . . .' She trailed off, trying to remember what she'd had for breakfast, and when. Oh yeah, the gelatinous mass of raspberry yogurt. She shook her head. 'Never mind. What's your question, Detective?'

'Tell me what you were doing yesterday, starting with the morning.' Nowicki didn't miss a beat. Some part of her brain told her this was an investigative tactic, to keep pressing for answers no matter how shocked the interviewee was.

'I spent almost the entire day at the shop.' Lydia recanted how she'd been preoccupied with the Easter orders, and her worry over having enough kielbasa on hand. 'I finished making the extra sausage sometime before nine or ten last night, then I brought it all home and got the smoker going.'

'What did you do after that?' Nowicki posed.

'After I hung the kielbasa, I made up several dozen chrusciki. That's the kind of cookie I already told you about. They have to be deep fried so I cooked them out there on the patio, with a hot plate. I didn't want to bother Mom and Pop. Then I went back inside, to my apartment over the garage. That would have been by eleven-thirty, because Grandma and I watched Johnny Carson together.'

'All right.' Nowicki scratched more notes on his pad. 'Did either of you hear anything strange, anything out of the ordinary?'

Nowicki glanced from Grandma to Lydia.

'We couldn't miss my other granddaughter coming home way past anyone's bedtime,' Grandma stated.

'We both heard the loud car, the one her boyfriend drives, at about two-thirty, right, Grandma?' Lydia looked at Mary, hoping her grandmother would read between her burning eyeballs. *Let's get this finished up. Stick to the same story.*

'I heard two cars. One at two-thirty and one after five.' Grandma's lips – which she'd coated with Posy Paisley, a godawful shade of frosted orange that reminded Lydia of Halloween waxed candy lips – pressed into a thin line. Grandma Mary wasn't budging. She knew what she'd heard and that was that.

'Where were you at that time, Lydia?' Nowicki asked.

'After five? I was already at the store. Grandma wanted to come in with me but I convinced her to go back to sleep.'

'So she was asleep before you left your shared apartment?'

'Yes.' OK, it was a little white lie. Grandma had been on her way back to bed. That was good enough for Lydia. She knew Grandma wouldn't kill anyone. At least, as long as she wasn't backed into a corner . . . Lydia exhaled. So she'd glossed over the truth. It wouldn't affect Nowicki's investigation. He still had to find the real killer.

'Lydia left well before five. That's why she didn't hear the second car,' Grandma said.

Nowicki kept scribbling, his pencil strokes decisive. 'Did

either of you notice any other sounds? Dogs barking, a garbage can tipping over, footsteps?'

'No.' Grandma answered first. 'I started saying my Good Friday rosary and let me tell you, when I take to my meditation practice, I'm on a different spiritual plane. Have you ever had your aura done, Harry?' Grandma inquired.

'Ah, no. No aura doing for me.' Detective Nowicki stopped taking notes. 'Wait. Back up. I thought you were asleep, but instead you were saying the rosary?'

'I told you, I go to a different spiritual zone when I meditate. Have you ever tried transcendental? I can guide you into it, Harry. Anyhoo, I fell asleep in the middle of the fifth decade. Of the beads. But that's OK, because—'

'Your guardian angel finishes it for you,' Nowicki finished. Grandma beamed at him as if he'd announced she'd won the million-dollar New York State Lottery.

'Yes. Sister Ann.'

Nowicki nodded. 'She was a tough old broad.' He chuckled, then turned his attention to Ned, who'd been coming in and out of the odd gathering, slipping notes to Nowicki.

'What time of death did the coroner estimate, Officer Bukowski?'

'Between midnight and five this morning.' Ned didn't flinch, as if he'd been investigating murders his entire life. The civilian murder rate in Cheektowaga is pretty low as far as Lydia knew. As in, she'd never, ever heard of one until this morning.

Why did she have to be the one to discover it?

'Between midnight and five o'clock, Louie McDaniel breathed his last.' Nowicki looked at Mary, then Lydia. 'Is there anything you want to change about your stories, ladies?'

'Why would there be?' Lydia couldn't stay quiet any longer. 'What possible reason would any of us have to kill Louie, Detective? He's our meat supplier and has been for years.'

'A meat supplier who' – Nowicki looked at one of the notes Ned gave him – 'you owed money to?'

'That's not true! We'd caught up with our debt.' It sounded like the police had interviewed Louie's wife, Charlotte, after they'd informed her of his death. She wanted to damn Charlotte to hell, but compassion for the new widow won out. It didn't stop her frustration, though. Charlotte always believed whatever Louie told her. When the issue of tainted pork arose, Charlotte had proclaimed Louie's innocence in the matter to Pop.

'How would you describe your relationship with Louie, Lydia?' Nowicki persisted.

Lydia knew her cheeks were red but she was not about to back down on this. 'OK, sure, Louie wasn't the nicest man in the world. He called and threatened me only yesterday, when I still have two weeks to pay our bill.' *Ouch.* A sharp kick to her shin made her gasp, but she covered it with a cough. Grandma Mary's annoyance was shimmering out of more than her aura, that's for sure. 'Um, he was our meat supplier for many years.'

Ned slipped away as she spoke, no doubt checking into headquarters on the radio in his police car. Or maybe it was referred to as a 'cruiser'? Or a patrol vehicle? Lydia wished she'd paid closer attention to the more subtle details the last time she and Grandma watched *Columbo.*

'Harry, dear, listen to me. Lydia may be my granddaughter but she's also my roommate. We are more like sisters than grandma and granddaughter. I know her heart and it's pure, even if her tongue is too sharp. She's always confided her troubles to me. Louie is like the boys we knew in school who couldn't help but be mean. Remember Chucky Jones, Harry?'

Nowicki allowed a soft smile to break through his interrogator persona. 'Chucky "the Candyman" Jones?'

'That's him.' Grandma pressed her hand atop Harry's and gave it a quick squeeze. 'He would sell us penny candy at recess for half of what Mr Stein charged at the corner store.'

'We were all so impressed with Chucky, weren't we?' Nowicki reminisced. 'I'd save my allowance so that I could buy enough to last the weekend for me and my brothers.'

Grandma nodded. 'But then we all found out that he'd stolen the candy from Mr Stein's storeroom, and when we confronted him he got all mean and nasty.'

'I remember that better than you realize.' Nowicki leaned over the table and pointed to his left ear. 'I still have the scar from when he clocked me with his ink bottle.'

Grandma tittered and Mom rolled her eyes. Pop's reluctant smile, still a bit lopsided, revealed his soft spot for his mother. As much as Lydia's heart warmed at how her family was banding together in such an unexpected circumstance, the tragedy of possible bad sales today due to poor customer service pushed her restlessness to the breaking point.

'Detective Nowicki, may I please leave? I've got to get to the shop. I promise I'll call with anything else that comes to mind.' Should she try to give him the doe-eyes like Grandma?

'You'll need to file a statement at headquarters, first, Lydia.' Nowicki didn't miss a beat, no matter how congenial he appeared in his banter with Grandma.

A cold blast of air preceded Ned's re-entry through the back door. Stashu shivered on Lydia's lap under the table, where he'd taken refuge.

'Dispatch sent a message for you from the lieutenant, Detective Nowicki. You're wanted back at the station.'

Nowicki drained the rest of his coffee, shut the tattered notebook. He stood, speaking as he shrugged into his suit coat.

'Tell you what, ladies. I'll take you both with me. One of our officers will give you a ride back.' He nodded at Lydia and Grandma, then turned to her parents. 'Mr and Mrs Wienewski, I see no reason to bring you in. Nor your home helper, Gladys. But I'm going to need official statements from all of you, so work with Officer Bukowski to set up a time in the next day to go into the station. Unless it's going to be too difficult for you, Mr Wienewski?'

Pop shook his head. 'Not at all. I'm a little slower but I can still get the job done.'

'Good.' Nowicki nodded.

'Wait a minute. Why do my grandmother and I need to go in right now? We're both needed at work. It's one of our busiest days of the year. Can't it wait until I close the shop, later this afternoon?' Lydia had told Ned and Nowicki all she knew.

'I need your prints.'

'But we're not being charged, Harry.' Grandma made it sound like a directive. 'You can't officially take our prints unless you arrest us, can you?'

'No, you're not being arrested.' He paused and Lydia was

certain he wanted to add 'yet.' 'But I expect that you'd both want to fully cooperate, since you're claiming you had nothing to do with Mr McDaniel's death. Do I have your consent to take your prints?' Nowicki's query seemed superfluous to Lydia. If she said 'no' wouldn't that give him impetus to arrest? To make the fingerprints a mandatory thing?

'I gave my fingerprints to the Feds when I was wrongfully detained at the Capitol in Washington, DC.' Mary sniffed. 'I was supporting my right to—'

'Grandma was an activist back in the sixties, when everyone was.' Lydia never interrupted her grandmother but they were speaking to a law enforcement officer and the less said about previous arrests the better. Even though said arrest led to dropped charges. Plus, she didn't want to risk Nowicki hearing one of Grandma's police slurs, outdated or not. She was certain any and all favor granted by Grandma and Nowicki's shared childhood memories could be erased with one ugly word.

'I'd still like to get fresh prints from you today, Mary. Who knows how long we'd have to search for anything the FBI has on file? How about you, Lydia? Have you engaged in criminal activity in the past?' Nowicki asked, ignoring her attempt to save Grandma from The Law.

'No, I don't have a record, I've never been arrested.' She thought she didn't have to answer any questions without a lawyer but she wanted to give all appearances of cooperation.

Thank Jesus, Mary, and Joseph that she'd not been charged for any of her teenaged stunts. Which amounted to underage drinking, smoking one joint, and getting threatened with a ticket the night she and Stanley decided to 'go all the way' in the back of his father's dairy delivery truck at Cheektowaga Town Park. She'd made two bad choices that night: venue and vehicle. The truck stank of sour cream and some local kids were playing flashlight tag. The same children reported to their parents when they heard 'unusual banging' from the windowless back of the truck. The parents had called the police, leading to one of the most mortifying nights of her life. Sadly, the only banging that occurred was tipping over a pile of aluminum trays.

Although, she and Stanley had managed to figure out how to be alone while his parents were out and had sex a few weeks later. Awkward as it had been, she still smiled at the tender memory. Her stomach did a few polka steps as she thought about the tingly sparks that had arced between them earlier.

Stop thinking about Stanley.

It was over between them, no matter how nice he'd been this morning. And comparing youthful misconduct with the possibility of facing a murder wrap was beyond the contrast of apples and oranges. Beyond the differences between Polish kielbasa and Italian sausage.

Lydia was in over her head.

SEVEN

All told, Lydia and Grandma only spent forty-five minutes at police headquarters. Ned drove them back afterwards, dropping them at their insistence in the alley behind the butcher shop.

A jumble of voices hit her ears when Lydia walked into the shop with Grandma, confirming that the chaos described by Vi hadn't abated. *Thank goodness.* Noise meant customers which meant cash in the drawer.

Lydia threw off her coat and donned a clean apron. Tying it at her waist, she watched Grandma do the same. As Grandma rifled through her purse for her beloved lipstick, Lydia marveled at how composed the older woman had remained throughout the entire morning.

'We've done a lot of things together, Grandma, but becoming suspects was never something I thought we would do as a team. Are you OK?'

Grandma paused mid-stroke above her lips with the frosty hue. 'OK? Are you kidding me? I'm more than "OK," I'm terrific! Better than ever. I've just closed one of my major rings of destiny.'

'What?' What was Grandma talking about? Lydia wondered off and on if Grandma would ever start to lose her grip, as some of her other elderly relatives had. Was this the first symptom?

'Harry, honey. We're soulmates.'

'Oh! OK. That's great, Grandma, that you think that about Har— Detective Nowicki. I'm a little more worried about you and I becoming cellmates, though. You know, locked up for a murder we didn't commit.' How could Grandma forget what they'd learned watching *Columbo*?

'Oh, phooey.' Mary capped the tube and dropped it into her apron front pocket. 'You worry too much. Why, when I was your age I didn't have a care in the world.'

'You had three kids by the time you were my age, Grandma.' That was a lot of cares, as far as Lydia was concerned. She wished she could retract her words, though, because ever since Uncle Ray died Grandma got sad at any reminder of only having two living children now.

There wasn't a glimmer of anything but feisty in Grandma's bright eyes, though. Maybe she was right; Lydia worried about everything, especially things she had zero control over.

'Exactly! I lived my life and loved it. You kids nowadays don't know how to embrace what you have. You're always searching for the next best thing. Stuff. A lot of stuff will get you more to dust. Look around you, Lydia. You have a family that loves you, you're using your talents to get this shop in tip-top shape, and you're going to have your very own restaurant by summer. Focus on that. Enjoy being young while you can.'

'What about Louie? And the murderer? Who, since we know it wasn't you or me, is still on the loose?' She couldn't stop the shudder that coursed down her spine, shooting right past the parts Stanley made hum and straight for her wobbly knees.

Grandma's eyes shone with wisdom. She placed her hands on Lydia's shoulders, waited for her to look into her eyes. 'It will all work out, my dear. Have some faith.' She kissed her on each cheek before embracing her. Lydia returned the hug, wishing she could indeed be as calm as Grandma.

'OK, Grandma. I'll try.'

'That's the girl I know. Now, tell me, what do you want me to do?'

'Give me a sec.' Lydia quickly scanned the back work area, peeked into the refrigerator, poked her head into the tiny office. Vi was nowhere to be seen, so she must be out front with Johnny. A first.

Lydia turned back to Grandma. 'Can you take the phone-in orders? I need you to turn on the tape recorder each time the phone rings, and repeat the customer's name and order, so that you don't have to worry about writing it all down.'

'Got it.' Grandma slipped into the office and Lydia headed out front. The clamor was exactly what Lydia had hoped for, and more.

Lydia took a moment to observe the shop activity before diving into the melee. Customers were jammed inside, reminding her of the meat she'd stuffed into sausage casings last night. Everyone seemed to speak at once and it was impossible to discern any individual conversations. The atmosphere was buoyant no matter that many were dressed in more subdued hues, traditional for the solemnity of Good Friday. Many were on their way to or from church, no doubt, and saving their spring outfits for Sunday Mass and the myriad family celebrations afterward.

Johnny sported dark rings under his eyes but he handled the onslaught with aplomb, belying any fatigue he might have. His easy smile and youthful demeanor had a calming effect upon the mostly female crowd. Vi was on the far end of the case, engaged in what looked like a confidential discussion with the single male customer in sight.

Figures. Vi was nothing if not a magnet to anything male. A beautiful woman was a draw no matter her age, and Vi was no exception. She may have sworn off men since she tragically lost Uncle Ray – and face it, they had all lost the most lovable man in their family when he passed – but that didn't stop men being drawn to her. And she hadn't honored her oath of permanent singledom as she'd married twice since, both ending in divorce.

'One-seventeen!'

She called out the number indicated on the ticket counter and stepped next to Johnny.

'Here!' A wide woman sporting a clear plastic scarf on her even wider hairdo – shellacked with the kind of hairspray that only came out of an aerosol can and indestructible for at least a week – waved a tiny pink ticket over her head. 'I'm one-seventeen.'

'What can I get for you?' Lydia asked, taking the ticket and throwing it in the nearby trash bin.

'Order for Majewski. I called in last week, for four pounds fresh, two smoked, and a ham, bone-in. Throw in one of those butter lambs, will you? And are those your angel wing cookies? I'll take a box.'

Lydia put aside the butter and chrusciki, then went to the

back and found Mrs Majewski's order in the refrigerator and noted that approximately half of the pre-orders were gone already.

The telltale clacking of her kitten heels on the concrete slab floor announced Vi's presence.

'Lydia! I didn't see you come in.' Vi's voice rasped through the chill air.

'Oh, hey, Vi.' Lydia straightened from where she'd found the heavy paper bag of meat and faced her beloved uncle's widow. 'You were busy with a customer. I didn't have time to interrupt.' Lydia didn't call Vi 'Aunt' in the shop and the moniker seemed to have faded from her lexicon once she became a teenager. Add in that Vi had become cooler, more distant, since Lydia took over the shop, but she was helping Lydia focus on the store when all she wanted to do was run away from the murder investigation.

'Well, I couldn't not listen to him, Lydia, even on a busy day like today. Mr Wojak is a dear old man who just wants to see his boy – you know him, Robbie, he's my age – married off. It won't be to me, though!' Vi's dedication to never remarrying was admirable. Lydia didn't think she'd want to be alone like Vi for the rest of her life if given the choice. Of course, she'd thrown away her shot at happiness, hadn't she?

'Well, back to your question on the phone, yes, we've been busy! I'm so glad I was here a little earlier than usual. Johnny would never have been able to handle this on his own, I tell you.' Vi sighed and her expression grew wistful, her bright lipstick highlighting the purse of her lips.

Uh oh. Vi was about to wax poetic.

'It's times like these that I can't help but wonder, Lydia dear. If only Ray had taken over this shop like his father intended, he and Victor would have put Cheektowaga on the map! And now your poor pop might never work here again.'

It was nice that she included Pop.

'He'll be back, Vi. Don't worry. In the meantime, thank goodness we have you, right?'

Lydia's stomach churned. She was going to have to go to confession for this whether she fired Vi next week or not. If she were the type to go to confession, that is. Maybe she needed to start paying better attention to the faith she'd been handed when baptized in the elaborate satin and lacy baby gown passed down from Grandma's side. Would better thoughts about the people who annoyed her prevent them from being murdered, though?

'Wait a minute, honey. Where on earth were you, exactly?' Vi's dark brown eyes contrasted with the icy blue eyeshadow caked on her lids, made more dramatic as her eyes narrowed. 'Is everything OK?'

'No, not really, but there's no time to worry about it right now. Not with all those customers standing in line outside.' She needed time to process the morning's events, to decide her next steps, before everyone found out about Louie.

'Oh, they'll wait, honey. Are you kidding me? People can't do Easter without kielbasa. Now, let me find Mr Wojak's order . . .' Vi ran her fingers over each bag on the lowest shelf. Her long acrylic nails – Teri was right – were the usual shade of mauve.

'The Ws are on the back wall.' Lydia gritted her teeth to keep from snapping. The morning was catching up to her.

'Thanks, hon.' Vi grabbed the brown paper bag and scurried out of the cold room, shivering as she went.

'Hon?' Lydia spoke aloud to herself and the kielbasa pre-orders. First Louie last night, and now Vi this morning, both referring to her as bee shit. No one but Grandma regularly called her 'honey.' Grandma usually said 'honey bunny' or 'honey child,' which was OK and most welcome – from her grandmother. It was the patronizing connotation from people she wasn't as close to that bothered her. She sighed. Chances were that everything was going to bother her today. The image of Louie's dead body burned into her eyeballs being one.

Johnny walked in, and he somehow must have sensed her disconcertment as his eyes were full of empathy.

'Rough morning?'

'Why do you ask?' She tried to smile, unsuccessfully.

He shrugged, shifted on his feet. She waited for the inevitable squeak of the rubber soles of his sneakers against the hard floor. Chirping footfalls were synonymous with Johnny, in her mind. At the unexpected silence, she looked down and saw that Johnny wasn't wearing his usual footwear. Instead, he'd dressed like every other Buffalonian at Easter and worn black snowboots, the kind with the metal clasps that rusted if you didn't wipe them dry after each use.

'You're never late, Lydia. And you seem . . . I don't know . . . upset.' Johnny didn't notice her inspection of his footwear, and his disconcerting stare unnerved her.

What was it that was bothering her? Lydia shook her head to clear it. She was letting everything get to her.

Well, duh, you've had a shock. She squared her shoulders. No matter what she had to get through business hours.

'Well, yes, it has been a long day and it's barely noon. But it'll get better.' She didn't want to risk slipping the news about Louie yet. 'Whose order are you looking for?'

'Lewandowski. I see it.' Johnny reached for a large package. But not before he gave her a long look, as if he knew she had bigger things on her mind.

As if he *knew*.

There was no way Johnny knew the first thing about what had transpired in the family smoker overnight, though. Paranoia was a by-product of her scare, was all.

Lydia then fell into the day's work as if she'd never found a dead Louie that morning.

EIGHT

t took another six hours, but finally, at precisely six p.m., Lydia locked the shop front door, turned the sign around to 'closed,' and tugged the chain on the Wienewski's Wieners & Meats glowing neon sign.

She thanked Johnny profusely for the extra-long day he'd put in, and Teri, who'd come in after her exams. Vi had left as soon as Teri showed up, hours earlier.

Johnny left, leaving Lydia alone with Teri for the first time since . . . since before she'd found Louie.

'Teri, we need to talk.' Lydia had to make sure Teri had her story straight.

'Can it wait? I'm so tired and we still have to stop by the tavern to get the fish frys for tonight. You know how Mom is.' Teri wasn't whining but it was close enough to make Lydia's irritation stir.

'I do, and we still have a few minutes.' Mom called in the order for five fish frys every Friday night at exactly five forty-five, for a six-fifteen pickup, whether it was Lent or not. The Buffalo staple was served by any self-respecting restaurant and even pizza parlors. The fancier places gave a choice of broiled fish, too, and baked potatoes in lieu of French fries. One scoop each of coleslaw and potato salad, a roll and butter, and plenty of tartar sauce in small plastic cups completed the meal. Lydia and Teri were going to stop by O'Callaghan's to get theirs on the way home. It was only half a block out of the way.

'Did you go home after school, before you came back here?' Lydia asked.

'No, how could I have? I scarfed down two donuts when I got here, and had a quick bologna sandwich in between filling orders.' The dark circles under Teri's eyes seemed to have darkened several more shades since the morning.

'Thank you for that. Listen, there's been a bit of bad news today I need to tell you about before you go back home.'

'Oh, my God, not Pop again? Grandma? Mom?' The words ran out of Teri's mouth like wieners off the sausage filler.

'No, no, everyone's OK. Well, everyone we care about, anyway.' Lydia winced. She cared that Louie had been killed, that some awful person thought it was OK to murder him like that. He'd been at her baptism, as he'd said, for heaven's sake. But her feelings toward Louie had never been warm or loving. Not since she'd become an adult and observed his true nature, anyhow.

'You better tell me what's going on or I swear, I'll f—'

'OK, OK, calm down!' Lydia cut her off before the f-word echoed about the shop. The last time she'd let out a stream of blue, Grandma had been here and had threatened to 'spank your f-ing *dupa*' if Teri ever swore like that again. Dupa being Grandma's favorite word for 'behind.' Grandma's father had been a Romano, but she was quick to remind the family that while she wasn't as Polish as they were, her mother had been one hundred percent Polish. There were other Polish swear words Grandma would let fly when she was particularly harried.

'Teri, it's about Louie. Louie McDaniel. He's dead.'

Teri's head tilted. 'The meat man?'

'Yes.'

'Huh.' The worry lines she'd sported all day eased, and her expression grew more thoughtful. 'Well, I'm sorry to hear that. I know he screwed Pop with that bad pork but he was always nice to me. Slipped me tens whenever he saw me, you know. Said he was making up for being a bad uncle. But he wasn't really related to us, was he?' Teri's smile was sad, small. 'Although I suppose it's not a surprise, since he looks, I mean looked, like a walking heart attack.'

'That's just it, Teri.' Lydia reached out and grasped her kid sister's hand. Teri tried to pull it back but then at Lydia's firm grip relented. 'Louie didn't have a heart attack. He was killed. Murdered.'

'Oh my f— Goodness. That's just awful. Was it when he was picking up his accounts?' Even Teri knew how tenacious Louie had been about collecting his due. Trichinosis or not.

'No. He was stabbed. In the neck. And I found him in our backyard smoker.'

Teri's eyes widened. 'Are you kidding me? Our kielbasa house? Where we played hide-and-seek? Where Stashu likes to sniff for old kielbasa bits?'

'Yes.' Lydia had forgotten about Stashu's habit of searching for scraps. If he'd found Louie before her, wouldn't he have alerted the family?

'When did you find him?' Teri's curiosity shook her from her musings.

'After I left you and Johnny here and went to get the extra kielbasa. I didn't see him right away. He was . . . a little further back in the smoker.' Where someone had probably intended him to be hidden much longer than a few hours, she realized.

Teri blanched, looked at the almost empty meat case. '*Ew.* You didn't sell any of it, did you? I mean, I won't say anything if you did but it's gross, is all. Cursed meat.'

'No, of course I didn't. And while I'm sad that Louie died like that, that's not the worst part.' It actually felt good to air the day's events with Teri. She was still a kid, but other than Grandma, Teri was the only person Lydia could be herself around. Mostly, that is. When she didn't feel compelled to play mother hen to Teri's immature impulses. Maybe this is why Grandma encouraged her to stop mothering Teri – so that they could rely on one another more as loving sisters than vying siblings. As friends.

'What's the worse news, Lydia? You can tell me.'

'He had the sausage pricker stuck in his jugular.'

'Wait – you mean Great-Grandpa Wienewski's pricker? Our family pricker? Or one of the cheaper, plastic-handled ones?'

'It was the Wienewski pricker, Teri. The murder, it was . . . it was made to look like I, or one of us, did it.' She wanted to protect Teri from the harsh truth as much as she wanted her to get what she'd experienced and was thinking deep down off her chest.

'That's crazy. Who would try to frame any of us?' Teri looked around the butcher shop. Through her gaze, Lydia saw

the paint peeling near the ceiling that leaked after last year's
ice storm, the battered floorboards, the linoleum flooring that
had been bleached from its original shade – of caramel? Nut
brown? – to a sickly yellow. 'We're barely scraping by, Lydia.
We don't have anything for anyone to take from us. And who
have we ever hurt or offended enough to make them try to
pin a murder on us?'

'I hear you, Teri, and I agree. But . . .' Lydia shook her
head. 'The police go on evidence. And right now it all points
to a Wienewski doing the deed. But don't worry, I'm going
to figure it out. I won't let this hurt us, or the shop.'

'Did you ask Stanley to help us?'

'No, why would I do that? We're not together anymore,
Teri. You know that. Besides, he's not a lawyer, not yet
anyways.' The Cheektowaga slang she'd prided herself on
discarding when she moved to Ottawa slipped back into her
dialogue as easy as putting on her favorite terrycloth seafoam
scuff slippers.

'What I know is that his rebound fiancée fling didn't work
out, and he's started making deliveries here again, even though
he's in law school.' Teri clamped down on the Stanley
bone. 'He wouldn't come by if he didn't want to see more
of you. He disappeared after you left and showed up only
when you moved back.'

'He's always worked for his dad – it's how he's paying his
tuition. And they've always supplied our shop with dairy
supplies.'

'Listen to me, sister. He didn't make any deliveries here
after you left. Pop would stop by their warehouse and get the
inventory, or send me.'

'Huh.' Lydia hadn't known that.

'I'm telling you, he still has the hots for you.' Teri smiled
and nodded as if she was an old sage and not all of eighteen
years old.

'Whatever.' Lydia wanted to be a cool older sister to Teri,
but her baby sister was still too starry-eyed when it came to
the male species. 'Heads-up, now. It's going to be hard,
but the police are going to question you and it's important
you try to stay calm.'

'You mean don't act like I did it.' Teri's chin jutted out.

'Well, yes. I'm a little surprised they haven't already interviewed you, frankly.'

'Why?' Teri's over-plucked brows tried to knit together.

'The police think Louie died in our smoker between midnight and five this morning. You'll need to verify that you came in at two-thirty and went straight to bed. Don't worry, both Grandma and I heard Dave's engine then. We're your alibis. And Mom and Pop heard you come in, too, I'm sure.'

Teri paled. 'Well, yes, I came in at two-thirty, when Dave dropped me off. And Stashu barked – you know how he does when it's one of us. One of those half-assed ruffs that wouldn't scare a flea away.'

Lydia laughed, surprised that she still had the capability after all that the day had yielded. 'Yes, I do know that particular bark. The little brat is too lazy to leave Mom and Pop's bed.'

'Yeah.' Teri seemed distracted as she started biting her nails in earnest. Lydia gently removed Teri's hand from her mouth.

'You don't have anything to worry about, sis. You'll tell the truth and that will be that.' Unlike for Lydia and Grandma. They had each other as alibis, which meant no alibi since they lived in the same flat. And it wasn't lost on Lydia that Grandma wouldn't hesitate to do whatever it took to protect her family. But would she actually murder Louie for being a terrible meat source?

Two large tears fell down Teri's cheek as she let out a sob. Lydia's stomach plummeted.

'What is it?' Why was Teri so upset about giving a report to the police, other than the shock of the murder? Or was this more about being too young to deal with the emotional fallout?

'That's not the whole truth, Lydia.' Teri sniffled. 'Oh, I didn't want anyone to know.' Her tear-streaked face struck a primal cord in Lydia's heart. Cold, brutal fear gripped her lungs, making it hard to breathe. First she'd suspected Grandma – but had she overlooked the possibility her sister or her sister's boyfriend could be a killer?

'Teri, what? What did you do?' Her throat ached.

'I did come in at two-thirty.' Teri nodded. 'That part is accurate.'

'Right. And Stashu barked.' Lydia sucked in a deep breath, expelled it.

'Yes. But then he barked again, around three-thirty.' Teri looked away.

'OK. That's good. You can tell that to the police, they need to know. Stashu may have heard the killer!' *Phew.* It wasn't Teri.

'No, no, Stashu didn't hear a killer. He heard me. I woke him up when I left the house again. To . . . meet someone.'

'Wait, what? You went out again? With Dave?' Lydia had done her share of sneaking out, so Teri doing the same wasn't odd. But did she have to pick the night Louie was murdered in their backyard to do it?

Teri shook her head. 'No, not with Dave. He dropped me off, yes, after we were at Fast Eddie's.' She refered to a large warehouse that had been converted into a popular dance hangout. 'I broke up with him.'

Lydia sat stock-still, praying the thoughts Teri's words triggered weren't showing in her expression. It was about time that Teri got rid of Dave – he was too rough around the edges for her baby sister. But Lydia wasn't concerned about Dave or the demise of Teri and Dave. Had her sister, her sweet, innocent baby sibling, had a close shave with a murderer?

'Teri, whatever you saw, no matter how awful, it's OK. We'll get through this. Keep talking, honey.' She patted Teri's hand, something that soothed her as a toddler.

'Calm down, Lydia. I'm not having a nervous breakdown or anything.' Teri squirmed on the stool. 'It's just that this is personal. Private.'

'I found a dead – no, make that murdered – body in our yard this morning, Teri. Nothing that you did last night or this morning is private anymore. If you don't want to tell me, I hope you'll be able to tell the cops whatever you saw. You don't want them looking at you funny. As though you're a suspect.' Lydia couldn't help herself, but didn't regret blurting out the truth. Better Teri accepted the kind of trouble she was dealing with here, with Lydia, than screwing up her statement to Ned or Nowicki in the near future because she was embarrassed or ashamed about something.

'I didn't see anything awful. Oh my God, you think I saw Louie get murdered! No, it wasn't that.' Teri's lips began to tremble. 'It wasn't anything bad, but you might think I was bad.'

Lydia's gut ached from allowing her emotions over Teri's antics to jerk it around. She gritted her teeth to hang onto the last thread of her patience. 'What is it, Teri? You're acting guilty and, in case you don't realize it, it's not a good look to have in this situation.'

Teri offered a meager smile. 'That'd be funny if we weren't in a shit ton of trouble, you know?'

'Keep talking.'

'Fine.' Teri let out a dramatic sigh. 'I didn't kill Louie, Lydia. I didn't see anything strange, either. I wasn't looking in the backyard, I was headed out.'

'I know you didn't do it, silly.' Well, not for all but a nano-second. 'You're my sister. You take spiders outside in tissues instead of smooshing them. There's no way you'd ever kill someone.' At least not Louie. Teri had no reason to be angry at the man; Lydia kept the business part of their family woes from Teri as much as she could. You were only a kid once.

'I went back out at three-thirty, like I said, to meet someone. I got back in just after five or so.'

'Who did you meet, and where, Teri?' Lydia really didn't want to know but had to. This was bigger than all of them. The possibility that Teri could have come face-to-face with a murderer made her neck tighten in a painful spasm.

'I went out through my window. That's when Stashu gave out a little bark again, but then he must have gone back to sleep. Johnny lifted me down. I did what I wanted to do, Lydia.' Teri crossed her skinny arms in front of her generous breasts. Both she and Lydia had inherited Grandma Mary's large bra cup size. Their mother was 'flat as a pancake' as she often joked.

Lydia silently congratulated herself for not reacting, for sitting quietly and keeping a neutral expression on her face as her sister revealed her more devious side.

I'm not mothering. I'm not mothering.

'Your eyebrow's twitching, Lydia. You think I'm troubled.'

OK, maybe her expression wasn't as neutral as she'd hoped.
'I'm not your mother.' Lydia admitted to herself that she
sure felt like a mother hen to Teri. What was her sister thinking,
getting together with Johnny when Dave was barely out of the
picture? 'This is about a murder investigation, not your social
life. How long did you stay outside with Johnny?'

'Um, uh, we, ah, you know . . .' Teri wound her hair around
her finger, looked everywhere but at Lydia.

'Just spit it out, Teri.'

'We weren't outside. We went to his car. Well, his dad's
station wagon. And he had the radio on, and it played our
song, and, oh, Lydia, we made love! I'm not a virgin anymore!'

Lydia stilled, sucked in another deep breath. Her baby sister
wasn't a baby any longer. Bittersweet tears threatened as happiness for Teri's evolution warred with sadness over how quickly
she'd gone from being a tiny tot to a disgruntled junior high
schooler to the woman in front of her now. She gulped.

Stay cool. Be a big sister, not a mother.

'OK, well, I'm happy for you.' And she was. Except . . .

'Before you have a fit, yes, we were careful. I'm not a baby,
Lydia. I know about birth control.'

'Obviously, OK, good. We sure don't need a baby Wienewski
right now, that's for sure.'

Teri shook her head. 'We have nothing to worry about. I'm
on the pill and Johnny had a rubber.'

Lydia nodded as if she heard first-time sex confessions on
the regular. Boy, she wished Mom was having this conversation with Teri instead of her, but nothing else in their family
was going as anyone ever expected, so why should Teri's love
life? And while Mom had been good about giving them 'the
talk' as she called it, Amelia Wienewski still gave off an air
of disapproval when it came to premarital sex. Sure, she
realized that Lydia and their older brother Ted weren't virgins,
but never made reference to her children's love lives, either.
Except to mention every now and then that she'd like a
grandchild sometime this century. Pop's stroke had put the
kibosh on any talk about their family's future, though. Except
for hopeful comments about the store coming back to life
under Lydia's management.

Keep your eyes on the prize. She had to solve this murder before it ruined business.

'Where, um, did you and Johnny go, and when did you get back home?'

'Oh, we didn't go anywhere. We were on the street. Parked.' Teri blinked, probably confused that she hadn't made this clear.

'In front of our house?' Lydia couldn't keep her tone neutral on this one. Really, did Teri and Johnny have to consummate their adolescent lust in the street? What if a lunatic had seen . . . She stopped her thought train. A killer had been about while Teri and Johnny were oblivious to the danger.

'Yes. Like I said, I went back inside around five or so.'

After Lydia left for the shop, but within the timeframe Louie had died. They'd both been up and about in the time window the police thought Louie had breathed his last.

Teri shuddered. 'But I can't tell the police any of this, Lydia. I'll die of embarrassment!'

'You have to tell them everything. Well, not the virginity or sex part. You can say you were making out. That's nothing they haven't heard before. They need to know you and Johnny were there and didn't notice anything. Unless you did. Did you hear or see anything?'

Teri's woebegone countenance morphed to sarcastic in two blinks. 'Really, Lydia? We were in passion's embrace, for God's sake. I didn't notice anything except Johnny, and the way we moved together . . .' To her credit, Teri stopped before she said anything that would make either of them cringe. Or throw up.

'OK, OK. We'll figure out what you can say. Give me a minute to think.' Lydia didn't want to alarm Teri, but was there a chance Johnny had done more last night than awaken her younger sister to the wonders of good sex? She couldn't shake the mental snapshot of his boots this morning . . . or of the sneaker imprints in the snow outside the smoke shed.

Rap rap. The chain holding the open/closed sign rattled against the front door's window from the determined knocks.

Lydia and Teri both startled, and Lydia looked to the front entrance. Detective Harry Nowicki stood in the darkened threshold, his stern face a beacon of dread under his fedora.

'Who the hell is that? We're done for the day.' Teri looked between the door and Lydia. 'Don't open it! I'll call the cops.' Teri stood and turned toward the wall telephone.

'It's all right, it's Detective Nowicki, the man investigating Louie's murder. And please, Teri, tone it down with the swear words, will you?' Lydia held her finger up so that Nowicki saw it, indicating she'd open the door in a second. She grasped Teri's forearm. 'Remember what we talked about. Just tell him the truth, and know you're good. It'll all work out.' If only she believed it.

Teri nodded. 'OK. Got it.'

Satisfied that Teri was on steady ground, Lydia walked to the door and unlocked it.

'Good evening, Lydia.'

'Detective.'

He looked past her to Teri. 'Are you Teri Wienewski?'

'Yes.'

'I have some questions for you, young lady.'

Lydia knew what Teri was going to say but it didn't stop her insides from doing anxiety gymnastics. Not when it sounded as though Nowicki already knew the answers to his own questions.

'Before you talk to my sister, can I talk to you privately, Detective?'

No need to upset Teri with any of this, not until her hunch solved the case. Telling Nowicki her footprint theory should prove that she and Grandma, and her family, were in the clear. None of them wore the kind of sneakers that Johnny did.

NINE

'Pass me the ketchup, will you, Lydia?' Mom asked from her spot next to Pop as she held out her hand. Lydia grabbed the slim glass bottle and handed it to her, noticing that Mom's meal was as yet untouched. As usual, Mom had made sure Pop and everyone else was all settled and had what they needed before she took care of herself. Lydia tried to ignore the tugs of worry on her conscience as she took in her mother's appearance. A once stunning and still beautiful woman, the stress of Dad's health and the family checkbook woes reflected in every new horizontal line on her forehead, the open and closed parentheses on either side of her full lips, the slight stoop of her shoulders. Another sign of Mom's exhaustion was that she'd remained silent as the rest of the family compared notes about the hardest day they'd ever been through, second only to Pop's stroke day last Christmas.

'What do you think, Mom?' Lydia asked, trying to turn their conversation back to Louie. Amelia Wienewski was nothing if not wise and naturally observant. Lydia wondered if her mother had seen or heard things she hadn't brought up, or only mentioned to Nowicki when he questioned her in private.

'What do I think about what?' Her mother's eyes filled with dread and Lydia realized her mistake. Mom thought Lydia was going to ask a question about the murder, and she was not interested in regurgitating those facts over her meal.

'Your . . . your fish fry.' Nice save!

'The fries are ruined.' Teri sniffed. After Lydia had relayed her sneaker insight to Nowicki – who'd not batted an eye at the revelation – Teri had been brave and told Nowicki everything, with Lydia at her side. It had felt like hours but had only delayed their exit from the store by another half hour. It'd been enough time, however, to make the fish fries soggy as hell.

'I was asking Mom a question, Teri.'

'It's OK, girls. None of us could have expected you'd be held up by the detective.' Mom fiddled with her drooping fries. 'Today's a wash, and it's no one's fault. Except for whoever . . .' She contemplated her macaroni salad and took a forkful.

'I think dinner's delicious.' Pop spoke.

'You're happy you can feed yourself again, aren't you, Vic?' Mom dredged up a weary smile for Pop.

'Damn straight.' Pop shoved another fry into his mouth. He picked up his knife and slowly, deliberately, buttered the large slice of rye bread served atop the boxed meal.

'I don't know, Lydia. What has been going on with Louie that someone would want to frame you or Mary, maybe any of us, for his murder?' Mom asked, revealing the source of her sour mood. Mom wasn't as shook by Louie's sudden demise as she was by her family finding themselves in law enforcement crosshairs.

Shame made Lydia squirm. She hadn't been giving her mother enough credit. Surprise deaths weren't new to Mom, or Pop, as they had grown up in an era where family and friends dropped dead with little to no warning, be it a heart attack or sudden onslaught of a bad flu. Add in the car crashes from driving home after tying one on at the local gin mill, and death was a familiar partner in the Wienewski dance of life.

'I haven't done a thing to Louie or anyone he deals with for our meat.' Lydia defended herself against Mom's misconception. 'It's more about what he did to us. He almost ran Pop out of business last Easter with that bad pork!'

'He's a longtime business colleague, Lydia. You can't erase that fact.' Mom didn't have a thing to do with the business, except when she had concerns, like now. Usually Mom found enough to do with running her side hustle. Mom cleaned houses for a few families in Amherst, an affluent Buffalo suburb. Her long-term clientele of two doctors and one high school teacher had paid for all three siblings' braces, as well as many surprise house expenses through the years. Broken pipes, a leaking roof, and a new furnace came to mind.

'You told me you wanted to cut ties with Louie, find a new

meat source. Did Louie know you were going to let him go?'
Pop spoke as he chewed his food.

'No, Pop. He had no clue what I was planning.' Nonetheless
she racked her brain for any missteps. She'd only discussed
her business plans with Pop. No one had overheard those
conversations, had they? 'Plus Louie's the one who's dead. If
he knew I was going to let him go, wouldn't he have come
after me?'

'Now you're saying that Louie had the potential in his soul
to kill *you*? You're just running things until Pop goes back to
work. I don't see either you or Pop being targeted by a
murderer.' Teri snorted. 'This is so messed up.'

'At this point it doesn't matter who would go after who,'
Pop said. 'Someone sure wanted it to look like one of us did
it, though. You're doing a good job with the shop, Lydia, and
so are you, Teri. I don't disagree with you about Louie's quirks,
but sometimes . . .' Pop trailed off and she didn't think it was
from how tired speaking often made him.

'What, Pop? You would have trusted him and watched your
customers get sick again? At least we don't have to worry
about that now.' Her words came out with such vitriol that
they shocked Lydia as much as her family. Ever since she'd
found Louie, saw their family antique pricker piercing his
jugular, she'd lost any sense of manners. Needing to be the
good girl, the responsible older sister, the woman in charge
of the shop, all took a backseat to survival.

There was no way Lydia could have imagined running the
shop or opening a café and bakery before her experience in
Ottawa. Madame Delphine's firehouse of a crappy attitude
toward her had stung so badly, coming from the woman she'd
idolized since reading a profile on North America's premier
pastry chef in *Gastronomy* magazine. The yellowed article was
still tucked away in her dog-eared copy of *Joy of Cooking*. It
hadn't taken her long to figure out that what she was searching
for – validation that she could run her own café and bakery,
serving her custom recipes – wasn't something Madame
Delphine or any fancy cooking school could give her. It had
to come from within. She'd been born to bake, born to cook.
Her newfound confidence, that she'd nurtured carefully since

leaving pastry school, had buoyed her through taking the steps to open her own restaurant by this coming summer.

But since discovering Louie's corpse, it was as though she'd gone backwards and lost whatever self-esteem she'd gained, as if she was operating from some primal level of her being. She felt stalked, accused. And the absolute worst – vulnerable.

Time to channel her own inner Angie Dickinson.

Lydia refused to be anybody's prey. She wasn't going to sit back and watch her family fall victim to a killer's twisted attempt to avoid capture, either.

'Pop, we've got to put ourselves first here.'

'That's enough, Lydia.' Mom sounded like the mom of her youth, after Lydia and Ted had beaten the crap out of each other over a toy – most often an irrelevant temporary tattoo – at the bottom of the Cracker Jack box. By the time Teri came along they'd each been given their own box as a treat. It didn't hurt that the boxes came packaged in sets of three, connected by a long length of sticky red tape.

'Lydia's on to something here. Whoever snuffed out Louie has a helluva resentment against the Wienewskis. Otherwise, why go to all that effort of killing him in the smoker with your weapon?' Grandma's support was unwavering but her truthful observation appeared to shake up everyone at the table.

'A sausage pricker isn't a weapon.' Pop said what Lydia hadn't been able to articulate all day.

'Exactly,' she replied. 'I mean, I never thought it was strong enough to poke through a neck like that, you know?' She looked at Grandma, at Pop.

'Why can't we let the police do their job?' Mom's exasperation made her voice reedy. 'They're the experts. I say we stick to sausage-making.'

'Yeah, Mom's right. Don't you have to get going, too, Lydia?' Teri's grousing was something Lydia usually brushed off without thought. But Teri knew how to pull on her last nerve.

'You're just sore, Teri.' Lydia shot Teri her best older sister glare. She wasn't above bribing Teri, or at least allowing her to believe she'd tattle about her rendezvous with Johnny, to get what she needed.

'Takes one to know one.' Teri's immature response was so ludicrous that after locking glares, they cracked up into a fit of laughter.

'Girls!' Mom tried for stern impatience but the tiniest of smiles peeked out from her worry lines. Sibling squabble territory was familiar to the point of being comforting.

'We're fine, Mom. It will all work out. We just have to get through the investigation.' Lydia knew that it was pointless to bring her parents into her plan to find the killer. Mom would only worry and Dad might suffer a setback, neither an option as far as she was concerned.

'Lydia's right. We're all going to be just fine,' Grandma said. 'It's time for a toast to Louie, then. We can't be disrespectful to the dead.' She got up and went to the tiny cupboard over the refrigerator. Taking the step stool from its place against the wall, she set it up and climbed to reach around the family's sacred ceramic cookie jar and its matching pieces. Sugar bowl, creamer, salt and pepper shakers, all shaped like a wide-bottom bell and painted as a Polish country girl wearing a white coat with a bright red hood, was pushed aside. Peering into the family liquor cabinet, Grandma withdrew an aged bottle of brandy. Lydia bit back a smile. It looked like the last time that particular bottle of brandy had seen the light of day was at least two if not three Christmases ago. Before she'd left for pastry school, well before Pop's stroke.

'Who's up for a shot?' Grandma asked, her brow raised in a challenging arc.

'No, no, no!' Amelia spoke harshly to her mother-in-law. 'Mary, you know Vic can't have booze. He's on too many meds as it is.'

'Victor's a grown man and can speak for himself. A tiny sip won't give him another stroke, if that's what you're thinking. It's the fatty cuts of meat that clog arteries, after all.' Grandma's mouth, wiped clean of her orange lipstick by the meal, set in a determined line. 'Life is short. We need to have some fun while we're all still here to do it.'

'I agree,' Teri said.

Lydia looked from Grandma to Mom, her teeth worrying

the inside of her cheek. 'Mom's right, Grandma. Dad shouldn't have one, but I'll do a toast with you.'

'Give me one!' Pop slammed his hand on the table, making it shake. Still on her lap, Stashu sprang up, shoved his head above the table, and went off like the fire station siren at noon, yipping and howling as though there was an intruder. His tiny feet and nails dug into her thighs as his entire body shook. He refused Lydia's admonition to *shhh*.

'Get that mutt away from the table!' Mom exclaimed. Lydia tensed. Mom only called Stashu a mutt when she was beyond breaking point.

Lydia's heart jumped into overdrive. Could Mom have gotten to a breaking point with all the trouble Louie had caused the family business? Was her mother a killer?

Naw. If someone had it in them to kill, it was definitely Grandma. And she had stayed behind after Lydia left for the shop. Grandma would never try to frame her own family with the sausage pricker, would she?

Stop it. Lydia's mind was tracking the wrong line of inquiry. Isn't that what the trial lawyers on TV said? Besides, the footprint didn't match anyone's size – or shoe type. Except, possibly, for Johnny. But did Johnny really have it in him to kill?

Lydia hated the way the murder made her suspect her own family of such an evil action.

'Come on, you little menace.' Lydia stood, holding Stashu in her arms. 'I'll take him in the yard for a bit.'

'You can't go back there yet, Lydia. Harry asked us to stay out of the yard until he gives the OK,' Grandma admonished.

'OK, then. I'll take him out front and walk him up the street for a bit.'

Stashu lay in her arms, immediately silent, his huge eyes imploring. As if he knew he'd gone overboard yet still was going to get a treat. The tiny dog was no dummy. He knew how to act apologetically.

'Hang on, Lydia. Go get the shot glasses from the dining room, will you?' Grandma asked.

Lydia complied and returned with the maroon hand-cut

crystal pieces her parents received as wedding gifts from the Wienewski side.

Grandma doled out the liquor and held up her glass. The liquid shimmered under the light from the smoked glass fixture above the table.

'To Louie . . . What was his last name, again, honey?' She looked at Lydia.

'McDaniel.'

'To Louie McDaniel. May God rest his soul.'

'To Louie.' Lydia and Teri concurred, while Mom and Pop silently held their glasses up. Mom put hers back down without a sip and Pop sloshed his over his mouth, much of it dribbling onto the felt-back vinyl tablecloth printed with tulips and gold chicks. Mom snatched her napkin up and wiped Dad's face. Dad pushed her hand away.

'Enough, Amelia. Leave it.' He meant more than the brandy stains on his shirt.

'It's bad luck to not at least have a sip, Amelia,' Grandma observed.

'Yeah, well, that man's brought nothing but bad luck to us already. Whether I drink that godawful swill or not won't change a thing.' Mom stood up. 'But it doesn't mean I can't make my own toast.' She went to the refrigerator and pulled out the plastic bottle of tonic water she kept 'for my leg aches.' In swift motions too practiced to be rare, she grabbed a different bottle from the high cabinet and poured herself a gin and tonic. Using the handle of her fork as a mixer, she swirled her cocktail, then took a sip.

'Ahh. Now, that's what I call a proper send-off. Rest in peace, Louie.'

'I'm going to w-a-l-k the d-o-g.' Lydia was careful to spell out the words – she didn't need Stashu wriggling in anticipation of his outing before she got the leash clipped onto his collar. Now that peace had been restored Lydia bolted for the door, before anyone got upset again.

Lydia didn't care how they sent Louie off. All she wanted was to figure out who had killed him. Before the killer struck again.

TEN

To Lydia's dismay her anxiety only ratcheted as she attempted to find freedom from the cloud of angst over her family's house.

Aftereffects of Louie's murder had rippled across her neighborhood, judging from the large group still loitering in front of their house despite the cold evening. She was smart enough to use the back door to sneak out and run through two backyards, over to their neighbor's driveway where she finally came out on the street, thus avoiding a run-in with either of the television camera crews and any random journalists from the *Courier Express* or the *Buffalo Evening News*. But she couldn't avoid the gawkers who stood in their driveways.

Lydia kept her chin high as she marched Stashu down the street. She offered a greeting to the people she knew and a quick nod and smile to those she was less acquainted with. Appearances were everything and she had no reason to behave any differently than usual – with a healthy helping of defiance sprinkled on top.

Once she turned off her street, she allowed her gaze to focus on Stashu. Large, fat snowflakes fell from the low clouds, and the dog did his business quickly. And then sat, refusing to move another inch, staring up at Lydia with his I'm-about-to-start-yipping expression.

'Come on, Stashu. Give me a break, boy.' Lydia shivered in her coat, determined to be strong. But after more shivers she bent over and picked up the dog, cradling him in her arms. 'You are such a baby. And I love you.' She kissed his head.

'How did the store do today, Lydia?' A deep male voice startled her, and she jerked herself upright, slapping her mittened hand over her mouth to stifle her scream.

Stanley stood in front of her, his unzipped parka revealing the navy blue lambswool sweater she knit him for Christmas three years ago.

'Sorry, Lyd. I didn't mean to scare you. Hey, little buddy.' He scratched Stashu's damp head. Stashu, always quick to growl at anyone who wasn't holding him, licked Stanley's fingers. *Traitor.* As if no time had passed since she'd left, since they'd broken it off, since he'd gotten engaged . . . *Don't you have a murder to solve?*

'Yeah. Um, the store did well, thanks.' Lydia sighed. 'I was afraid sales were going to bomb, after the events of the morning.' She assumed the entire street knew about Louie by now.

Stanley's eyes were pools of concern. 'I heard. About Louie, that is. The police came over to our house, spoke to Mom, then came to the office to question me and my dad.'

'Why would they—' *Oh.* Nowicki was asking what others thought about her family. Looking for motives. At least, that's what the cops did on TV.

Stanley shrugged. 'My mom said she told them that she heard your sister's boyfriend Dave's car sometime before three o'clock. But other than that, no one heard anything else.'

'Huh. Did . . . did Detective Nowicki question you?'

'No, I don't know who that is. Ned's the officer they sent.' Stanley had played Little League with Ned. 'Sometimes it's hard to see him as a cop and not the kid who used to grease his baseball.'

'Did he seem to think they have an idea of who did it?' Lydia didn't care about Ned's childhood pranks. Not today.

'Not from what I could tell. But you know Louie, he wasn't the friendliest guy except for when he wanted something from you. My father had a run-in with him last year, over our egg supplier, you know.'

'No, I didn't know that.' Lydia's breath caught in her throat. Was Stanley's father capable of murder?

Or worse – was Stanley?

She forced herself to breathe. Her heart immediately started pounding, racing to keep up with her thoughts.

'Why would you? You weren't here.' Stanley's tone wasn't accusatory but his words cut just the same. Guilt hit her, hard. Guilt over wasted time away, guilt over the money she'd so carefully saved for years, almost a decade, in fact, and then blown on tuition at the culinary school. She didn't even have a degree of completion to show for the expense. Her heart and her conscience ached at how the nest egg she once had could have helped the family shop now. If she'd been able to keep them out of the red, and let Louie go sooner, would he have still shown up dead in their smoker?

Lydia squared her shoulders. She needed to grow a thicker skin if she was going to figure out who killed Louie. And survive these close encounters with her ex. Maybe if she repeatedly reminded herself that Stanley was nothing but an 'ex,' it would go a long way in getting over the loss of their relationship.

But all hasn't been lost, has it? Not if they were able to have civil conversations with one another again, and not when her body betrayed her with its longing for Stanley's touch every time they spoke.

Still, she'd best keep her emotional distance here. Stanley had to be on her suspect list, as did his father. Her fingers itched to squeeze dough. She'd make a loaf of dark rye the next chance she got. Baking always helped her work out her troubles.

Murder was trouble, indeed.

'No, you're right, I wasn't here, I was in school. There's . . . there's a lot I've missed. When you say "run-in," what do you mean, exactly?' Had Stanley's father, Mr Gorski, gotten physical with Louie?

'Louie decided to switch suppliers without telling Dad. You know my dad, Lydia. He's no-nonsense. Just give it to him straight. If Dad finds out you've been lying to him, you're on his crap list. End of story.'

'Right.' A list she was certain she was on after supposedly breaking Stanley's heart. The last time she'd run into the Gorski patriarch had been at Mass, and he'd avoided eye contact. Thankfully Stanley was giving her these details because Mr Gorski wouldn't be as forthcoming.

'One of our most loyal customers – Kalinski Bakery, you know them – said their cakes weren't coming out good. Mrs Kalinski said the eggs were the only thing they could trace it to, and sure enough, the boxes were marked "extra-large" but they were medium-sized. Plus the yolks were a different shade of yellow. Dad was royally pissed off.'

'Cheaper feed is probably what made the eggs a different color.' Lydia knew eggs, too. Next to quality butter, they were key ingredients in her Polish baked goods.

Stanley nodded, placed his hands on his hips. She looked at the still-falling snow, the flakes on Stashu's eyelashes, the slushy sidewalk. Anywhere but at the man in front of her. When had Stanley become so masculine, so chiseled?

'Yeah, everything about Louie was cheap,' he observed.

'So what did your dad, um, do to him?' She held her breath.

Stanley's eyes narrowed, the way they used to when she really made him mad. Which almost always was about her not standing up for herself with her family, or doing too much for others. Stanley had always been her biggest champion. But now she saw him through the eyes of a woman who'd found a murdered body. One who believed that anyone – Stanley included – was capable of murder, given the right circumstances. She took a half-step back, hoping he didn't notice.

'"Do?" What the hell, Lydia? Are you asking if my father assaulted Louie? You've really let this get to you.'

'I'll be the judge of that, Stanley.' She jutted her chin.

'You've changed, Lydia.' He shook his head. 'I never thought you'd get cynical.'

His words cut but she shoved through her heart's turmoil. 'Answer my question, Stanley.'

Stanley didn't reply, his hands balled at his sides and his mouth turned into a sour line. He wasn't going to stalk off, was he? She had to know what had happened between Mr Gorski and Louie.

'Please, Stanley. I need to know.' He didn't hear that tiny tremor in her voice, did he? She shook inside her parka, in disbelief that she had to question the man she'd once – and maybe still – loved like this. Surely she hadn't loved a murderer? Or the son of a killer?

Stanley let out a heavy sigh. 'He didn't do anything to him, but they sure had words. Louie's lucky my dad didn't do more than cuss him out, believe me. It's a tough spot that Louie put my family's dairy business in, because for years my dad relied on Louie for the best quality and best priced eggs. Louie was reliable, until he wasn't.'

'A lot of people look for ways to cut corners,' Lydia said. Pop had said as much to her when they'd worked together in the shop.

'Tightening your belt during hard times is one thing. Cheating your most loyal customers the way he did both of our dads? I'd say he finally crossed the line with the wrong person. By that I mean whoever killed him.' Stanley's opinion of Louie was clear.

'I don't disagree with you about the cheating part. You know he sold that bad pork to Pop, and I felt like I could strangle him for that. Not that I would, of course.' She looked past Stanley's shoulder to where Mrs Snyder was standing at the end of her drive. Staring at them. Turning her head, she caught the Arkowskis' drapes falling shut. Who needed the local television news crews, or papers, with this neighborhood?

'Did you or your father ever report what Louie did? To either the police or to the Department of Health?'

Stanley let out a harsh laugh. 'Did your dad ever report Louie over the bad pork?'

They locked stares, and Lydia's blood chilled at the steel glint in Stanley's eyes. It wasn't like him to put blame back on her, or on anyone. She'd never seen him get so defensive, either.

'How about answering *me* this time, Lydia?' Stanley pressed.

She took a step closer to Stanley, keeping her voice low in acknowledgement of the nosy neighbors. 'No, of course we didn't report him.' It just wasn't done, reporting a family friend, no matter that they screwed you with business. Plus Pop always worried that he'd ruin all chances of getting any supplies if he angered any of his source connections. It was super old-school but Lydia had never questioned it. 'No matter what he did with his merchandise, Louie didn't deserve to die like that. People treat their pets better. He was left to rot with our sausage pricker in his throat.' The words slipped out before she remembered that it was important to keep details on the down-low, so that the killer could never be sure how the investigation was moving along. It prevented a crook from going on the lam, according to Grandma and reruns of *Police Woman* aka Angie Dickinson, with added validation from a recent *Charlie's Angels* episode. Now that Lydia had added Stanley and his father to the possible suspect list she had to improve her interview technique.

'What?' Stanley's dark brow rose. 'I thought he was shot. In fact, I'm positive that's what Ned said when he first came by. That Louie had been shot in the chest, in your shed. Ned never mentioned a sausage pricker.'

Shock shook off any reserve she'd mustered. 'What? First of all, Louie was in our smokehouse, not the tool shed. And he wasn't shot, not as far as I know. I'm the one who found him, and believe me, those tines were stuck deep into his neck. It was so gnarly. We'll never use it again, of course.' She held Stashu tighter, her shoulders hunching over him. The shivering creature was her only anchor to life before finding Louie. Well, besides Stanley.

'Ned never mentioned the sausage tool to me, Lydia.' He grasped her shoulder, gave her a reassuring squeeze. She swore it warmed her through her thick coat. 'Hey, I'm sorry I got defensive a moment ago. You know you can be an independent woman and still rely on a friend, don't you? I mean, you and I, there's a lot of water under our bridge, I get it. But it doesn't change how I feel about your family, or that we've been friends our whole lives. I'm on your side, Lydia.'

The intensity of emotion in Stanley's eyes made Lydia's heart pump with all the regret she'd been running from. This wasn't the time for her to bare her soul or try to figure out her own life. *My family needs me.*

She set Stashu down. 'Let's walk. There're too many eyes and ears around here.'

'Good idea,' he agreed. 'This weather is nuts, isn't it?'

'Tell it to Old Man Winter.'

Stanley matched his stride to hers, but they both were at Stashu's mercy. Competing thoughts battled for priority as Lydia's stomach churned with worry. She waited to speak until they were around the corner, walking alongside the cemetery. Away from the busybodies.

'I don't get what on earth was Ned trying to accomplish by

telling you that Louie had been shot. Why on earth would he lie like that to you? To any of us? He knows us. We're not unknown suspects, at least.' Was there information he thought he'd glean by suggesting that Louie had died from a gunshot instead of the meat tool?

'Um, well, I don't believe my dad or I are suspects, either. We have no reason to be.' Stanley politely stood to the side as she cleaned up Stashu's doo-doo with an empty bread bag. 'Honestly, Lydia, I don't think Ned made it up. Isn't it possible that you missed a gunshot wound? They're not always so obvious. Why don't you ask the detective in charge what they've found out so far?'

Lydia paused in her squat next to where Stashu did his business, frantically trying to make sense of this new information. Had Louie really been shot, not stabbed? That meant there had to be a gun somewhere. And it automatically cleared her family as they had never owned a gun in her entire lifetime. Except for her great-grandfather's antique hunting rifle that, as far as she knew, was still shoved away in an attic chest.

She stood, her composure regained. 'I'll have Grandma ask him. She went to school with him, and apparently they were once . . . friends.' She wasn't ready to admit that Grandma's past romantic life might have an effect on the investigation. Not aloud, at least. 'If what you're saying is right, I don't want to talk to Detective Nowicki, or Ned, or anyone else in uniform until I figure out what the heck is going on. I'm telling you, Stanley, from what I saw, the man was stabbed to death.' Doubt began to seep in through her belief, though. She stopped slushing through the messy precipitation and stood under a huge oak tree at the cemetery entrance gate. Stashu, intrigued by the scents on this unusual route, sniffed away at the ground.

'I believe you, Lydia. I do. But tell me something, how much blood was there?'

'Blood?' She flashed back to the awful sight of Louie's corpse, mentally skimmed over what she was certain was forever etched on her memory. 'There was a darker spot on his shirt, under his parka. It would have covered his chest, maybe his stomach. It was too dim to see it, to be honest. I thought it might be blood, you know, where the stab wounds dripped.' Her voice faltered.

'Did you notice any blood pooling around the body?' Stanley's eyes implored her to tell him everything.

'Ugh. Gross. No.' She stared at Stanley as her mind sifted through the awful details. She sighed. 'No, I didn't notice any blood. In fact, the smoker's floor was as clean as always, except for his body.' Why hadn't she thought of this sooner? There hadn't been any blood around Louie's neck, either. In her panic and shock she'd assumed the blood on his shirt was from the stab wounds.

'Holy cannoli, Lydia. I'm thinking that Louie's body was put in the smoker after he was already dead. I mean, think about it. He would have bled to death on the smoker floor if he was shot there.' His conviction stunned her as much as his theory made total sense.

'How do you know this?'

'A case study for class. Dead bodies stop bleeding when the heart stops pumping.'

'But I was sure he was stabbed . . .' She'd made a big mistake! Sure, Louie had the sausage pricker in his jugular. But it didn't mean he'd been killed with the family's tool. If there'd been a pool of blood under his neck, she hadn't noticed. She'd been so focused on the sausage pricker, and had all but closed her eyes when she'd leaned in to press her fingers on his jugular. Plus it had been so dark in the shed.

Lydia puffed out her frustration with a forceful sigh. She wasn't a medical expert. How was she supposed to know a body didn't bleed after it died? It made sense, though.

'I know what it must have looked like to you, Lyd. I wouldn't know about the pumping blood part unless I'd done a criminal case study for school.'

'Oh. My. God. I am so dumb. Detective Nowicki acted as if he believed our story. Mine and Grandma's, I mean.' She'd thought that because Grandma seemed to have an 'in' with Nowicki that maybe they'd be in the clear. That Nowicki might be their ticket to being off the hook for the murder. But Nowicki wasn't their friend. Proved by how he'd kept basic facts and findings from her family during the questioning.

'Wait a minute. Have you or your family been accused of the murder, or told that you're suspects?' Stanley asked.

'No. Yes?' She bit her lower lip. 'I'm not sure, really. Detective Nowicki told Grandma and I not to talk about it – the case, or how or why we think Louie got killed.' Lydia stared at Stanley. Didn't he notice the snow landing on his brows, drawn together as he stared back at her? Her fingers itched to . . . *No.* She swallowed and curled her hands into fists.

Stanley placed his hand on her shoulder again. It took every ounce of her will to resist leaning into him this time. It had been the longest day of her life and Lydia needed a friendly hug.

Careful. Everyone's a suspect.

She stood straight, completely avoiding an emotionally needy lean-in.

'Lydia, you have to watch it. You might be the prime suspect, since you're the one who found Louie. This isn't one of your grandmother's TV shows.' Stanley's pronouncement blew away any thoughts of getting comfort from him under the dark spring sky.

'Tell me something I don't know. I mean, Grandma was in our apartment by herself after I left for the shop, which was during the last bit of the time span they think he was killed, so I'm sure she's on their list. And then Teri was out dancing at Uncle Sam's all night, and then . . .' She stopped. Teri's story was Teri's, not Lydia's to tell. Except Teri didn't know what Lydia had told Nowicki about Johnny. Was Johnny wearing his sneakers when Teri snuck out?

'What aren't you telling me?' Stanley always knew when she was holding back. But she was glad she had. If Johnny was the killer, the last thing she needed was Stanley going after him out of a misplaced sense of loyalty to her family. That was something a partner did, and they were definitely no longer together.

'Nothing.' She stood firm.

Stanley shook his head. 'Listen to me, Lydia. Promise me you won't talk to the police any more without your lawyer. You have one, right? Your folks do?' He took his hand back and shoved it in his pocket. She tried not to visibly shiver at the loss of its warmth. Tried to remind herself again that Stanley was a suspect, too. Except a killer wouldn't be able to look at her with such concern, would he?

'Our family doesn't have a lawyer. Besides, we can't afford one right now.' They were going to need a half-dozen attorneys at the rate things were going.

'Then at the very least, call me when they come around again. I'll ask one of my profs if they'd recommend someone to defend you guys right now.'

'None of us did anything wrong, Stanley!'

'I'm sure you didn't. But the cops and the law don't know that. Until they actually find the real killer, you have to have your guard up. Trust me. You need help with this, Lydia. Let me help you.'

'I can't imagine why the police would come back to talk to us again. They're still there, collecting evidence, but we already spent all morning talking to them. We told them everything we possibly know. There's nothing left to say. I'm not waiting for the police to return, anyhow. I'm going to do what I can to find out who did it. I can't have Wienewski's Wieners and Meats associated with this.'

'First, that's a bad idea, to appoint yourself as an investigator. From what I can tell, this killer is not someone who'd hesitate to murder you, or your family. Second, you can't make any of this go away no matter what you find. Louie was found in your backyard. Third, you can count on the police coming back. It's what a homicide investigation's all about. Put yourself in their shoes.'

She had, a thousand times over since Nowicki had walked into their backyard. 'I know, I know. But the sad thing is that no matter how I look at it, Grandma and I don't have solid alibis. Not foolproof, anyhow. I can't trust local cops with this. I need answers now.' In truth, none of her family had a decent alibi. They were backing each other up, and not very convincingly at that. If she were Nowicki, she'd be suspicious.

'It's OK for now. Unless they have your prints on the weapon, anything they claim is all circumstantial.' Stanley had

always been a bit of a geek when it came to the law, way
before anyone suspected he'd go to law school. Everyone
thought he was destined to go to the Police Academy, like
Ned had, since along with his top grades, Stanley had always
been a decent athlete. She stared at him, wondering when
Stanley had become the epitome of a solid legal defender.
Swap his winter jacket and jeans for a tailored suit and tie
and he'd be Cheektowaga's Perry Mason.

'Circumstantial? The sausage pricker – that I know has my
prints on it from last night – is enough to convict.' Unless
Stanley was right and Louie hadn't died by pricker.

'You haven't been accused yet, and if you are, I'll see to it
myself that you get cleared. I know you're not a murderer.'

'I appreciate it, Stanley. Thank you. But I'm not waiting on
Detective Nowicki, or Ned, to come after me, Grandma, or
anyone else in my family. Like I said, I'll solve this myself
if I have to. It won't hurt to poke around a bit.'

'Please don't. You know Louie was involved with some
unsavory people, right?'

'How do you mean?' She knew the dead man had been a
jerk at times, but never saw him as an outright criminal.

'The only way he made enough to drive his fancy cars and
live in that humongous house on the other side of town was
by doing the bidding of crooks more powerful than him. Plain
and simple.'

'You learned all this in law school, too?' she asked.

'No, no way.' He chuckled.

She'd missed Stanley's laughter.

'We don't have time to study local crime and politics cases
– not that many, anyway. Sure, lots of local trials are used for
our class case studies, but they're from years ago. I read the
paper every day, that's how I know. The *Courier Express*.'
Buffalo's morning paper.

'Oh.' Lydia's family got The *Buffalo Evening News* delivered, as the late afternoon paper was more suited to their
family business schedule. Pop spent his evenings in his circa
1968 recliner with the lifetime guarantee that the family
begged him to replace with a new one, his face behind the
open paper while Mom ironed and watched her shows.

'Louie has skirted the law for years. I'm surprised you weren't aware of this.'

'I guess I just never put two and two together.' With sickening clarity, Lydia realized she hadn't wanted to believe someone Pop did business with was a real crook. The more she thought about it, the more she saw that there was more than one possible motive for someone to kill Louie. But whoever had done the deed had decided to try to pin it on the Wienewskis. Which made it her problem.

Worst of all, she had no idea if anyone in the family was in the killer's bullseye. Had Louie's killing been a warning?

No matter what Stanley said, or what her heart still held for him, Lydia had to stay objective. Which meant Stanley remained on her suspect list, along with his dad, until she found and stopped the killer. She knew the cops were busy with the case, but it felt as though it was on her to solve the crime before anyone else wound up like Louie.

Dead.

ELEVEN

'I don't want to upset you, Grandma, but I think you need to be very careful around Detective Nowicki. He's not the boy you once knew. It's his job to pin the murder on somebody as quickly as possible.'

'Lydia, you're overtired, honey, and you let Stanley's opinion trigger you. It's making you paranoid. I know about paranoia, trust me. I had a puff of some wacky weed once.' Grandma Mary peered at her over her reading glasses, long lengths of hemp in each hand. She was bent over her latest macrame plant hanger, the finished ends draping past the edge of the folding card table. Lydia was making dough for rye bread in their tiny kitchen with the standard-size stove and oven that Pop had installed for her as a surprise on her eighteenth birthday. The family understood that baking and cooking was how Lydia had coped with her often overactive imagination as a child, and she'd carried the coping technique into adulthood. She grinned, probably her first since finding Louie's body. Who would have guessed she'd turn a childhood hobby into her own business?

A pang of longing squeezed her heart. Was it only a day ago that she'd been balancing the butcher shop's management with planning the grand opening of Lydia's Lakeside Café and Bakery? She'd not glanced once at her draft menu, or the stack of recipes she'd yet to test on a larger scale.

Soon. They'd get to the bottom of Louie's murder and then she'd once again be able to focus on her new life. Patting the firm dough into a ball, she placed it in a greased, white, oven-proof bowl and covered it with an old but still usable linen towel. The red polka dots had faded to pink along with the pompom trimming. Her grandmother had been big on Polish-American styles and themes when first married to Grandpa Wienewski. It was incredible to think of Grandma as anything but the wild child elder Lydia had always known her as.

They'd been watching *The Love Boat* on their small TV, but it was a commercial break. Lydia wiped her floured hands on her apron and watched as one of the Charlie's Angels pranced across a New York City street, and thought about when Stanley gave her a bottle of cologne. She was long over that kind of scent – she'd discovered French perfume in Ottawa – but Stanley still occupied space in at least one chamber of her heart. Obsessing over which, she reminded herself, was going to do nothing to solve Louie's murder.

'I'm not paranoid, Grandma. And just because I never smoked bad pot doesn't mean I don't know what paranoia feels like.' In truth, she didn't smoke weed, and had no interest in it. Although the last thirty-six hours of questioning her sanity – as the world as she knew it turned upside down – made her understand the temptation to puff one's worries away. She walked to the oven and lit a match, turned on the gas, and lit the pilot light. Setting the dial to its lowest setting, she placed the dough bowl atop the stove. With the draftiness of their flat and cold temperatures outside, she wanted to make sure the rye bread had every chance of rising.

'Honey, I'm sorry. I'm not patronizing you. I'm proud of your conviction to be drug-free. Even though I don't see the harm in something that grows from the ground. You and me' – Grandma motioned her hand between their hearts – 'we're kindred souls. Ancient. We've seen a lot of life and death in our many, many visits here.'

Great. Grandma was retreating to her supernatural-explanation-for-everything beliefs. Lydia was cool with that, usually. But sometimes things just were what they were. Like needing to figure out who killed Louie, while avoiding becoming a prime suspect, or worse. The killer was still out there.

'I'm not imagining things.' She explained why she was worried about Nowicki's motives, since he hadn't told them that he knew Louie was killed by a gunshot. 'Don't you think it's odd that neither he nor Ned mentioned it? Face it, Grandma, they wanted us to admit we'd killed Louie.'

'No.' Grandma shook her head. 'I don't believe that. If Harry was holding back it's because he's an experienced investigator and it's how he usually does business. He's bound to tell us the real cause of death, I'm sure.'

'Don't you think you're being a little one-sided here, Grandma?' Lydia wanted Grandma to let go of her affection for Nowicki long enough to acknowledge their predicament.

'I'm sure I am seeing it how I want to see it. But what you – this entire younger generation – doesn't understand is that people my age are friends for life. We may not see one another for years, but when we do, we're there for one another. Harry's on my side, which means he's on your side, too, Lydia.' Grandma set down her ropes, placing individual strands atop the numbered pieces of masking tape. Lydia shook her head. Macrame was too involved for her, especially while watching a show. She preferred knitting or crochet.

Not that she'd gotten anywhere with her craft project this weekend. A pile of bright pink, turquoise and yellow granny squares stared forlornly at her from their clear plastic tote bag on the floor. She needed twice as many to sew together into the Afghan she was giving Mom for Mother's Day and her birthday, a week apart, next month.

Warm hands held her face as Grandma forced her to meet her gaze. Lydia blinked back tears. It was as if only Grandma could enable her to open her heart, make her see the emotions she'd been avoiding.

'Lydia, you've got to stop carrying the weight of the Wienewskis on your shoulders. No one here killed Louie and Harry knows it.'

'How can you say that?' Big tears plopped from her eyes and onto Grandma's hands. She pulled away and swiped at them. What was she, five years old again? They were talking murder, not a skinned knee. 'We're in big trouble, Grandma. Stanley wasn't making things up; he's a smart guy. And he's right about the police's way of thinking and how they do things. Everything Stanley asked me, and told me, lined up. He's learned a lot in law school.'

'So what? You and I are going to solve this before long, don't worry,' Grandma soothed.

'How? It's not going to happen sitting around watching TV.' She motioned at their living area. Her half-eaten aluminum pie tin of stovetop popcorn sat on the coffee table, next to the half-full avocado green glass of instant iced tea. 'He's been dead almost twenty-four hours and we haven't found anything out.'

'That's not true. You found out that he was killed by a gun. No one in the family has a gun. So that rules us out.' Grandma could be so stubborn when it came to her decisions. Especially if said decision involved a man of current romantic interest.

'OK, so who do we know who has a gun, but more important, who would want to kill Louie?' Lydia reached for her steel three-inch-by-five-inch index card file. She'd used it for her secret Polish baked goods recipes – now transferred to a three-ring binder – then as an address file, and now it would hold their murder investigation notes. She opened the lid and placed the M divider in front. M for Murder. Taking out several empty cards, she grabbed a pencil, ready to begin. 'I'll write while we brainstorm.'

Grandma sat next to her on the sofa and took a quick sip of the lukewarm 'iced' tea. She grimaced. 'This powder stuff is truly awful. Remind me to make us real tea tomorrow. Let's see . . . we know that Ned and Harry and all the cops in the neighborhood have guns, right? And what about the hunters?'

For the next several minutes they listed all the possible gun owners they knew of. Lydia wrote the names on the lined cards while Grandma looked up exact addresses in the phonebook.

'We've listed people with hunting rifles and pistols but we don't know what kind of gun killed Louie.' Lydia's knowledge of firearms was nil.

'I'll ask Harry.' Grandma pursed her lips, then let out a chuckle. 'He can't resist me. Did you see the twinkle in his eyes at the kitchen table?'

'Let me handle this one. I'll ask Ned.' Lydia knew Grandma could coax clear water from a rusty spigot but Nowicki, in charge of the investigation and a seasoned law enforcement veteran, knew how to play all the cards better than they did. 'Now, let's come up with every suspect possible. I'll start. Stanley and his father.'

Grandma gasped so Lydia quickly explained her reasoning.
'OK, I see why you need to have them on the list. Add in
your sister's boyfriend.' Grandma paused. 'Both of them.'

It was Lydia's turn to gasp. 'What, who . . . how do you
know, Grandma?' She'd kept Teri's secret, and the only other
person who'd know, besides Johnny, was Nowicki. Detectives
didn't have loose lips, did they?

Grandma winked. 'I see things, and hear things, my dear.
Which is why I know you don't for one minute want to believe
Stanley did it. But he could have.'

'I haven't told you everything, Grandma. You know those
footprints outside of the smoker? They seemed similar to
the kind of sneakers Johnny wears. I told Nowicki.'

'He mentioned you were trying to do his job but made sure
he knew that you're cooperating when you tell him things.'
Grandma ran her fingers through her hair. 'That would make
it too easy, Lydia. I noticed those prints, too, and they were
from a very big man, if you ask me. Johnny's tall, but I don't
think his feet are as big. I double-checked when I saw him in
the shop.'

'You did?' Bemusement lifted her heavy heart, gave her a
more optimistic view of their ability to solve the case. 'We're
thinking like detectives, aren't we?'

'We are. Let's keep it up.' Grandma was back to the business at hand. 'Write down Charlotte, Louie's wife. I've actually
had occasion to know her more than I ever did him. She's a
regular at my favorite bingo hall. It took me a bit to put them
together, but after listening to you talk to Harry and then
asking around, I figured it out. She's a sweet woman with a
spine of steel, let me tell you. Knows the bingo rules inside
and out. You always have to suspect the wife. Isn't the murderer
someone the victim knows, most of the time?'

'If television shows are to be believed. But you're right,
Charlotte needs to be on the list. Anyone else?'

'Well, your brother Ted is out. He was working in the
hospital that night from what your father told me.'

'And he doesn't even live here. He didn't know about Louie
until Mom called him.' She'd overheard her mother talking to
her eldest when she'd ran back into the main house for some

extra butter after the fish fry tonight, before coming back up to the apartment.

'I get the feeling you don't like Harry, Lydia. You need to separate the man from his societal role.'

'"Like" has nothing to do with it.' She mentally patted herself on the back for not rolling her eyes. 'No matter what we think we know from TV shows, this is our real life, Grandma. We're the prime suspects for murder, no matter what Detective Nowicki is saying in private to you. Like I said, give me a chance to get whatever information I can out of Ned first. We'll save Nowicki for more important clues as we need them.'

'Well, OK.' Grandma leaned back. 'But I'm still going to keep a dialogue going with Harry. I'll keep my questions more on the vague side, get him to open up about the broader issues of the case if I can.'

'Sounds good.'

Phew. She'd rarely convinced Grandma Mary of anything in her life to date. But she reminded herself that this was a small victory. There was no telling what Grandma would say to Nowicki the next time she saw him.

'When do you think you'll run into him again, Grandma?'

'Harry? We're meeting for bingo on Tuesday night. I thought I told you.'

No, she hadn't.

Bingo raised money for the Catholic school that stood adjacent their family parish, and was the main happening on the east side of Cheektowaga besides the plaza kitty-corner from the church, across the town's main intersection. Bingo was a favorite distraction from all kinds of Buffalo woes, from bad weather to its often poor economy. Its only competition in Lydia's mind were the airplanes that took off and landed at Greater Buffalo International Airport, its main runway only a mile from their living room. The noise! It wasn't unusual to miss full swathes of dramatic dialogue during summer afternoons when the windows were open and the roar of the jet engines obliterated any sound coming from their Zenith television. They'd all learned to read their favorite actors' lips.

Lydia was no fan of bingo. She knew she was sentencing

herself to two-and-a-half hours of choking cigarette smoke in the parochial school's basement gym/cafeteria/auditorium, awaiting the painfully slow announcement of which row and column she could either slide the red plastic cover over, or dab out with one of Grandma's multi-hued bingo markers. Louie's murder investigation was ongoing, though, and she had to squeeze information out of Nowicki in any way she could.

'Would you mind if I come with you, Grandma?'

'Lydia, are you kidding? You know I love it when we go together. But you hate bingo. You don't trust your sweet grandmother alone with the detective, do you? What, do you think I'm going to jump him?' Her grin would be malicious on any other face, Lydia thought.

'I trust you, Grandma. It's just that I want to be there in case he says anything significant. Two sets of ears are better than one, you know? And how about you give him one of the loaves of rye bread, too?'

What Lydia didn't add was that she was concerned Grandma would let it slip that not only were they aware they were the top suspects, they had also decided to solve the murder themselves. That would not enamor them to Nowicki.

And they needed all of law enforcement on their side.

TWELVE

Holy Saturday morning Lydia stared at the Bukowskis' side door a full minute before she knocked on the aluminum storm door. She'd peered through the sheers covering the kitchen window and saw the light on. Hopefully it was Ned and not her aunt or uncle. Contrary to what she'd told Stanley, she apparently did need to talk to an officer of the law again.

The sound of a chain lock dropping followed by Ned's blonde head appearing on the other side of the outer door both exhilarated and surprised Lydia. Surprise because he startled her from her thoughts, which ran way too deep since finding Louie. Exhilaration because she had found who she'd come here for and might just get some information out of him. It was like waiting for a new cookie recipe to bake – wondering if she'd get a tender, mouthwatering product or the consistency of a hockey puck – only more intense. Cookies didn't usually come with life-or-death stakes, however.

Was this how real-life detectives felt each time they questioned a witness?

'Lydia. Is everything OK?' Ned's face and voice reflected alarm. Seeing his cousin on his doorstep wasn't a usual occurrence.

'Yes, no, I mean, yes. I mean, nothing new has happened. I just need to ask you some questions. If you're not too busy?'

'I'm getting ready for work. I'm not even dressed yet, Lyd. Can I stop by your place in a few?'

'No. I won't be home anytime soon. I have to open the shop.' She stared at him, tried to employ that unrelenting stare Nowicki wielded so well.

Ned continued to stare at her and she realized her cousin wasn't kidding: he didn't want to let her in or talk to her now. But she needed answers from him.

'Oh, Ned, I'm sorry. Did I wake you up?' She knew she hadn't, but maybe he'd only been up for a bit.

'Not quite, but . . . oh, hang on.' He disappeared for a few moments, and when he returned he unlatched the outer door and held it cracked open for her. 'Come on in. I'm making coffee. Want some?'

'Ah, sure.' She didn't think a real private eye would take a beverage from her subject but Ned was her cousin and not a suspect. She needed him to think nothing of this and give her the goods before he thought twice about it.

Sitting at the small kitchen table with a Corelle mug of coffee, she poured from the pint container of half-n-half. 'Where's Aunt Dot and Uncle Jim?'

'Groceries.'

'Oh.' She searched for something relevant to say, in a most casual manner. 'Is the basement warm enough through the winter?' Ned still lived at home, but in the basement and not the attic bedroom he and his brother had as kids.

Ned looked at her as he took what had to be his first gulp of coffee. His eyes brightened and one side of his mouth lifted. She swore she saw him wake up right in front of her. He set his cup down.

'Lydia, just spit it out. What are you trying to find out?'

'I heard that Louie was shot to death. I thought he was stabbed. What's really going on, Ned?' So much for playing it cool.

'He was shot, of course.' He tilted his head. 'Didn't Nowicki mention it?'

'No. He didn't.'

'Huh.' Ned took another slug of joe. Lydia would have believed that his surprise was genuine, except for the way he refused to meet her gaze.

'Why would you keep this from us, Ned? Do you really think that I, or anyone in my family, is capable of committing such a crime? We don't even have a working hunting gun that I know of.'

'Rifle, you mean.' Ned didn't question her meaning of 'working,' thank the Virgin Mary. 'No, I don't think you're capable of hurting a fly, Lyd. But as an officer, we have to keep all of our options on the table. It's the way we do things, is all.'

'Louie's body might have been moved after he was shot, is what I figured out, from what I heard.' She kept Stanley out of it.

Ned winced. 'OK, so it sounds like details are getting out there.' He shook his head. 'People can't stop from opening their traps in this place, you know?'

'Seems not.' Man, she was better at this skating along the edges of the truth than she'd expected.

'Yes.' His decisive nod made her sit straight up.

'Yes, what?'

'Louie was shot. One bullet, right in his heart. He was probably dead before he hit the ground. A blessing amidst the tragedy.'

'How do you know this?' And when had her cousin become so philosophical?

To his credit Ned didn't sigh, roll his eyes, or laugh at her ignorance. 'The coroner's report. We got the rest of it late last night. An autopsy can reveal a helluva lot about a case, you know? Tell you things you might not see at the scene.'

'If Louie was shot, and killed by a bullet, why would someone stab him, unless they were out to frame me or my family? Before you answer, Ned, I need to know something else first, about dead bodies. I, ah, watch a lot of detective shows with Grandma. Is it true that a dead body doesn't bleed? Do you know?' Lydia thought she was being smart, keeping her secret source of information – Stanley – hidden.

Ned's eyes narrowed. 'What I do know is where you're going with this. No, dead bodies don't bleed, not after a few minutes. As you may have noticed yourself, there was no blood on the shed, er, smoker, floor. We think someone moved Louie's body to your smoker after he was killed. The neck jab' – he motioned sharply at his own jugular – 'was for effect. Why they stabbed him, well, your guess is as good as mine. A twisted sense of humor? Anger? A fit of rage?'

'For effect?' Her words came out on a whisper and nausea threatened. Someone *had* wanted to frame her family! It wasn't news, but the validation of her fear stung nonetheless.

'Yeah. Like a Hollywood special effect, you know what I

mean? Some killers like to do that. For show.' Ned shrugged,
stood. 'I'm going to make breakfast. Do you want any eggs?'

'No, thanks. I ate.' Her stomach growled, catching her in
her lie, but she didn't think eating his food was appropriate.
Coffee was one thing. Sharing a meal with someone who had
the power to put you away in the slammer, though? Lydia
drew the line. No eating with persons of interest. Not that she
suspected Ned of the murder.

Don't you have to keep every possibility on the table?

'Ned, did you know Louie personally at all?'

'Me? Not really.' He shrugged. 'I avoid troublemakers as
a rule.'

'What about Aunt Dot and Uncle Jim?' Uncle Jim worked
on the railroad, often gone for a few days at a time, while
Aunt Dot served food at the elementary school cafeteria.

'Mom saw Louie every week, when he came to school to
get the meat contracts signed.'

'He supplied meat to the school?'

'The entire school district. You don't think he'd afford that
nice car and big house from butcher shop sales, do you?'

Tears burned her eyeballs. Lydia blinked, and quickly swallowed around the lump of defensiveness in her throat. Ned
didn't mean anything by his comment, but she couldn't brush
aside the harsh reminder of how precarious Pop's business
was. She needed to get back to the store.

Just one more question.

'I told Detective Nowicki that Johnny, our employee,
wears sneakers that I thought might match the footprints by
the smoker.'

'So I heard.' Ned's professional demeanor returned in
the tight-lipped expression she glimpsed before he turned
to the stove.

'Did you . . . hear anything more about that, Ned?'

Ned banged two pans atop the gas burners and didn't seem
to notice, his back to her. She watched him reach for the
bacon, already on the sideboard, and into the refrigerator for
a carton of eggs. As he pointedly ignored her request
for information. He shot her a glance over his shoulder.

'Sure you don't want some? Last call.'

'I'm sure, but thanks anyway. Ned, I don't know anything about guns, so I'm sorry if my questions sound ridiculous to you. But can you tell what kind of weapon the bullet was from?'

Ned didn't answer right away but whisked eggs in a chipped bowl as bacon sizzled.

'If you can't tell me anymore, that's OK, I understand.' She stood up, rinsed her empty mug in the sink next to where Ned worked. 'I'm sorry I barged in on you so early, especially after yesterday.'

'Long days are part of my job.' He deftly turned the slices of bacon with a fork. 'No apologies needed. And yes, we can match the bullet to the barrel it came out of. Louie was killed with a handgun.' His quiet statement belied its gravity.

Double phew.

'No one in my family has ever had anything but a hunting rifle, and Pop got rid of his father's rifle when Grandpa died.' They were cleared! Wait until she told Grandma.

'That doesn't mean you didn't use a handgun to kill him. People steal weapons all the time.'

'Oh.' Back to square one, then.

Ned put the fork down, placed both hands on the small counter, and looked at her. 'I know you didn't kill Louie, Lydia. But you can't rush these things, make it all neat and tidy to fit your schedule. An investigation has to run its course.'

'The "course" needs to hurry, then, before our business suffers.'

'We're doing the best that we can, Lydia. Louie deserves justice.'

Sorrow hit her and she bowed her head. 'Of course he does. Please don't misinterpret my need to solve this as soon as possible for not caring about Louie. We weren't very close, but I've known him my whole life.'

'I don't take you the wrong way. But I'd appreciate it if you stop trying to break the case yourself. If there's one thing I've learned since joining the department, it's that you never know what's going to come to light in an investigation. Most things are straightforward. Kids pulling pranks. The DWIs. A domestic dispute. But every now and then there's a whole lot more under the surface.'

'How do you mean?'

'People you think are regular guys can end up having ties to things you'd never imagine.'

'Like the mafia?'

Ned grinned. 'Yeah. But not really. Usually a criminal's motive is more basic, to be honest.'

'Can I ask you more questions if I have any? I'm not looking to do your job.' She lied. Wasn't that exactly what she was doing?

'Of course. Though I can't promise I'll always be able to answer them, you know?' He removed bacon from the pan, placed it atop paper towels. Without draining the grease, he poured the eggs into the hot oil and stirred with the fork.

'Do you like it, Ned? Being on the police force?'

'I sure do. There're slow days, sure, and lots of boring paperwork. But every day is different, and I know I'm making a difference. Keeping the bad guys off the streets.'

'Thanks for that, Ned. Doing your job. I'm proud you're my cousin.' She grabbed her parka from the back of her chair. 'I'm heading out. Appreciate the coffee. Tell your parents I said "hello."'

'Will do.'

Her hand on the door, she opened it.

'Lydia?'

'Yeah?'

'Try to have a happy Easter. Don't worry about Louie. This is ugly stuff. We're working on it. Let us.'

'Thanks, Ned.' She let herself out, and was halfway down the driveway when she realized that Ned didn't think a murder investigation was something she, a woman, should worry about. Before now, she would have spun back around and set him straight. But time wasn't on her side. The constant worry over getting to the truth before the shop went under, or her family suffered needlessly, was more pressing.

I'm not worrying.

Lydia was problem-solving. Ned claimed he didn't suspect her of the murder, but he hadn't said he was certain Grandma, or Pop, or Mom, or Teri didn't do it, either.

Nope, she didn't have worries, not a single one. Simply more reasons to keep digging.

*   *   *

Lydia left Ned's in time to open the shop early, as she'd planned, at eight o'clock. It was her father's custom to stay open for the last-minute Easter shoppers until two o'clock. Usually they were open all day on Saturdays, but today most people were back home by early afternoon. There were four dozen hardboiled Easter eggs to dye in all shades of pastel with expired food coloring, and Easter baskets full of sponge candy, orange chocolate, and locally made jelly beans to be prepared. And hidden for the Easter Bunny to deliver tomorrow morning.

By noon the small stream of customers who'd stopped in earlier had trickled to none. There were at least two dozen pre-orders left in the refrigerator room, with no sign of their buyers. Which meant no money in the register. Lydia tried to shove the panic down as she mentally calculated the losses. There was still two hours left. Plenty of time for people to come in, right?

'If you don't need me, I'm leaving.' Vi spoke up, standing next to Lydia and Teri. All three stared out over the gleaming refrigerator case, into the empty room that only yesterday had been jam-packed with yakking customers. But that was before the Cheektowaga nosy bodies got going. Lydia sighed. With her luck going the way it was, she wouldn't be surprised to hear that they'd found a dozen dead bodies in their smokehouse.

'That's fine, Vi. See you on Tuesday, then.' Lydia needed to check on the books without Vi peering over her shoulder, anyhow.

'I usually come in on Dyngus Day. It's not a holiday for me, you know.' Vi never missed an opportunity to underscore that she'd married into the Wienewskis and wasn't Polish by birth. Except when she'd begged Pop for a job all those years ago.

'No, I don't need anything until Tuesday.' Lydia faced Vi, and willed herself to not take the tank in sales out on her estranged aunt. 'It's been a rough weekend. We all need a rest.'

'Too bad my Ray's not still here. The shop wouldn't be hurting, you wouldn't be worried about losing customers.' Vi sniffed, held her lace-trimmed handkerchief to her face. 'He and your pop would have worked together, been a real team, you know?'

'I'm sure you're right, Vi.' Lydia's jaw clenched. She didn't want to snap at her.

'It's the truth,' Vi replied.

Lydia opened her mouth to fire off a smart alec remark, but shut it just as quickly. She still had to check the books and make sure her suspicions about Vi were warranted. No way did she want Vi to suspect what she'd planned, or that she didn't trust her aunt-by-marriage.

She and Teri silently watched Vi leave. Only Vi could make exiting a butcher shop a major event. She tossed each fringed end of her magenta scarf over her shoulders, settled her navy leather purse straps on her forearm, and clicked her kitten heels across the backroom floor as she left.

After the door shut behind Vi, Lydia turned to Teri. 'Kinda like you were getting at yesterday. She's not the nicest person all the time, is she?'

'Real family is supportive in tough times. Vi's anything but nice underneath her nice clothes these days. She used to be OK, but I don't know what her deal is lately.' Teri's somber expression underscored her observations.

Lydia nodded. 'Enough about her. We'll close at one if it stays this quiet.'

'We can't do that! You told people on the phone orders that they could come by until two. It'll ruin our reputation if you close early.'

'I don't disagree with you, but I have to face facts. People have found out about Louie.'

'Just make sure that they know you didn't sell them sausage from the backyard smoker.' Teri's persistence lit a warm ball of comfort under Lydia's ribs.

'I wish I could laugh at your joke, sis.'

'Yeah, it was lame.' Teri grimaced. 'I don't understand, Lydia. We had a record-breaking crowd yesterday.' She unnecessarily rearranged a stack of Grandma's horseradish as she spoke. Grandma had mercifully agreed to stay back at the house. Mom needed help preparing for their family celebration tomorrow, and Lydia wanted Grandma there to keep an eye on the backyard. The police had cleared it, removed the yellow tape almost as quickly as it had been hung. But both Lydia and Grandma agreed that the police might come back for another look, depending on what they uncovered during their investigation, and it would be an opportunity to ask for more information from Ned, Nowicki, or any other police officer.

Lydia smiled as she remembered how disheveled Ned had been at his door earlier. Until Teri's petulant sigh registered.

'Hang on. I need to check something out.' Lydia walked to the back of the shop, to the workbench where she'd dropped the rolled copy of the *Courier Express*. She'd taken it off their house porch, meaning to see what it said, if anything, about Louie. Nothing of detail had been printed in the *Buffalo Evening News*, except to say that police were called to a home in the neighborhood adjacent St Ursula's parish to 'investigate an ongoing matter.' So as long as her customers didn't watch the evening and eleven o'clock news on TV last night, there was a good chance they wouldn't know what had transpired at 10 Pulaski Place.

'I already checked. It doesn't say that a mutilated body was found in our smoker, if that's what you're thinking.'

'He wasn't . . .' Lydia couldn't argue with her sister. Louie's body had been left in a horrific manner.

'Yeah, you got it, sis. Having Great-Gramps's pricker shoved in his throat is the definition of "mutilated." And super gross.'

'I found out that he died from a bullet wound, Teri. Ned confirmed it to me this morning.'

'What? So the killer shoots Louie then jabs him in the neck with our family pricker? Great. Nothing personal there.' Teri succinctly summed up what had taken Lydia more than a few heartbeats to figure out.

'I wish I could have made sure people didn't find out . . .' Lydia ran her hand over her face, uncaring about her mascara. Oh, wait – she hadn't put any makeup on this morning, save for her shiny pink lip gloss. Even the strawberry scent didn't give her the usual lift. She still felt too raw from yesterday. Would this awful sense of foreboding, of danger, ever leave?

'What do you mean? You don't have anything to do with Louie's death, the news about it getting out, or the store's sales.' Teri moved on to the display of horseradish mustard, a Western New York specialty. Most folks used it on their ham, and saved pure, sinus-clearing horseradish for the kielbasa. And roast beef, at Christmas time.

'Maybe not, but getting the shop back in the clear is my responsibility.' She racked the timeline since she'd found Louie. No, there was no way she could have kept it quiet from the newspaper or TV stations. Her little sis was correct.

'I think you need to stay focused on your own business. Not in a mean way, Lydia. I'm talking about your café. It's opening soon, right?' Teri appraised her with a measured gaze that belied her years. 'Pop is going to have to close this shop someday, one way or the other. None of us want to keep it going, you know?'

'I want to make it a success for Pop to come back to. I know Ted will never work here' – Ted was finishing up his surgical residency – 'and you have other plans, as do I. But Pop's young – as long as he takes care of himself and doesn't have another stroke, he could work at least until retirement.' Pop would start drawing his Social Security in five years. Lydia wanted him and Mom to be able to retire on their own terms.

'Look around you, Lydia. Times have changed. Weren't there like a million butchers and delis in Cheektowaga, or Buffalo at least, before I was born?'

'Not a million. But more, yes.'

'Stop stressing yourself, I say. Work on getting your own career going. You know, like in *Fame*.'

'I'm not a dancer and no one's telling me what to do, Teri.' They'd gone to see the movie together and stuffed their faces with faux buttered popcorn, sharing a bucket and extra-large sized cola.

'Exactly. Make your own way. Focus on your next steps.' Teri's analogy might be wonky but she had a point. Lydia wasn't helping anything with her worry.

And she sure wasn't getting any closer to Louie's killer.

THIRTEEN

After closing the shop Lydia went back home, hoping to relax a bit before dinner. But she had hours until then, and even the sacred scent of fresh baked rye bread – Grandma had taken care of baking them after Lydia had punched down the dough and shaped it into two large, round loaves – couldn't keep her in the garage flat. Not sure of what her next steps in the investigation should be, she opted to focus on her future – her café and bakery. Tired of simply writing up the menus, Lydia longed for more direct inspiration. She was going to the lake.

Grandma joined her and they made the half-hour drive west through several Buffalo suburbs, the views to the south growing hillier and more scenic the closer they got to the shore of Lake Erie. Not for the first time Lydia wondered how anyone could call the vast great water a lake when it behaved more as an ocean for all of Western New York. Their seasons were dictated by the tilt of the earth – she'd paid attention to Mr Rosetti's eighth-grade science class – but Buffalo embodied its weather. Lydia agreed that Buffalo was a friendly place, as touted by locals and PR firms alike. Neighbors helped each other out through the worst storms including flooding and blizzards. But long grey winter days couldn't help but affect one's mood, no matter how cheery and bright their usual disposition. Buffalonians were tough.

Which is why she was willing to risk her new business on the belief that they'd venture out to the lake front for her food all year round. She dreamed of an establishment that attracted locals and tourists alike, in mid-summer when the sun dappled Lake Erie into a pool of crystalline aqua, and in the winter as well, when the lake often froze solid. As did the water spray on the homes and businesses that lined the shore, but she'd picked a spot that curved inland just enough to hopefully offer protection from the Arctic cold.

'*Make your own way.*'

Teri's words rang in Lydia's mind as she unlocked the front double door of the lakeside café. It was the perfect building in the perfect location as far as she was concerned. Less than thirty minutes from her current home, the property boasted a small cottage adjacent the restaurant where the previous owners had lived for decades. It could serve as another income flow if she chose to rent it out, but Lydia planned to move in as soon as Pop was back to work.

She'd signed the mortgage papers mere days before Pop's stroke. Her constant imaginings of how she'd set up her first business had been derailed first by concern for Pop's survival, followed by taking over the butcher shop. Why let a little bump like a murder investigation stop her now?

She let Grandma and herself in, and they shivered in unison. Grandma tugged her red beret over her ears and stomped her feet on the ancient commercial entry mat.

'Sorry, Grandma. I've kept the heat at the absolute lowest setting to save money.'

Grandma nodded in approval, eschewing any thoughts of how uncomfortable the temperature made her. No matter that her finely chiseled nose was turning a vague shade of periwinkle. 'Smart girl. You don't want the pipes freezing before you even get started.'

'No.'

They grew silent, their footfalls soft as they walked through the entry hall, past a coat check complete with a framed rectangular opening cut from the varnished paneling. The shallow counter and box with its scrolled tickets label reminded Lydia of a carnival trailer at the Erie County Fair, the kind where you tossed rubber rings at empty soda bottles in vain, all for a fuzzy stuffed animal you didn't know you needed. Rows of coat rods emerged from the shadows behind the counter, the remaining few forlorn wire hangers listless in the frigid air.

A stalwart walnut podium greeted them at the dining room's entrance. The tiny reading lamp was missing a lightbulb but Lydia didn't care. She planned to either repurpose the hostess stand or get rid of it. She wanted her patrons to feel as though they were coming home, only better, more welcoming. Self-seating required less staff, too, less drain on her initial cashflow.

'It's awfully dark in here. The real estate agent sure didn't show it to us like this, did he?' Grandma squinted. 'Where are those windows?'

Lydia laughed. 'Yes, it was blinding when we looked at it last fall. Let me open the drapes.' She walked around the circumference of the room, pulled open what had to be the heaviest draperies this side of Lake Erie. 'The curtains are weighted, and insulated, which is great for the winter.'

'So you'll close it up every year?'

'I don't know yet. I want to keep the bakery going all year, even if I have to find another kitchen in the winter.'

'These places right on the water can end up coated in inches of ice, Lydia. Maybe you'll make enough in the warm months to last you all year.'

'Hmmm.' Lydia didn't want to think about closing her café, not even for valid seasonal reasons. Not when she hadn't opened it yet.

'Here we go!' She pushed back the last set of drapes. White light spilled into the room, immediately dispelling the foreboding darkness to reveal a cheerful setting for any meal. Lydia envisioned tables covered with white and red polka-dot linens, customers marveling at fresh salads and sandwiches as they sipped made-to-order milkshakes from fountain glasses with red-and-white striped straws. A display case of her baked goods would encourage dessert and coffee sales. Her red-and-white theme, based on the Polish flag, was her only concession to the menu. It was Lydia's belief that the food would make diners come back again and again, but the décor needed to be as up to date as she could afford if she wanted to attract all generations of patrons. Grandma's peers expected the pressed linen napkins and tablecloths, while her parents and their friends would appreciate a well-stocked bar as cocktails had always been part of their dining out experiences. Lydia planned a true contemporary redesign including the dozen fake ficus trees she'd wrangled at the local decorating store's yearly half-off sale in January. Bright white twinkle lights – not the heavy, ugly outdoor lights she'd grown up with – could brighten the ficus trees at Christmas, and she'd get several large white vases to keep seasonal fake flowers in. Live flowers were out of her budget and too much work, in her opinion. She needed as much time as possible to run the restaurant.

'I can feel the draft all the way over here!' Grandma laughed from her spot across the large dining area. 'We've got some caulking to do around those windowsills.'

'I need to insulate things better, for sure.' Lydia tried in her own way to remind Grandma that she didn't expect her to do anymore than she already had. Lydia counted her blessings down to her toes that Grandma had footed the down payment for the property and the first few months' mortgage.

'We all need help at times, honey. There's no shame in accepting it. In fact, it takes a bigger person to take things gracefully than to refuse an offer.' Lydia acknowledged she'd heard her but wasn't at all inclined to agree.

'I'm going to paint the room white, and hang sheers during the summer. I'll get pull-down woven shades for the afternoon sun.' She stared out the humongous glass panes, watched the agate blue waves that were speckled with white foam. 'People will come as much for the view as the food.'

'That's a fact, but they'll come back for your cooking, Lydia. I like your idea for the windows, too. You can clean and store the drapes over the summer.'

'There are plenty of storage shelves off the kitchen.' Although the heavy fabric would require dry cleaning, not in the immediate budget. Lydia hoped to eventually have the best of the best for her place, but Grandma was right. She had to start somewhere. Maybe this first year she would be open during the summer and early fall, then re-open in the late spring next year.

'Thanks for coming out here with me, Grandma. I needed to get away to clear my head.'

'No problem, I get it. We both needed a break from the case.' When Lydia had asked if she'd like to join her this afternoon, Grandma had at first refused, insisting she needed to stay by the phone in case 'Harry calls. He's very busy, you know.'

But then that familiar gleam of compassion had entered Grandma's eyes and she'd all but jumped in the car. Lydia would have been fine coming out here alone, but Grandma saw what she didn't want to admit to herself. Lydia needed someone else to share her joy with.

The water's smell permeated the aged building, but it wasn't unpleasant. Not to Lydia. The Great Lake scent added to the waterfront ambience of the place that had begun as a local 5 & 10 store in 1925, morphed into a family restaurant twenty years ago, and was about to become Lydia's Lakeside Café and Bakery.

Waves crashed against the large boulders and decaying pylons from a long-ago pier, echoing through the main dining room. The sounds were louder the further back she walked, through the host station and into the kitchen.

The kitchen would be too small, too cramped for Madame Delphine, but it was a slice of heaven to Lydia. Like the other good ideas she'd brought back from Ottawa, she knew she'd have to enlarge the kitchen at some point. It all depended upon the first year or two and how it went.

'Where will you store your baked goods?' Grandma's keen gaze took in the stainless steel commercial refrigerator, the practical shelving, the charred griddle.

'You know the coat check on the way in? I'm going to knock down that wall and put in two large display cases.'

'Where will you get those?' Grandma's gaze scanned the room, looking for equipment left behind by the previous owners.

'I already have them ready to go. Kalinski's old bakery recently replaced theirs but their old cases are perfectly fine. Mr Kalinski sold them to me for a song, and agreed to store them for me until I can borrow a truck to bring them here.'

'Wonderful!' Grandma clasped her hands in front of her, as if they were looking at one of the seven wonders of the ancient world and not a rundown building. 'Just imagine, I could very well be coming here with Harry on a date this summer!'

The reminder of the investigation jarred through Lydia's contentment. It had been wonderful to escape the onerous threat to her family, if only for the drive out here and back.

'Do you think Detective Nowicki is just as interested in you, Grandma? Not to be a negative Nelly but I don't want you to get hurt again.'

'And I love you for that, honey child. But Harry's nothing like that sonofabitch who left me high and dry without a pot to piss in while he raced down to Miami. Moving into a garage apartment had to be the worst moment of my life, except for when my beloved Joseph died, may God rest his soul.' Grandma made the sign of the cross, as she always did when she said Grandpa's name. 'No offense, dear, you know I adore bunking with you, but let's just say it wasn't my plan A.'

'I get it, Grandma. Being back over the garage wasn't in my plans, either.' As soon as Lydia was confident in her earnings she'd move out. There were plenty of houses for rent only a few miles from the lake, which would reduce her commute to minutes instead of half an hour.

'To be honest, though, my dear granddaughter? I'm glad I didn't move to Florida, after all. I'm a Buffalo gal and I'm where I belong. Harry's got deep roots here, like me. And he's not looking to take off anywhere. His wife's been gone for over five years now. He's ready for love. For me!' She smiled, the sunlight bouncing off both her teeth and eyes in equal measures of sparkle.

'I didn't realize he'd been married. What did his wife die of?'

'A cop half her age.' Grandma must have read Lydia's confusion. 'She cheated on Harry with his rookie. They divorced.'

'That's – that's awful, Grandma!'

'Not as far as I'm concerned. Harry's free to follow his heart. And trust me on this, Lydia. A woman knows when a man loves her. Harry's got the hots for me, sure, most men do. But he cares about me, too. I'm telling you, Harry's a keeper.'

'Whatever you say, Grandma.' Lydia smiled, enjoying the moment with Grandma in the place unmarred by recent murderous events. She didn't disagree about Harry being a keeper. It was the timing that bothered her. Detective Nowicki hadn't become the lead detective of the Cheektowaga Police

Department by accident. The man had to be intelligent, thoughtful, deliberate. Maybe even calculating.

And wouldn't wooing a lead suspect be the perfect way to verify they'd killed Louie? She wasn't going to voice it, not yet. But it wouldn't surprise her to see Nowicki go his own way after he realized Grandma, and in fact the entire Wienewski family, was innocent.

'What are you going to do with the soda fountain?' Grandma asked, pointing to a long ledge that the hostess station backed up to.

'What do you mean?' Lydia stared at the paneled room partition.

'Oh, honey, you don't know what that is?' Grandma walked to the far end of the divider and kicked it, hard. 'Hear that? It's hollow. These cheap fake wood panels are covering the original soda fountain. I'm sure of it.'

'How do you know this?' Lydia joined Mary and peered at the paneling, and one spot where the edge molding had cracked off. 'The seller didn't mention anything about the original service counter still being here.' A furl of excitement brushed against her ribcage. If there really was a counter under there . . .

'Here, hold my purse.' Grandma handed her the beaded macrame bag she insisted was 'perfectly fine for year-round.' Grandma Mary wasn't one to follow Western New York fashion edicts. Point in fact was her white bag, going against the rule that forbade wearing white pants, shoes or purse before Memorial Day at the end of May and after Labor Day, the first Monday in September. No exceptions unless you wanted to stick out like a pariah at the A&P grocery store.

'I don't mess up anything I can't fix, Grandma. I'm running on a shoestring until I open.' The last thing she needed was to have to hire a contractor. 'My priority has to be the safety and health inspections. I have to pass them.' Heaven only knew what a kitchen that hadn't been used in two years would yield.

'Don't you wor—' A large crack rent the air, followed by Grandma being shot backward and landing on her bottom, clutching a length of the tan molding.

'Grandma!' Lydia reached for her but Grandma shooed her away.

'I'm fine.' With zero preamble Grandma was at once on all fours, then back to her feet, a grin splitting her face. 'Aha! See what I mean! Look at that chrome. And the water hasn't touched it! No rust.'

'Hang on. Are you sure you're OK? You might have bruised your tailbone.'

'Nonsense. I wasn't born with a one-hundred percent Polish *dupa* but I got it through osmosis, being married to your grandpa for so long.' Grandma Mary's mother had been of Polish descent and she used the Polish slang for buttocks with aplomb. 'Plenty of padding here.' She patted said dupa with unadulterated affection.

Lydia knew arguing with Grandma's ping pong logic would prove futile, so she turned her attention to the large hole in the room divider. Grandma hadn't merely pried a length of molding away from the structure, but freed an entire three-foot-by-five-foot portion.

'You were right!' Lydia stared at the silver-toned trim on what appeared to be the counter wall, the brass kick plate that lay behind the ornate footrest that she'd bet ran the length of the structure. If the entire room divider was indeed the original soda fountain, they were looking at a small portion of it. Even from this limited perspective, Lydia could make out a uniquely Art Deco pattern – in red and white!

'Of course I'm right.' Grandma set the molding down and brushed off her hands. 'My grandparents would bring us out here in their buggy when my sister and I were tiny. I have few memories of our horse-drawn rides, but more of when my parents drove us in their first Ford, for a Sunday drive. If we behaved, we could have root beer floats, or a sundae. Sometimes I got an egg cream.'

'Did you ever not behave?' Lydia said the thought aloud and Grandma chuckled.

'Are you kidding? And miss watching the man make our treats?'

Tears welled and Lydia swiped at her cheeks.

'What's wrong?' Grandma looked closer at her. 'You're happy here, aren't you?'

'These aren't sad tears. I'm overjoyed. I mean, I had no idea you'd been here as a girl when I found this place. You'd said you remembered the 5 & 10 but I didn't put it all together. This means there's a family connection here.'

'I should have made it clearer, honey. There was a lot going on when you came back and told me about it. I would have been happy to give you the down payment on whatever building you chose. But this one is special. You have a lot of work in front of you, but it'll be worth it.' Grandma beamed with pride, yes, but there was more. Satisfaction. Love.

Lydia had missed this. Believing in her dream, going after it, and enjoying the satisfaction of knowing she'd found her place in Western New York, too.

'Yes, it's going to take a lot of elbow grease.' Between the butcher's shop and finding Louie's killer, she had no idea how she was going to get it all done in less than two months. *Just a few weeks.* But she kept her thoughts to herself. The café and bakery was her place, her chance to build the life she'd only dreamed of until now.

The last thing Lydia wanted was any mention of Louie's murder intruding on her solace.

FOURTEEN

'Thanks for going along with me, Grandma.' Lydia turned onto their street, savoring the last few moments of peace before returning to the specter of Louie's murder.

'Anytime, sweetheart.' Grandma peered through the windshield. 'Look, that's Harry's car. It's unmarked, you know.' With practiced efficiency, she flipped down her visor mirror to freshen up her lipstick.

Lydia noted the battered brown sedan, and tried to ignore the resurgence of her agitation. Quiet time at the café and any of its lingering effects disappeared more quickly than chocolate bunny ears after the Easter Vigil Mass.

'Maybe he has some news on the murderer.' She voiced her thought, hoping to remind Grandma that Harry wasn't here for romantic motives. Unless she was wrong. Lydia conceded that she didn't know a whole lot of things, hadn't she learned that much from her abbreviated foray into pastry school? But she knew that Nowicki was a detective on the hunt for a killer.

Grandma darted from the car before Lydia had put the parking brake on, and hurried up the drive toward the back door. Lydia followed, albeit at her own pace. She entered the house and instead of the furnace heat washing over her still-chilled skin, the din of several voices in the living room reached her, and she wasn't even in the kitchen yet.

Slipping off her boots and parka, she told herself she was going to stay calm, no matter what Nowicki had come to tell them, and observe. If she was lucky, he'd let some vital clue slip, giving her and Grandma a leg up on the case.

When she walked into the parlor, however, it was Grandma's leg that was up, on the back of the sofa. Did Grandma think this was a good time to do some of her fancy aerobics dance moves?

'Harry, look at the bottom of my pants. Do you see that?'

He leaned in, took a good look. Jesus, Mary and Joseph, if

Harry got any closer to Grandma's leg he'd tip over. Seeing her parents express more affection than usual since Pop's stroke had taken enough getting used to. Dealing with the mental image of her grandmother with Nowicki in any capacity other than talking was too much.

'I see what looks like splinters,' Nowicki observed.

'Because we were where I said we were. Tell him, Lydia.'

Nowicki's gaze took a beat longer than necessary to shift from Grandma's dirty pants leg to Lydia. He blinked.

'Why are you here, Detective?'

'He's been here the last two hours wondering where the hell you two went. We all have.' Pop spoke from his recliner. 'You didn't tell anyone you'd closed the shop early, and Vigil Mass isn't until eight-thirty.'

Lydia opened her mouth to respond that Teri had known where she was, but shut it just as quick. No doubt Teri and Johnny had used the unexpected free hours to continue where they'd left off in the wee hours of Friday morning.

'What if we needed you?' Mom walked in with a tray of snacks that Lydia knew she'd been saving for tomorrow's family feast. A large serving bowl overflowed with Bugles, a horn-shaped corn snack, which she set in front of Nowicki. 'Here you go, Harry. Try them in the French onion dip, it's divine.' She set down the faux silver bowl she'd filled with the Bison brand dip her family used on everything from potato chips to baked potatoes. And now . . . deep-fried, horn-shaped, cornmeal snacks. Lydia had never developed a taste for them; to her they were like eating salted Styrofoam. But she had a sweet tooth longer than a saber-toothed tiger's eyetooth, and eschewed salty snacks as a rule. Give her a plate of butter cookies, though? She'd scarf them down much as her family did potato chips and the like.

'Thank you, Amelia.' Nowicki accepted the cocktail-size paper napkin and plate, both imprinted with jelly beans, and helped himself to the spread. Lydia waited while he sampled the hors d'oeuvres, not quite sure whether to be furious that the enemy had infiltrated the Wienewskis twice – first with Louie's corpse and now with a cop who sought to pin one of them with the crime.

'Detective?' Lydia prompted.

Nowicki took his time loading up the paper plate that looked like a toy tea set in his huge paw of a hand. Lydia's jaw ached from the smile she refused to relinquish, needing whatever information Nowicki might give up. Finally, he nodded at her.

'Let's take this in the kitchen, Lydia. If that's OK with your parents?' Nowicki smiled at them.

'Of course, go ahead.'

Grandma started toward the kitchen with them, but Nowicki rested his free hand on her arm. 'I need you to stay in the parlor, Mary. I'll question you after I talk to Lydia.'

Lydia didn't wait for Grandma's response and left the room. Back in the kitchen she put the tea kettle on to boil, plopped a tea bag into her favorite yellow smiley face mug, and sat in the chair closest to the stove. This forced Nowicki to awkwardly maneuver his large frame between the table and window that overlooked the backyard. The kitchen smelled like the lasagna cooling atop the stove, Grandma's contribution to their before-a-holiday meal. She'd made it last week and froze it so that Mom wouldn't get all stressed right before the big party.

'Let me get right to it, Lydia. When I asked you and Mary – your grandmother – to stick around, I meant it. Since it's Easter weekend, I expected you to be either here, in your home, or at the butcher's shop. Maybe a few errands here and there. Nothing that would keep you away for hours.'

'I'm sorry, I didn't realize that.' She hadn't. OK, well, maybe it had crossed her mind for a split second that they needed to check in, at least with Ned, but she'd been desperate to get out of the empty store. Away from any reminder of what now appeared to be the death knell of Pop's butcher business.

Nowicki stared at her, and she stared back, refusing to move her gaze, not even to the crumbs that sprinkled his silver mustache. Why did bald men sport bushy mustaches, anyway?

The tea kettle screeched. Lydia jumped up and shut the stove burner off, poured the scalding water over her bag. She sat back down and started dunking the bag, her fingers needing a task.

'Why don't you tell me where you were, and with whom?'

'I think my grandmother already told you that.' She added

three cubes of sugar from the bowl that sat in perpetuity on the kitchen table's lazy Susan, alongside matching salt and pepper shakers and Pop's post-stroke medications.

'Lydia.' Nowicki's tone was no-nonsense.

'All right. The butcher's shop wasn't doing any business. People hadn't come in to get their orders. Word obviously got out about Louie. I decided to close the shop early.'

'Why not wait to close when there were only two hours left?'

'I told you, no one came in.' The silence of the telephone, usually ringing itself off the hook on a holiday Saturday, had been stifling. 'There was no sense in keeping everyone there, so I decided it'd be a good time to make a quick trip to my café.'

'Your café?' His brow, as bushy as his mustache, rose incredulously.

'Yes. I bought a building I'm in the process of redecorating. It's opening at the end of next month, hopefully by Memorial Day.' The last full weekend of May had seemed perfect when she chose it. Before she knew that a murder investigation would take up the time she needed to devote to her menu, cleaning and decorating, and advertising in the local papers.

'Did you go alone?' His question with such an obvious answer annoyed her.

'No, I asked Grandma to join me.' She spoke slowly. Two could play at obvious.

'Why?'

'Why? Grandma and I, well, we're close. She likes the drive out there. And she's the one who helped me with the financing.' The reminder of the looming mortgage payment made her stomach curl. If the falsehoods being associated with her family meant the end of Wienewski's butcher shop, was Louie's death going to end her dreams of Lydia's Café, too? Before it even opened?

'What time did you leave?'

Lydia told him, and proceeded to give Nowicki a blow-by-blow account of the drive to and from the lake, how long they'd stayed in the dusty building, and what they'd accomplished in their short half-hour there.

'It just seems strange to me, Lydia, that you'd leave town on a holiday weekend just to, ah' – he looked at his notes – '"check out" a business site you won't be opening for well over a month yet.'

'Since when is driving to the lake leaving town? I needed a break from this whole mess, OK?' She shook with embarrassment, with shame, at admitting she wasn't the calm, cool and collected woman she wanted him and her family – hell, the world – to see. 'I'm the one who's supposed to be getting Pop's shop out of the red, and I'm about ready to start my own business. Louie's murder may be the end of it all.' Her bottom lip trembled but she would not cry. *Nope, no bawling.*

She'd learned well in pastry school to never let her challengers see her sweat. Breaking down in front of Nowicki wasn't something she wanted to do, ever. But stumbling over a dead body hadn't ever been on a wish list, either.

Nowicki nodded. 'All right.' He drummed his fingers on the table, momentarily lost in thought. 'Do you have the keys to the restaurant? I'll need to borrow them.'

'Um, sure.' She stood and walked the short distance to the entryway, dug into her parka pockets. 'Here.' She placed the entire set of keys on the table. The Strawberry Shortcake key ring looked up at them, her expression seeming forlorn to Lydia and not the fun encouragement it was meant to be when Grandma gave it to her after she'd signed the contract for the café. 'I need to go back soon and get the soda fountain cleaned up, and give the place an overall scrub down. Can I have permission to do that this week?'

'We'll see. You won't be going back for at least the next few days. I need to have my team go inspect it. Don't worry about it, it's just a formality. Check back with me midweek if you don't have your keys by then.' Nowicki had finished his snack. 'Stay close to home until then, Lydia. *My* definition of close, OK?'

'So you don't think me or Grandma did it, then?'

'I don't "think" anything, Lydia. I collect the facts. But off-record? No, I don't think anyone in your family did this.' He paused. 'We've found Louie's car.'

'I didn't know it was missing.'

'Well, it was, until an hour ago.'

'Where did you find it?' she pushed.

Nowicki's eyes narrowed. 'Let me ask you something first. Do you have any knowledge of who Louie worked for?'

She blinked. 'I thought he ran his own business. He's a middleman between shops like ours, and product suppliers, right?'

'Not wrong. So you've never heard him mention that he had a boss of any sort?'

'Do you mean like the mafia?' Western New York had its own mob scene but no one she knew, not even Louie in his scuzziest moments, was involved with them.

'No. If we thought Louie was involved with organized crime, trust me, there would be more law enforcement agencies on the scene, working his murder.' Nowicki looked down at his notebook but she sensed he wasn't reading. He was collecting his thoughts. She had to give the detective credit for his steadfastness. No matter her misgivings about his motives, the man displayed zero evidence of doing anything without forethought.

'Would you like more to eat, or how about a cup of tea?' Had Mom or Grandma already invited him to stay for dinner, too?

He looked back up at her. 'No. But if you remember anything, the least little detail, about Louie, call me.'

'I will. I promise.' She added the last to assuage the remaining bit of her conscience that knew she should tell Nowicki she was working on the case, too. That she and Grandma had a list of all gun owners within their neighborhood, a three-block enclave of sorts.

'I'll hold you to it. Please send your grandmother in. See you tomorrow.'

'But tomorrow's Easter.' Was he really going to encroach on the family holiday?

Nowicki grinned. 'It is, and your parents have invited me to join you.'

'Oh.' Lydia clamped her mouth shut. It was Mom's and Pop's doing, not Grandma's. She gave Nowicki a quick nod.

Easter dinner was already going to be awkward with Vi there
. . . why not make it a stew of uncomfortableness?

'I'm looking forward to more of the placek. Your mother
said you baked it?'

'Yes.' And she was going to have to either stay up really
late tonight or get up early tomorrow – on Easter Sunday, for
God's sake – and make another batch. They'd gone through
two of the three loaves she'd made last week, thinking it was
enough for Easter. If she had known her great-grandmother's
recipe would be used to cajole a suspicious homicide detective
she would have doubled the recipe.

As she left the kitchen Lydia realized that Nowicki had
never said where Louie's car was found.

FIFTEEN

Saturday night Lydia couldn't get to sleep as early as she'd hoped. Since Grandma was still over at the main house doing her laundry – she liked to work alone in the basement after everyone was in bed – Lydia turned on the eleven o'clock news.

She folded her own laundry and cleaned up the minuscule kitchen area as the anchorman's deep voice intoned the most serious local news. Which of course had Louie's murder as its lead.

'The body found one block off Union Road has been identified, and Cheektowaga Police are treating it as a homicide.'

Lydia dropped the dish rag and stared at the television screen. Video footage of their street, a zoomed-in shot of the smokehouse, made her blood boil. It was one thing for the local gossipers to spread the news but now the entire Buffalo metro area knew about Louie's death, that it was murder. She listened for more details but the anchorman switched to other, more mundane reports. Lydia put the last iced tea glass upside down on the drainboard at the same moment the anchorman pronounced, 'An abandoned vehicle was called into West Seneca Police, near Cazenovia Creek, by a concerned citizen. We have a reporter on the scene and will bring you the full story tomorrow.'

Cazenovia Creek, particularly the area that bordered both Cheektowaga and West Seneca, wasn't unfamiliar to Lydia. Heat warmed her cheeks as she remembered the nights, and one particularly fun summer afternoon, when she and Stanley had driven there to have some private time. It wasn't Lovers' Lane, per se, but it offered local teens privacy.

Was the car the anchorman mentioned Louie's car?

There was only one way to find out.

* * *

Lydia turned her headlights off once she pulled into the back parking lot of the Christmas novelty store that was all Christmas, all three-hundred-and-sixty-five days per year.

'Over there, between the truck and the building.' Grandma pointed to a commercial van bearing the name of the Christmas store.

'I'll back in, in case we have to leave quickly.' As Lydia maneuvered the Gremlin, she hoped no one caught them prowling about, not with how nuts they both looked. Dressed in dark clothes to include full-face, knitted ski masks, she questioned her sanity in agreeing to let Grandma come along. But Grandma had walked into the flat right as Lydia was leaving, and refused to let her go alone.

Once out of the car, Lydia led the way as they'd decided she would on the fifteen-minute drive over.

'I don't see any sign of the police.' She whispered loudly to Grandma, who seemed to be a natural at the cat burglar deal, skulking next to her like Cary Grant in *To Catch a Thief*. The roar of the creek made quiet communication nearly impossible. It also masked any sounds from the depths of the trees, which concerned Lydia. Unless they saw lights, they could end up on top of a police team without knowing it.

'See that car parked across the street?'

Lydia did. 'With the guy leaning against it.' How had she missed it?

'He's a cop, I'll bet, and it's his unmarked car. See how it looks exactly like Harry's car?'

'You think that's Detective Nowicki?'

'No, I know it's not. He and I talked after he left and he was in for the night because he said it's going to be an early morning. They're dredging the creek.'

'Why didn't you tell me—'

'Who's there?' A deep, ragged voice cried out. Lydia froze, holding her breathe. Grandma shoved her in-between the shoulders.

'Keep going. My bet's on closer in to the water.' Grandma gave her a second prod.

Lydia kept toward the woods that lined the creek, each step a test of her courage. All she thought about was being swarmed by officers, guns drawn. She really should have thought this through before committing.

'I'm calling the police! Get out, you youths!' The man's pronunciation of 'youth' was more like 'ute,' identifying him as a local of a certain generation. Grandma's, in fact.

A gunshot rang out. Lydia grabbed Grandma's hand and tugged. 'That's it. We're going back home. Let's get back inside the car, now!'

But Grandma literally dug her boot heels into the graveled parking lot and refused to move.

'No, not the car. We're heading for the creek like we planned. That's just crochety old Elvis Jones, being his usual cranky self. He lives in the old farmhouse back here and thinks he owns it all.'

'But he said—'

'Never mind what he says. He never leaves his porch, and the gunshot was fired into the air, over our heads. He's harmless. I took meals to him when I volunteered for the county shut-in outreach last winter.'

'He's calling the cops on us! We can't be caught out here, Grandma.' Nowicki had been adamant that they stay close to home. She didn't think a suburb over counted as 'close,' not by Nowicki's definition.

'We're fine, believe me. Let's go, Lydia! Less flapping and more running!'

Against her every instinct, Lydia ran in the opposite direction of certain safety, into the dark forested land adjacent Cazenovia Creek.

They didn't have to go too far in to come upon what they were looking for. The worn, narrow road that Lydia knew as the Lovers' Lane stand-in came into view under the half moon, as did the shape of a large, long-bodied car. Along with two persons standing next to the familiar vehicle, both wearing unmistakable uniform hats.

'It's Louie's car, all right,' she whispered.

'And those are the cops guarding it until their forensics team gets here.' Grandma's high-pitched voice seemed too loud, even as the creek rumbled with snowmelt. Lydia pressed her index finger to her lips, making sure Grandma saw her gesture in the pale moonlight. Grandma nodded, and motioned for them to stay right where they were.

Lydia nodded back, and turned her attention to the scene.

'I have to go pee-pee, honey. Keep on the lookout,' Grandma whispered into her ear, and Lydia nodded. They'd been sitting or standing and at times squatting in the same area alongside the creek for the last twenty minutes. Lydia thought that patrol cars would have arrived on scene by now, but getting a car into the area wasn't a direct route. The roughhewn road, made from years of 'clandestine' use by enamored couples, could only be accessed from a subdivision of a subdivision – one of the many residential roads that crisscrossed former Western New York farmland. The post-World War II housing boom had initiated the developments, and subsequent generations seeking a private home and small backyard to raise their families had added onto the site of many American dreams.

'Boy, do I feel better!' Grandma returned to her previous spot, a seat on a gnarled tree stump. 'Any action?'

'Not yet.'

'Maybe it's time to think about going back home.' They hadn't come prepared to camp out and the damp cold had seeped into her every pore, not helped by the fear sweat she'd produced earlier. Her black turtleneck clung to her skin like a heavy wet towel that had sat out in the freezing rain.

But as she spoke, light flooded her peripheral vision and she followed its source to where the officers guarded Louie's car.

'Hey, they're going through the glove box!' Grandma spoke as she used her birdwatching binoculars to monitor the scene.

The crackle of the officer's walkie-talkies, followed by low male laughter, alerted Lydia that something had been found. But what would make the police laugh, at the car of a murder victim?

'What is it, Grandma?'

'Here. Take a look for yourself.'

Lydia grabbed the binoculars with frozen fingers and adjusted them to her much wider face. Grandma had the most petite frame.

'I see that the one officer is holding up something.' It didn't look like a gun, or any kind of weapon. 'It looks . . . flimsy.'

'Keep looking.' Grandma's voice sounded on the verge of laughter. What the hell was so funny?

And then Lydia saw what the fuss was about. As the officer holding the object held up his hand, his partner shined his flashlight on it, revealing a very small pair of black lace panties.

'You've got to be kidding me. We've been staking out a rendezvous spot?' Louie's last rendezvous, at that.

'Don't sound so down about it, honey child. Now we can assume Louie was having an affair! Unless he and his wife came out here to liven things up. Why, Joseph and I used to—'

'Not now, Grandma!' she hissed, right at the same moment the walkie-talkie chatter stopped.

'Did you hear that?' the officer holding the sexy underwear asked.

'What?' The flashlight clicked off.

Lydia thought she'd never had to stand so still for so long ever before. Even when she and her girlfriends had played pranks on the boys they liked throughout early high school, like ringing a doorbell and waiting in nearby shrubs until the object of one – or all – of their affection opened the door.

Finally, finally, the officers went back to their job and continued to clear out the car, placing items into plastic bags that Lydia knew were to keep the evidence clean. As she allowed herself to breath normally again, she heard several motors along with the sucking sound of tires on mud.

'It's definitely time to leave. That's the rest of the police coming in. We'll never be able to get out of here unless we go now.'

Grandma nodded, and relief gave Lydia the courage to ease out of their hideout and slowly, silently, walk out of the woods. Once they were at the grassy albeit muddy stretch between the parking lot and the trees they made a beeline for her car.

Only once she'd gotten them back onto the main drag did Lydia turn the headlights on and let out a huge sigh of relief.

'Not so heavy on the pedal, honey. We don't want to get pulled over now.' Grandma fiddled with the heater, blasting still-cold air onto Lydia's face. She didn't care, all Lydia wanted to do was get home.

'I'm sorry but I'm in a hurry.'

'For what? We can analyze our new clues as you drive.'

'It's my turn to need to pee, Grandma.'

'You should have gone in the woods!'

'Maybe.' But if they'd both taken potty breaks, they may have missed out on a potential case-solving clue. 'Grandma, if Louie was having an affair, then his wife Charlotte would be the prime suspect, right? If she knew about it, or suspected it and was spying on him, that is.'

'Sure thing. Crime of passion. And with our sausage pricker in his neck, she made sure she wouldn't get caught,' Grandma observed.

'But that doesn't make sense. Charlotte's only been to the butcher shop a time or two that I can remember. I saw her more when I was in high school and she still worked there. How would she know about the sausage pricker and where it was hanging? Or about our backyard smoker? That reminds me. We still don't know where Louie was killed.'

'No, but I know who does, and he's coming over for Easter dinner tomorrow.'

Lydia bit back a groan and it wasn't from her complaining bladder. Grandma was going to pump Harry for information. It could be a very good thing.

Or it could go wrong in the very worst way.

When they returned from their investigative foray, Lydia set the Baby Ben clock for four hours of shuteye before she arose to make the placek, but awoke an hour before the alarm. Grandma's snoring was probably what had done it, but she couldn't muster a drop of ire toward her partner in crime-solving. Grandma needed her rest.

It was an ungodly hour, true, but it was the best time to bake. She'd better get used to the early rise if she was going to make a go of her café, anyway.

Look at it as practice for Lydia's Café and Bakery.

Cursing Nowicki's zeal for the coffee cake and her mother's over-eager people-pleasing character, she made her way from the loft apartment and into the house. Not a peep from upstairs, so even Stashu was still asleep at this hour.

Lydia pulled the recipe card from her mother's index card box. It was the exact replica of the card she used to keep in her box, except it was in her great-grandmother's handwriting. She had transcribed the card with her mother's handwriting to a full-sized sheet of paper using her typewriter. All of her recipes were in clear page protectors, organized by meal course, and stored in her master recipe binder. She knew the placek recipe by heart, of course, but it was part of her ritual, a way of feeling connected to the women who'd passed the placek secrets down through the Wienewski tree.

First she preheated the oven to 350 degrees Fahrenheit. There wouldn't be any baking for a couple of hours but the kitchen had to be warm for the dough, and eventual loaves, to rise uniformly. The *woosh* of the gas flames igniting under the stove comforted her, as did the very act of baking. Each of the women in her family coped with life in their own way. Grandma meditated, Mom worried over everyone but herself, Teri retreated into herself. Lydia baked.

She plopped the sticks of butter into her mother's heavy, copper-bottomed saucepan along with the milk and lit the burner on low. Counting out a dozen eggs, she cracked each in half and used the broken shell to separate the yolks from the whites. She'd save the whites for a lemon meringue pie, Pop's favorite. Not that she knew when she'd whip up a pie. To be honest with herself, Madame Delphine had turned her off making pastry, and she'd avoided baking anything but breads and cakes – with several dozen cookies thrown in – since her return.

'Just look at it as *your* pie, not pastry,' she whispered to herself as she measured the flour, sugar, salt, yeast, and raisins, separating out the portions of flour and sugar she'd need for the crumb topping.

She had no choice but to soak a new batch of raisins as the ones she'd prepped the other day in front of Nowicki were beyond soaked and more appropriate for fruitcake than placek. It didn't usually take that long for the dried fruit to rehydrate, thank goodness. This was her secret ingredient in her placek.

Secrets were great in recipes but not in life, or with lives. Already soothed by her baking ritual, Lydia paused and thought about what she knew so far.

Louie had been murdered, but not in the smoker where she'd found him. Thanks to Stanley's insight and Ned's input, plus all the clues she'd picked up by watching Nowicki and talking to Grandma, she knew that Louie had in all probability been shot and bled out somewhere else, and then his body had been moved to their backyard.

Who had the gun or where they got it was a question she was least likely to figure out. A gun could be thrown into Lake Erie or the Niagara River, both literally minutes away, and never found again.

No, her special ingredient in the investigation was getting people to open up to her. So far she'd talked to Stanley, which she considered almost as good as talking to Mr Gorski. Stanley's father was a man of few words as his son had said, and she didn't think she'd pry more from him. Despite Grandma's certainty that his feet were too small to match the backyard footprints, Johnny remained her top suspect. He'd interacted with Louie recently and picked up on how rude – if not plain abusive – Louie was being to her. Johnny's interest in how Lydia was doing the morning of the murder raised her red flags, too. Add in the fact that Johnny wore boots to work on Friday, instead of his usual sneakers, which might have the exact same pattern as the footprints she saw, and it looked more like Johnny did it with each passing moment. If only she could find out from Ned if the footprints matched.

The reality of how Johnny and Teri's rendezvous coincided perfectly with Louie's estimated time of death, or when he was moved to the smoker, was a fact she couldn't overlook, either. No way did she consider Teri a suspect, but her sister may well have been with the murderer. The possibility stilled her hands, and she let the wave of revulsion travel through her shoulders, down her back. After a moment she refocused, thought of the suspects she and Grandma had discussed.

That brought her back to their other number one suspect, especially if her and Grandma's suspicions that Louie was slipping someone his salami on the side – just plain gross to even contemplate – proved true. Charlotte McDaniel had to be the next person she spoke to. She could do it under the guise of paying a sympathy visit, and see what sweet-talking would yield. She had to be prepared to not only play it cool, but to keep her opinions hidden. If Charlotte was Louie's killer, she knew she was being looked at and would no doubt do everything to protect her freedom. If Charlotte was a killer, she'd be a liar, too.

Lydia's nerves settled now that she had her next objective: interview Charlotte. But when? Tonight was out, as was the holiday tomorrow. It would have to be Monday, after she took care of the fire hall's Dyngus Day catering order.

Monday would be the start of the week and maybe this most unwanted mystery would be solved before Tuesday.

'Let's leave Monday until Monday.' She spoke quietly to herself as she whipped the egg yolks with a dinner fork. The longer the tines, the smoother the consistency.

Was there anything richer than egg yolks beat into creamy perfection? She didn't think so as she took the saucepan from the heat and stirred the yolks into the hot milk and butter concoction with her favorite wooden spoon.

Mom's Sunbeam stand mixer stared forlornly from the corner of the tiny counter that it occupied, as if judging her for not using the electric tool for such a laborious job. Mixing the sifted flour and sugar into the liquid was not for the weak, but Lydia had tried many different ways to make the placek, and while using either an electric hand- or stand-mixer took way less time, she found that hand-mixing the batter into pliant dough gave the best results. The Wienewski women that had landed at Ellis Island the better part of a century ago had never seen an electric kitchen appliance, yet from what Pop remembered of his childhood, no baked goods have ever tasted better than those made by his grandmother. With this in mind she kept stirring with her mother's ancient wooden spoon until the batter was thick and smooth, and then added the well-hydrated golden raisins.

'*Grrr.*' Stashu greeted her from the kitchen door.

'Happy Easter to you, too. Did you see the Easter Bunny come, sweetie?'

Stashu issued a short *yap*, then sat and scratched his ear.

'Let me get this covered and we'll go for a walk.' She greased a second large bowl with more butter, placed the dough inside, and set the stove timer for an hour. Swiping her hands together, she cleaned up. All that remained on the counter was the crumb topping ingredients and three banged-up loaf pans. She planned to purchase all new tools for the café, but the Easter rush had precluded her preparations.

Not to mention Louie's murder.

The reminder broke the mental respite baking had granted and she wasted no more time in the kitchen, alone with her thoughts.

'Come on, Stashu. We both need a walk.' They could walk to the shop and back, take their time. She grabbed a quart of milk. The kitties deserved an Easter morning treat.

Lydia entered pure chaos when she walked into the Wienewski kitchen late Easter morning. Familiar aromas of pork sausage, smoked and fresh, marjoram, and sugar from her placek baking hit her nose first, quickly followed by a tinge of . . . burning. She found the source with little effort. The large, enameled pot of fresh kielbasa was overboiling, hitting the gas stove flames with loud hissing. She quickly turned the burner down, leaving the pale grey sausage to simmer. Their family always parboiled the fresh kielbasa, then roasted it in the oven, covered, at a low heat. She preferred it right out of the cooking water herself, smothered in ketchup. She checked the oven and saw that the smoked kielbasa was done, as it only needed to be heated, and pulled it out and placed it atop trivets on the kitchen table.

The entire time she worked at keeping the main meal on track, she absorbed the verbal zingers that flew between her sister and parents. Ted was, as usual, nowhere to be found as he had hospital duty today.

'Pop, you've got to talk some sense into her!' Teri's voice reached an octave that hurt Lydia's ears.

'You know your mother.' Pop shook his head and slowly left the kitchen.

'Come on, help me get this ham in the oven. Get out of the

way, you damn dog!' Mom was in pre-party mode. She'd buzzed about the kitchen all morning in preparation for their family event.

'Mom, calm down. He's just a dog. And the ham will be ready when it needs to be. We have enough sausage to keep people happy when they first sit down.' Lydia scooped Stashu up and handed him to Teri. 'Here, you take him for a walk, then lock him in Mom and Pop's room. We don't want anyone stepping on him.'

'Fine. But I still have to curl my hair,' Teri complained. 'She hasn't let me do anything but fix platters since I got up.'

'If you'd gotten up in time to go to Mass with us you'd be ready.' Mom, still in her robe with pink sponge rollers in her hair, swigged back some coffee.

'You didn't go to Mass, either,' was Teri's parting shot before she and Stashu slammed out the back door.

'Mom, you didn't go to Mass?' Lydia asked. She'd gone back to bed herself after she'd left the placek to cool.

'How could I? I wanted to go to Vigil last night but it's too long for your pop. He's a lot better, Lydia, but don't be fooled, he's still not completely himself.' Pinching a whole clove between her fingers, Mom carefully pinned a canned pineapple slice to the ham Lydia had smoked two weeks earlier. It felt a lifetime ago. For Louie, it had been.

'What are you saying, Mom? Do you think he's not going to go back to work soon?'

Mom plucked a maraschino cherry from its jar, sliced it in half, and stabbed another clove through it.

'I don't know what I'm saying, Lydia. Between your sister's crazy behavior, Louie's death, and worrying about your father, I don't know which end's up. Detective Nowicki seems like a nice man and I'm glad he's on our side. But it's made this weekend a little more nuts than usual, you know?' Mom didn't have the concerns about Nowicki that Lydia did. Lydia let it go, for now. Mom's shoulders were weighed down enough.

'Here, let me.' Lydia washed her hands then took the jar of cherries. She couldn't recall when she'd worked alongside Mom last, and she'd missed it. Just not all the drama.

'It's something, though, that someone has it in for your father or me enough to put a dead body in our yard,' Mom said. 'It makes me sick to think about how much hate that takes.'

'Do you have any inklings on who'd do it, Mom?'

Mom shook her head. 'No. Believe me, if I did, I'd already have killed them for what they've done to our family and the shop. The Easter sales weren't good, were they?'

'They started out strong. I'm betting that Friday's business was enough to make it a success.' Lydia flat-out lied, and on Easter Sunday, too. No guilt or remorse pierced her soul, though. Sometimes positive thinking to the point of fabrication was necessary to survival.

'Mmm.' Mom was on to her but let it go. 'Tell me something. What are you and your grandmother up to? Is she getting information on Louie's killer from her old flame?'

Lydia stared at her mother. As usual, Mom hadn't missed anything, no matter how flustered she appeared.

'We're working on what we can, without interfering in the police's job.'

Mom held up her hand in classic 'stop' sign. 'Spare me the rigamarole. What are you and Mary up to?'

Lydia's face grew hot. 'We're going to solve this as soon as we can.'

Mom nodded, satisfied. 'That's my girl. Just be careful, will you? Whoever did this isn't stable, or predictable. You don't want to be next.'

'We're not doing anything dangerous, Mom.' Not another lie, not really. Last night had been risky, but neither she nor Grandma had been in harm's way.

Unless the killer was there too, watching you.

A shudder ran down her back and she moved to the sink with the empty jar to hide her reaction. As she rinsed out the bright red syrup, Mom paused over the ham, a clove in one hand and pineapple slice in the other. The line between her brows had turned into two but her mouth was in a soft line.

'Do you have any idea what's going on with your sister? Teri has been avoiding me. I know she's busy with school and working in the store, but she and I used to at least spend some coffee time together every day. Lately she's gone before I come into the kitchen.'

Lydia weighed her reply. 'She's not a kid anymore, Mom. I do know that she and Dave are on the outs.'

'Tell me about it. She's already invited a new boy to dinner. Today!' Mom's bemusement forced a giggle out of Lydia.

'Johnny was coming anyway, wasn't he?' Johnny and Vi, and even Louie for that matter, weren't strangers to a Wienewski holiday meal. Mom ran an open house on Christmas Eve and Easter Sunday every year. It was how things were done.

'It's Johnny? Johnny Bello's her new boyfriend? *Our* Johnny? Son of a b—' Mom cut her words off and shook her head again, this time hard enough to make her curlers bounce. 'That child of mine.'

Lydia held her breath, waiting for Mom to explode into a tirade of how young women should be more worried about getting an education to support themselves than finding a boyfriend to scratch a biological itch that once activated would forever need attention. Yes, Mom had said that to Lydia.

Silence grew, broken by the soft *plod* of the paring knife against the worn wooden cutting board as she split the remaining cherries.

'*Pffffft.*' Mom's emotional dam burst.

Mom's outburst wasn't what Lydia expected, though. Laughter filled the kitchen until Mom was bent over, her hands to her stomach. Lydia stared at her mother, usually the most un-amused member of their family.

'Oh, my God, Lydia. Do you know that when I was Teri's age, I started dating your father? My parents were fit to be tied, me bringing home a butcher man after dumping a fancy school teacher and all.'

'Really?' Lydia knew that her maternal grandparents, who died when she was a toddler, had never been enamored of Pop but neither parent had ever spilled the beans about the particulars.

'Oh yes, really. My father threatened to kick me to the curb, told me I'd better not let that "no good bum who smells like sausage" knock me up.' The sponge curlers bobbed with Mom's giggles. Lydia winced.

'That's mean, Mom.' No wonder Mom was rough around the edges when disciplining her kids. She hadn't had the best examples.

'Hey, it's how it was back then. Do you think school taught us anything about sex? He was worried for me, is all. And look, your pop turned out to be a winner.' She grew thoughtful as she finished dressing the ham and lowered it into the oven. 'Maybe Teri's found her Pop.'

Lydia couldn't comment without risking blowing Teri's confidence so she busied herself with scrubbing down the counters. 'Mom, people are going to start showing up in twenty minutes. Go get ready. I'll take care of the rest of this.'

'Is Stanley coming over today?'

Lydia straightened at the sink. 'He mentioned it, yes.'

'Don't let your pride get in the way of that, Lydia.' Before she could ask for clarification, Mom was gone, off to tease out her curls into their fluffy pixie 'do. Which left Lydia alone in the kitchen with her thoughts of Stanley. Her stomach churned and did a flip as she replayed how he'd been so determined to convince her that she had to protect herself, her family, from Nowicki. She was glad her mom had left the room before she said anything about looking at Stanley differently from how she'd always thought of him. She had to. He was a suspect until she found the killer. Could it be him? It would mean she hadn't seen what she thought she had in his eyes when he looked at her the other night.

Concern. As if he still cared.

Nope. Not going there.

The distraction of solving Louie's murder didn't seem so awful, after all.

'Mrs Wienewski, this is the best ham I ever tasted!' Johnny carefully wiped his mouth with the gold-embossed paper napkin. It matched the paper plates and cups, staples at any meal involving more than the six dinner plates in the kitchen cupboard.

'I'm glad you liked it, Johnny.' Mom was playing it cool about Johnny's sudden appearance as not simply an employee and family friend, but Teri's new squeeze. She deserved a gold star for her verbal restraint as far as Lydia was concerned. Teri and Johnny were all but glued together as they sat side-by-side at the main dining table. It had been elongated with card tables on either end to allow for the crowd. A kiddie table was set in the kitchen, where the battered oak highchair that Mom had fed all three of the Wienewski babies was being used by Lydia's cousin Joy, Aunt Dot's oldest. Six-month-old Amber mashed potatoes with both her gums and chubby hands, to the delight of the older kids.

'Harry sure enjoyed it, didn't you?' Grandma asked.

'Mmm.' Nowicki was still chewing. The man had a bottomless pit. Or was it all a show for Grandma?

'We'll have dessert after we get this cleared away,' Mom announced.

'Not me. I don't touch that white stuff. You know that sweets are bad for you, right?' Vi's voice sliced through the holiday cheer. Lydia had hoped against hope that the woman wouldn't make it, but as usual, she'd slid in late, making a big deal of the plastic-wrapped crystal dish of olives and mini gherkins she'd brought.

Vi stood and stretched, arching her back. 'I'm going outside for a breath of fresh air.'

'And a smoke. Now, that's real good for you,' Grandma observed. Her former daughter-in-law had never been Grandma's favorite person.

Vi landed a steely gaze on Grandma, which got Lydia's hackles up. She'd managed to give Vi a wide berth today, and had postponed looking at the accounts until after the holiday. But no one went after her grandma.

'Mary, you have your opinions of what's healthy and I have mine.' Vi cast a glance at Nowicki. 'And I'm not just talking about food. How many does this make since you lost Joe? I know I wasn't able to look at another man for years after I lost my dear Ray.'

'You're right about that, because those losers you paraded around after my dear son died weren't by any definition real men,' Grandma said. Lydia wondered if both Grandma and Vi had been nipping a little too much of the family brandy.

Vi leaned over the table and sneered. 'You know yourself

I never found a man who could replace *my* Ray. How many
times do I have to tell you that? There is never any pleasing
you, Mary. Why do you think Ray and I moved all the way
to New York City?'

Lydia stood and faced Vi. She'd fire her right here and now,
Easter dessert and Pop's approval be damned.

'Enough. Let's keep it nice. We're family.' Pop spoke more
slowly than usual, as if he'd not had several months of speech
rehab. Lydia suppressed a sigh. He was drawing on his mother's
sympathy to distract her. She wasn't thrilled with how he let
Vi's rude comments go, but then again, no surprise there. Pop's
way of honoring Uncle Ray's memory was wrapped into how
he treated Vi. He couldn't separate the pain-in-the-dupa woman
from his former sister-in-law. Pop was too nice.

But he wasn't stupid. Vi had left and once again the happy
din of multiple conversations going at once filled the house.

Grandma returned her attention to Nowicki, wiping a smear
of mashed potatoes from his cheek. 'Can I get you a coffee,
or do you want something stronger?'

'Coffee's good. Still on the case, you know.'

'Has there been anything new, Detective?' Lydia used the
cover of other people talking to seek out a clue.

'Nothing that you probably don't already know. We're
working on it, tracing down several leads. That's all I want to
say right now.'

'Several leads?' she asked. Were the footprints involved?

'Hmmm.' He nodded, giving her zero hints, then turned
back to Grandma. 'Why don't we go into the kitchen and get
that coffee?' Nowicki's focus on Grandma was so sweet it
made Lydia's teeth hurt. A pang shot through her. Stanley used
to look at her like that.

Stanley. He'd never shown. He'd said he'd stop in for Aunt
Dot's cheesecake, nothing more. Had that been an empty
promise? And why was she even worrying about it? He had
his own family to have Easter with, and she had hers. They
weren't together anymore.

Keep telling yourself that.

'Here, help me with this.' Mom was next to her, scooping
the used paper plates into a large plastic trash bag.

'Sit, Amelia. Let everyone else take care of it.' Pop put his good hand on Mom's forearm but she brushed it away. She was in full entertaining mode.

'I've got it! Sit down, Amelia.' Aunt Dot jumped up, eager as ever to get her prized cheesecake served. No question, Aunt Dot's dessert was the tastiest Lydia had ever tasted, except for her own recipe. Cream cheese and eggs beat together with sugar couldn't be bad in anyone's estimation, but then add in Aunt Dot's vanilla that she made herself from vodka and vanilla beans, and the sour cream glaze topping, and you had perfection. Lydia liked to include ricotta cheese in hers, which made her cheesecake a unique combination of the traditional sweet she'd grown up with and Grandma's Italian roots, where ricotta was the only cheese considered worthy of cheesecake.

'I'll help, too.' Lydia stood and reached for the used flat-ware just as they were all interrupted by the roar of a very un-muffled motor and screeching tires.

'Someone's burning rubbers,' Pop said.

'Rubber. They're burning rubber, honey. You mean their tires,' Mom corrected, agitated by Pop's obliviousness.

Teri's high-pitched gasp sliced through the commotion, but it wasn't at Pop's unintentional funny turn of phrase.

'Oh, no!' she cried. Her gaze met Lydia's. Lydia tried to look supportive of her little sis, but really, did Teri think she'd switch out boyfriends as easily as she changed her clothes? Especially when the guy she dropped was the likes of Dave?

'What?' Johnny, his arm still draped around Teri's shoulders, wasn't so quick on the uptake.

The back door slammed open, feet pounded on the three steps. Lydia silently counted. One, two—

'I need to speak with Teri!' Dave burst into the dining room. Or at least, he tried to, but the ferocity of his entrance was stymied by the sheer mass of overfed guests crowding at the same entry, hoping to move about before the sweet treats came out. He brought with him the waft of either too much drugstore cologne or booze, Lydia couldn't be certain. She knew he was a nasty drunk from Teri. Had he driven here while tanked?

'You can say anything you need to, to me.' Johnny shed all

vestiges of the ignorant new boyfriend in one fluid move, pushing back his folding chair and standing to face Dave. Johnny had dressed for the occasion. Lydia couldn't recall ever seeing Johnny in anything but work or casual clothes before and she had to admit, Teri's taste had improved. His pressed white dress shirt offset a festive yellow and violet paisley tie, and both complemented his dark features.

Dave, by comparison, looked like a degenerate with his over-styled mullet, black leather jacket worn over too-tight acid-wash jeans – Lydia remembered he'd asked Teri to bleach them for him – and white high-top sneakers. Johnny stood maybe an inch shorter than Dave but his confident bearing and wide shoulders made Teri's ex look like a bad version of a Tolkien character.

No contest there.

Lydia bit the inside of her cheek. The room had grown quiet and guests had cleared from the entry. This was the best surprise drama since her brother Ted had sliced his hand with the electric knife he'd bought their parents for Christmas two years ago. Pop had roared in protest – 'Whatsa matter with you, getting that piece of gimmicky plastic for a butcher?' – and Mom had driven Ted, hand bleeding, to the ER for thirteen stitches. Fortunately the accident hadn't affected Ted's surgical skills.

'I came here to talk to Teri.' Dave wasn't backing down but Lydia gave him thirty seconds more, max.

'Maybe you and I need to discuss this outside?' Johnny asked. It didn't sound like an invitation to Lydia. So Johnny was a tough guy. She'd never seen Johnny as her sister's protector before.

'I'm not *talking* to you about anything.' Dave's hands fisted and he took a half-step closer to Johnny. 'Allow me to introduce myself. I'm Teri's boyfriend.'

'No, you're not, Dave!' Teri screeched.

'I've got this, OK?' Johnny spoke to Teri in a firm but kind tone. Sexy, even.

'O-OK,' Teri stammered.

Johnny refocused on Dave. 'You're an ex. Ex-boyfriend. Go home,' Johnny growled.

'I'll tell you who's an ex!' Dave's mullet vibrated with his rage.

'I asked you once. Now I'm telling you. Let's take it outside. This isn't the time or place for this nonsense.' Johnny's voice had lowered two octaves and were his nostrils flaring?

'I don't take orders from you!' Dave swayed, identifying the whiff Lydia caught when he walked in. Definitely alcohol.

Lydia looked at Pop, who'd chosen this moment to make a show of getting up from the table. He was interested in how this was going to play out, too. Or maybe he wasn't concerned because he knew Johnny and loved him like his own son. Pop had never hesitated to refer to Dave as 'that bum you're dating' in front of Teri.

'Here's the dessert!' Aunt Dot stood at the entry, looking expectantly at Dave and Johnny. She held her legendary cheesecake in both hands, her pride evident in a beaming smile.

Johnny turned to Aunt Dot. 'Excuse us. We'll get out of your way.' He faced Dave. 'Right?'

'Wrong.' Dave grabbed Aunt Dot's beloved confection off her Easter Bunny serving dish and smashed it to pieces.

All over Johnny's face.

Lydia felt a cold *splat* of cheesecake on her cheek as Aunt Dot's stunned sputters turned into big tears, cascading down her powdered face and dripping from the tip of her nose onto the empty platter.

Indignation whirred with rage at the blatant lack of respect for the Wienewski family gathering. With Teri frozen like a fawn in the road and everyone else watching the show, Lydia saw no other option but to act.

'Enough!' she yelled as she rounded the table, reaching for Dave's shoulders. But Johnny beat her to it, taking Dave by the scruff of his neck and forcing him across the living room to the front door. Lydia scuttled alongside them and opened the oak door, holding the outer storm door wide as Johnny half-carried, half-shoved a red-faced, screaming Dave outside. She and several guests watched as Johnny threw Dave onto the wet lawn.

'Go home. Now!' Johnny roared.

Dave scrambled back up to his feet. 'Never!' He bent over

and aimed his head into Johnny's midsection. Johnny side-stepped, and Dave ran headfirst into their crab apple tree trunk. The impact sent him backward onto his ass, which Lydia thought commensurate with his behavior.

'Look, he's going to be in trouble now!' Mom exclaimed, pointing at Nowicki as he strode across the lawn. He must have gone out the kitchen door when he heard the commotion. His grim expression told Lydia all she needed to know. Nowicki would take care of it. If Dave had committed Driving While Intoxicated – DWI – coming over here, it was a police matter now.

She turned around, searching for Aunt Dot. She was right next to her, wiping the last of the cheesecake remnants from her pleated blouse.

'Aunt Dot, I'm so sorry!' Lydia plucked a graham cracker crumb from the edge of her aunt's eye glasses. 'I know how much work you put into your cheesecake.'

'Oh, phooey. We've got your placek – I love how you make your Polish coffee cake with the golden raisins, they're always so moist! – and all that orange chocolate your mother bought for us. I mean, I'm sad about my dessert but I have to admit, I haven't seen a show like this since your uncle took me to Shea's Theater downtown. The Rockettes were touring. They've got nothing on Teri's love life!'

Teri coughed and Lydia saw she was busy cleaning up the framed photo of Pope John Paul II that usually hung on the dining room wall. Even the first Polish Pope hadn't escaped the melee.

And now Nowicki was handling a DWI instead of finding Louie's killer. Lydia scoured the room for the only thing that would help her now.

A chocolate bunny. Or at least its ears.

SIXTEEN

Lydia awoke with a headache on Dyngus Day. Tired from being out all night at the creek Saturday night with Grandma, followed by the Dave and Johnny show, she'd indulged in too much orange chocolate last night. Mom still insisted on making all three of her grown children a bountiful Easter basket, filled with local treats to include sponge candy – spun sugar foam cut into cubes and coated with creamy chocolate – and the ubiquitous, orange-flavored molded chocolate figures.

Her brother Ted had missed all of the festivities as he'd been on call and slept over at Sisters Hospital, in Buffalo proper. Mom had insisted Teri and Johnny run a 'little something' down to the hospital for Ted. Lydia suspected Mom was doing her part to show her support of the new relationship by entrusting them with the honor. In fact, Mom had put together an over-the-top care package for Ted, filling an empty dozen egg box with enough kielbasa, ham, rolls, cheesecake and jelly beans to feed the entire hospital staff. Or at least half-a-dozen of them.

Grandma and Lydia had continued to 'play it cool' at the family get-together, and not reveal how tired they both were from the wee hour excursion the night before. Lydia had been relieved to see Nowicki leave – the last guest – and promptly gone to bed.

Good thing, because getting the fire department's order delivered had taken a better part of this morning.

The truck was almost empty after an hour of unloading.

'Let us get that for you.' Two volunteer firefighters took over unloading from the back end of the Wienewski's Wieners & Meats delivery truck.

'Thanks, you guys.' Lydia stood aside and began checking off the delivery receipt she'd prepared ahead of time. She'd loaded the Cheektowaga FD's large order beginning at six this morning, on her own. Grandma and Teri both needed sleep, and Johnny wasn't scheduled today, anyway. She'd decided to keep the shop closed today, as well, with nary a complaint from her family. Pop normally took Dyngus Day off.

She had hoped the time to herself would help her figure out why Easter had been such a disappointment for her. It would be easy to blame it on the Dave-Johnny-Teri drama, fatigue, or on the fact that while she now had another suspect in Louie's wife Charlotte, she didn't know much more than she had before she and Grandma did their own version of *Mission Impossible* in the woods.

Lydia was upset with herself. Over one person. One man. *Stanley.*

He hadn't shown for Easter, after giving her every indication that he would. Not that she was his keeper, of course. But had she misread his intentions? Was her gut instinct skewed? If she'd read Stanley's signals wrong, was she overlooking the real killer, risking another person might be murdered in the meantime?

'Is this the last of it?' A young firefighter with beefy arms bulging under his uniform jacket nodded at the three trays of kielbasa he held. Lydia smiled. She could carry one tray at a time, two if she absolutely had to and it was the short trip between the refrigerator room and the truck.

'Yes, that's it. Oh, wait. Here. Let me.' She grabbed a box of jarred horseradish and fell in step next to him. They entered the building through the open garage doors, walked past the bright red trucks, and up the stairs to the event hall that occupied most of the second floor.

'Wow.' She stared at the long tables covered in red-and-white checked cloths, the piles of baked goods from Kalinski Bakery, the pyramid of beer glasses awaiting ale from the kegs stamped with the Genesee Cream Ale logo.

Next year the sweets will come from Lydia's Café and Bakery.

All of the food and beverages were lined up against the nearest wall, with tables and chairs arranged throughout the rest of the hall. The dance floor and small stage where a polka band would play later, well into the night, were in the dead center of the tables.

'You can put the horseradish right here, Lydia.' Jenny Macki stood at a table laden with utensils, napkins, and condiments. She'd married Patrick Macki, whose surname was a shortened version of whatever it originally had been. It was common for a Polish name to be abbreviated, either at Ellis Island generations ago or more recently. Lydia had wished as a girl that their family name was easier on the tongue, easier to spell, but now it was a source of pride. She wouldn't want to be anything other than a Wienewski.

Except maybe a Gorski. Not while both Gorski men were on her suspect list, though.

'Hey, Jenny. I didn't expect to see you here.' She set the box down. 'I thought you'd be at work.'

'I got the day off.' Jenny grinned. 'How the heck are you? You've been quiet. Come to think of it, all of us have.'

'No kidding. We need a catch-up girls' night, like, yesterday!' Lydia gave Jenny a hug and was grateful for the warm squeeze she got back. 'It's been nuts!'

'So I hear. I wanted to call you but Patrick told me that you needed room to breathe, with Easter and . . . all.' Jenny looked away.

'Stop it! I know you know about the body in our backyard. Everyone does.'

'Well, it was on the news.'

'And since your husband is on the PD, he has the inside scoop, right? Let me guess, he talked to Ned?'

Jenny blushed. 'Actually, it was your neighbor who told him all about it. The department put him on the case right away.'

'I never saw him, ever.' Of course, she'd been distracted by Nowicki's constant presence, and what had turned into abysmal Easter sales.

'Pat says half of the department is assigned to the investigation. It's a number one priority.' Jenny's rapid fire use of the words reminded Lydia of the dialogue she and Grandma heard on *Adam-12*, a police show. Her husband Patrick had recently been promoted to corporal after being a detective in the Cheektowaga Police Department. Lydia knew that he'd had to have trained under Nowicki, as the man had been there for decades and was the lead homicide detective. 'It's been too long since we got together. When you came back I thought we'd go back to how we used to be, you know? You, me and Becky, hitting all the bars every other Friday night.'

'I know. Me, too. I guess we've all got a lot on our plates now.' Lydia sighed. Jenny and Becky were her two closest girlfriends and they'd all cried in a group hug when she'd left for Ottawa. Since she'd been back, though, getting together had been tough, especially since her time was soaked up by the butcher shop and her business. And now, Louie's murder.

'We'll fix this, trust me. I'll have everyone over for a girls' night soon. So tell me, Lydia, what can Becky or I do for you now? You're in a world of hurt, from what people are saying.'

'How do you mean?' Lydia knew her face had to be red. Her insides sure were red-hot.

'Well, I've heard that someone you know might be the killer.' Jenny never sugar-coated anything; why start now with the first murder either of them had ever been affected by?

Dread wound around Lydia's heart, followed quickly by ire.

'Who? Who said that, exactly? And who did they say did it?' Lydia's cheeks were hot, and she knew her eyes probably bulged.

'Hey, I don't know! I just heard that the murder was personal to your family. Chill out, why don't ya?' Jenny held up both hands as if Lydia were about to assault her.

'Everything OK over here, ladies?' One of the firemen stared at them.

'We're fine,' Lydia and Jenny answered in unison.

Jenny stepped closer, leaned in. 'Lydia, hon, I'm only telling you what's going around. I know you couldn't kill a fly. No Wienewski could.' Jenny's sincerity reflected in her brown eyes.

'Unless it'll look good in the meat case,' Lydia deadpanned. They both laughed, breaking the tension. 'I wanted to call you as soon as it happened, but I can't talk about the case. The lead detective told us that mum's the word.'

'OK, got it.' Jenny waggled her brows. 'Blink once for yes, twice for no. Did you find the body?'

Lydia blinked before she could think. 'No, wait, I didn't mean that . . .'

'So you didn't find the corpse?'

An involuntary shudder ran across Lydia's shoulders.

'Aha! So you did.' The polka band chose that moment to begin warming up. The boisterous strain of 'Beer Barrel Polka' playing across accordions, drums, and a clarinet made normal conversation impossible. Jenny grabbed Lydia's elbow and ushered her into a side room, closing the door behind them. The hushed quiet wrapped itself around Lydia like a hand-crocheted Afghan.

'There, that's better.' Jenny motioned at one of several folding chairs set up around a gargantuan metal desk. 'Take a seat.'

'What is this room used for, usually?'

'It's where they play cards, when they're on duty overnight. They're not all allowed to sleep, you know. Two have to be awake at all times.'

'That makes sense.' Lydia nodded. Jenny's pale skin sported two bright pink spots over her cheekbones. 'What's going on? I know you're dying to tell me something.' Jenny never could hide it when she had news.

'I'll tell you in a bit. First, you have to tell me what you need. Not just from me, but from all of us Misfits.' Jenny used the moniker their group of three close friends had settled on during junior high school, grade seven, Mrs Beasley's Home Economics class. They'd been the only three in the class of thirty to not pass the sewing course, thanks in part to the overly strict grading of the teacher they'd called 'Mrs Beastly' behind her back. The other reason for their poor tailoring skills had been lack of ambition, due in great measure to having discovered their blossoming hormones, thanks to the David Cassidy vinyl record Becky had cut from the back of a Raisin Bran cereal box.

'I promise I'll tell you if I need anything. Right now I'm more worried about the butcher shop than anything.'

Jenny nodded. 'Did you have a drop in Easter sales?'

'You know it. But wait – how did you guess?'

'Between what I saw on the news at eleven that night, and the rush on canned ham at the store, I put two and two together.' Jenny worked at Tops Supermarket on Genesee Street, a block from the shop.

'There were several orders that were never claimed.' Lydia's stomach plummeted. 'How can people think the worst of Pop, my family, without all the facts?'

'As much as people want to be all holy on Easter, they're a superstitious lot. One woman even said . . .' Jenny slapped her hand over her mouth, her eyes wide.

'Spill it, Jenny. Nothing is too hard to hear, believe me. Besides, it's better I know it all.'

Jenny slowly lowered her arm to the table. 'It was one of my cranky customers. Remember when I told you about the lady who took off without paying for her order at New Year's? It was her, but I can't prove it since I didn't alert management right on the spot. I didn't realize my drawer was short until it was too late. Do you know, she still comes back into the store every week, as though she's not a thief?'

'Maybe she's poor?'

Jenny shook her head. 'Oh, no. She's one of the boss's aunts. So she thinks she can get away with it whenever she wants to.'

'What did she say?' Lydia pressed.

'That death rubs off on everything. She said she'd never step foot in Wienewski's again. And she mentioned the pork incident.'

'Who was she talking to?' Lydia prayed it hadn't been in earshot of a crowd.

'Herself, mostly, as I rang up her three Polish hams.'

Lydia's mind flashed on the image of a large brown paper bag, filled with ham and kielbasa, the name DeLuca scrawled in grease pencil across the sales ticket. No one had come in to claim it, along with over two dozen additional Easter pre-orders.

'Wait, it was Mrs DeLuca, wasn't it?' Married to an optometrist, Maria DeLuca was a prized customer of Pop's. At least, she had been.

'Yes, it was her. I'm sorry, Lydia.' Jenny put her hand on Lydia's forearm. 'I know it's hard to see your family's business between a rock and a hard place, but you have to stay focused on your own goals. You're going to have your own place open by summer!'

Lydia raised her chin. 'I know. Grandma and I went out to the lake late on Saturday, actually. To take some notes, see what has to be done first. It's going to be great, Jenny.' She went on to detail the discovery of the original soda fountain and her plans for a budget-friendly renovation.

'I'm so happy for you!' Jenny enthused. 'So why are you hanging out here? You delivered the order. Go fix up your café.'

'I can't, not right now.' Not since Nowicki dressed her and Grandma down about leaving Cheektowaga. 'I need to stay close to home base. For my pop.'

'I know you, Lydia Wienewski. You're involved in this murder somehow. Oh, I know you didn't do it, but what's going on, besides you finding the dead body?'

'You mentioned the bad pork situation from last year. The dead body was the person responsible for it.'

'That Louie guy you told me about?' Jenny's eyes widened. 'Oh my goodness. I had no idea it was that crook! Patrick didn't give me any names, of the deceased or of the suspects, in case you're wondering. He's very good about following the "loose lips sink ships" rule,' Jenny explained. Jenny and Becky had heard all about the bad business deal, how Louie had left Pop and several other customers in the lurch, for his own profit.

'Yeah, that's the one. Well, our shop isn't the only one he was cheating. Which means there are a lot of people who didn't care for him.'

'And that means the police will need longer to complete their interviews and evidence collection.' Jenny mused. 'It makes sense that they have to keep you and your family on the suspect list, but no one around here believes you did it for one second, Lydia.'

'The thing is it doesn't matter what people think. It's what the police come up with.' Lydia sighed. 'And the longer it takes, the longer the butcher shop loses money.'

'You're not thinking of doing something stupid, are you, Lydia?'

'By "stupid," do you mean "figure out who killed Louie" myself?'

'That's exactly what I mean! Listen, let me ask Patrick for some details. It's against the rules, sure, but whatever it takes to help you. Just don't go sticking your nose into beeswax that isn't yours. It's dangerous out there.'

'What was the news you were going to tell me?' Lydia wasn't about to reveal all she'd already checked into, and how she and Grandma were going to solve this crime before any more damage was done to the Wienewski name. Jenny was married to Patrick, after all. Lydia wouldn't blame her for repeating what she heard to her husband. Jenny also would do anything for her friend, which Lydia didn't want. It was bad enough that Grandma was putting herself at risk. It was for the best to not tell Jenny anything, for both their sakes.

'You won't be surprised at my news.' Jenny glowed.

'Try me.' Lydia already knew but wanted her dear friend to have the joy of announcing what her too-tight designer jeans had already revealed.

'I'm pregnant.'

'Oh my gosh, congratulations!' Lydia embraced Jenny in a tight hug, both of them laughing until they cried. 'Did you tell Becky yet?'

Jenny nodded. 'I wanted to tell you together but I found out on Friday. But when Patrick came home for lunch that day he told me about the murder. He said it wasn't the time to get ahold of you. Then it was Easter, and well, you know how nuts it gets with my family.'

Lydia nodded. 'I do. This is going to be so exciting!' And she meant it, really, she did. Getting married and having babies had never been her top priority, not with her career goals and then going off to Canada.

It was then that Lydia realized how deep her feelings still were for Stanley, suspect and all. From her new vantage point, Jenny's life didn't look like any version of entrapment to Lydia. It looked like a future Lydia had lost to her single-mindedness over believing she needed a pastry school degree, fueled by her stubborn pride.

Either way, Lydia couldn't dwell on her sorrows or contemplate her future. Not until she cleared her family name.

It didn't keep her heart from weeping just a little bit, though, as it was a sad day when she couldn't celebrate having such deep feelings for someone.

Why, oh why, did her 'someone' have to be a murder suspect?

Lydia walked back out into the event hall and winced. The polka music echoed about the still-empty room. She looked at her watch. Mickey indicated it was still an hour before the doors officially opened.

'Lydia!' The familiar voice sounded in her ear and she turned to face Stanley's bright eyes. Funny, he looked as though he was thrilled to see her. Unless he'd found out something to tell her about the murder?

'Oh, hi!' she shouted over the music, pointed at her ears. 'Can't hear!'

He motioned for her to follow him and she complied. They didn't speak until they'd entered the kitchen, where volunteers were placing the fresh kielbasa she'd provided into commercial pots of boiling water.

'Let's go over there.' He pointed to a side room lined with mostly empty shelves and housing two refrigerators. 'It's the spare pantry.'

'What's up, Stanley?'

'I wanted to apologize for missing out on your aunt's cheesecake.'

'OK.' Really, what else could she say? 'Turns out you didn't miss it.' It couldn't hurt to tell him the funny story, could it? Not as far as the murder investigation went, anyhow. She briefly summarized the cheesecake showdown.

'I'm sorry to hear that but good on Johnny. I always thought Dave was a jerk. But it's still not OK that I didn't show.' He looked up at the ceiling as if counting the popcorn-textured tiles, then down at the fire hall reception room's floor, then finally, his eyes met hers. 'We're having a hard time at home. With my dad.'

Fear sliced through her center for Mr Gorski but more for Stanley. Apparently knowing she considered someone a murder suspect didn't prevent her from having feelings for them. 'Is he all right?' She'd never known Mr Gorski to be anything but the picture of health. But so had Pop.

'He's fine, really. It's just that . . . he's been really upset since Louie was killed.'

'Oh?' Her nape prickled. Mr Gorski certainly had motive to kill Louie. Was a guilty conscience at play?

'Stop it, Lydia. I can see you're doing the Inspector Clouseau thing again.' Was his reference to the movie they'd made out to in the theater's back row deliberate? She all but smelled the scent of Stanley's cologne mixing with the aroma of popcorn.

'I'm not some rank amateur, Stanley.' Well, actually, she was, but it felt like she'd been beating the pavement for clues a lot longer than four days. 'Why is your dad so upset over Louie? They weren't friends, right?'

'You've got that right. No, not friends. He's mad at himself for not speaking up about Louie being such a bad businessman sooner. Dad thinks that someone Louie was in business with killed him over money. If Louie had been forced to work elsewhere, or had to find a different job, he might still be alive today.'

'That's ridiculous. First, no one knows who killed Louie or why. Second, if he thinks he has a theory he should call Ned and tell him. It can't hurt. Do you want me to tell your father that myself?'

'No. But I thought you should know that I didn't just blow you off. I tried to call, twice, but the line was busy. I didn't feel right ducking out of our family dinner when he was that upset over a guy I thought he despised.'

'Your father's always been a kind soul. There's nothing he could have done. None of us saw this coming.'

'You're being too nice about this, Lyd. I mean, it wasn't a date or anything, but I was looking forward to seeing you yesterday.'

'Well, you're seeing me today, right? And I had a lot of things going on yesterday.' More like in the wee hours of Easter morning, but Stanley didn't need to know about her foray into the creekside forest. 'I wouldn't have been good company.' And wouldn't be, not until she solved the case, and then only if Stanley proved innocent.

Please let him be innocent.

'You're always the best company, Lydia.' He took her hands. 'Why don't we help the band practice?'

Lydia could not turn down the best polka partner she'd ever had. Keeping a suspect open to her, trusting her, was important, wasn't it? She gave Stanley a small nod, and they headed back through the kitchen and out into the dance hall. With no preamble, they one-and-a-two-and-a-three-stepped the first Dyngus Day circle around the parquet dance floor.

Lydia had never considered 'Clarinet Polka' romantic, but in this moment the polka band may as well have been playing 'Just the Two of Us,' her current favorite.

That's how it was with Stanley, and always had been. He made something usual something special. For the short length of the dance, Lydia allowed herself to put all thoughts of Louie McDaniel's murder on her mind's back burner.

SEVENTEEN

I t seemed like eons since she'd baked the Easter placek and formulated her method of questioning Charlotte when Lydia finally got into her car later on Monday as she drove out to Louie's house, replaying her time in Stanley's arms most of the way. As she turned onto Louie's street she refocused on the case and looked out the windshield for Louie's place. Well, now it was his widow's home. Getting used to someone having passed wasn't easy, and she found a sudden, tragic death like murder made it worse.

Mrs DeLuca's unclaimed, unpaid-for kielbasa was in a pretty Easter basket on her Gremlin's passenger seat, ready to be gifted to Charlotte McDaniel, Louie's widow.

You're visiting a widow, offering sympathy.

Hopefully the reminder would keep her from messing this up. She pulled into the long, unusual gravel drive, up to a large white-brick house that boasted elaborate wrought-iron railings around its front porch. Large, blow-up, vinyl Easter Bunnies stood sentry, their noses still covered in a thin layer of ice left over from the weekend's ice storm. And were those pink plastic flamingoes between the glider and front wall?

Lydia gathered the basket and potted Easter Lily, and got out of her car. There was a single car parked in the driveway besides hers, with Georgia plates. Louie's daughter Cindy had come home, of course. She'd gone to school with her, and knew Louie's wife, Charlotte, because she'd been the high school secretary for over thirty years. Lydia had no idea if Charlotte still worked at the school, but she'd be home now, planning for Louie's funeral.

His funeral. Lydia hadn't given that a thought. Louie alive was someone she had avoided as much as possible. But she supposed going to his funeral was important, to show respect for the entire family. As he'd loved to remind her, he'd been at her baptism. Louie had been a family friend for a long while, before his morals had taken a sharp wrong turn.

Plus there was the art of appearances, as Grandma liked to say. The Wienewskis had nothing to hide, no reason to not hold their heads high. Lydia was not going to stay home and cower from real or imagined gossip.

The door opened the second after she pushed the doorbell, and she faced Cindy.

'What do you want?' Cindy spoke through the storm door, the glass festooned with colorful cardboard Easter eggs taped to the surface. Charlotte had gone all out for the holiday, with no idea that her husband would be slain before it ever came.

Lydia held up her offerings. 'I wanted to tell your mother – and you – how sorry I am.' Could Cindy ascertain the real reason she was here?

Cindy looked over her shoulder, and Lydia suspected Charlotte sat out of sight, in the front parlor. A sudden movement in her peripheral vision confirmed her hunch when she caught the sheers covering the large picture window that ran the length of the full porch dropping back into place.

'Let her in, Cindy.'

'I brought you some food from our shop.' Lydia stood awkwardly in front of Charlotte, who was nested into an overstuffed recliner. It was the same brand as Pop's, but a much newer model. She knew her words were lame but there was over thirty dollars' worth of kielbasa and ham, along with a butter lamb and horseradish in the basket. No small gift from her family, never mind that it was a shop leftover order.

'Thank you, Lydia. Cindy, put it away.' Charlotte made a shooing motion as she issued the directive, revealing a wrinkled lace handkerchief in her clenched hand. 'Sit down, Lydia. It hurts my neck to look up. All the years hunched over that damn school typewriter.'

Lydia looked for a place to sit amidst the piles of flowers, gift boxes, and papers that cluttered the living room. She shoved a stack of rectangular boxes embossed with the upscale department store AM&A's aside as unobtrusively as possible and took a seat on the avocado velvet love seat across from Charlotte.

'Careful with those boxes. They have the last gifts Louie ever gave me, God rest his soul.' She made the sign of the cross.

'I'm so sorry for your loss, Mrs McDaniel. Our whole family is. Pop especially.'

Charlotte didn't meet her eyes, nodding and rocking as she played with her handkerchief. Its violet print reminded Lydia of her great-grandmother, who'd lived to almost one hundred, dying only after she'd decided to take to her bed and 'go to the Lord.' Lydia had been eight years old and put in charge of taking her dirty handkerchiefs to the laundry for Mom. She'd vowed then to never use anything but disposable tissues.

Charlotte's silence lay heavy on the room, broken only by the rustling of paper and the opening and closing of the refrigerator door as Cindy put the meats away in the kitchen. Lydia realized that the house was too quiet.

'Have you had, er, many visitors?'

Charlotte's gaze, still the beady dark brown one Lydia remembered facing down whenever she'd arrived late to school, sharpened. 'For a man who was squeezing every last penny out of his buyers?' Her snarl morphed into a laugh.

Is this what it means to come unhinged?

'Um, well, Louie certainly had his own way of doing business.'

'Yeah, well, if you've come here to try and get any sympathy out of me for losing your supplier, take a ticket. This is about my family, the loss that Cindy and I are suffering. I can't worry about what all of the businesses Louie's been so loyal to are going to do, you know? Who's going to be loyal to us now?'

Lydia was glad she'd learned that the first skill needed by a good detective was listening. It was all she could do to sit still when she wanted to share what she was hearing with Grandma. Charlotte might very well be the murderer!

'Yeah, that's right, no one.' Charlotte didn't seem to notice Lydia's reaction, or attempt to hide it. Louie's widow shook her head, motioned at the boxes she'd admonished Lydia over.

'You know what's in them, Lydia? What my husband thought was an appropriate anniversary gift to me after forty-five years of marriage?'

Lydia shook her head, afraid that if she spoke she'd stop Charlotte's words.

'A negligee set. A gown, robe, slippers, the whole shebang. He didn't even present me with the gift; I found them under his workbench in the garage. It'd be nice to think he'd hidden my anniversary presents because he was trying to surprise me.'

'That's romantic.' Lydia was game to play along. If Charlotte either wanted to pretend she didn't put two and two together about who the underwear was for – not her – or she was genuinely naive about the fancy AM&A's lingerie, it wasn't Lydia's place to break it to her.

'Romantic? Not when the nightgown's in the size I wore at our wedding.'

Lydia stared at Charlotte, saw the deep anger and betrayal in her eyes.

Charlotte knows.

'You're mistaken. You are a beautiful woman. I'm sure Louie meant well. You can exchange the clothes if you never wore them.' And never would, at least, not for Louie.

'Do I look like a negligee-wearing woman to you?' Charlotte's ruddy cheeks contrasted sharply with her bottle blonde up-do. The same one she'd sported the entirety of Lydia's high school career.

Lydia shook her head. 'I don't know.' She didn't. What was Charlotte getting at – Louie's most probable indiscretion?

Charlotte's exasperated sigh was followed by her clenching the arms of her chair. 'No, you don't know! No one knows how hard it was on me being Louie's wife. This is just one example of how difficult he made it for me. Forty-five years and he didn't know to buy me what I really wanted? Didn't know the one hobby that makes me happy?' She pointed to a large – gaudy, in Lydia's estimation, with its white wooden frame and gold gilt trim – curio cabinet. Lydia turned her attention to the display of Hummel figurines. She knew about them only because both Jenny's and Becky's mothers collected them. But they each had maybe half-a-dozen figurines, tops. Charlotte's collection was . . . jaw-dropping. Now wasn't the time to try to calculate the dollar value on them, but Lydia would bet her butchering arm that Charlotte's hobby could have paid for Stanley's law school tuition.

Why are you thinking about Stanley right now? Keep your eyes on the prize.

'It must be hard, dealing with all of this and the investigation, too.' And knowing that your dead husband was cheating on you. Because whether or not Charlotte killed Louie, Lydia was convinced she knew her husband had strayed. Or maybe it was that she'd accepted he'd want to? As much as Lydia didn't like to think about her parents having a romantic side to their relationship – or rather, the sex part – she knew that a long-term relationship like marriage needed physical expression. If Charlotte's rejection of Louie's intimate gift was any indication, physical relations weren't part of their marriage most recently.

'It is hard on me, thank you for acknowledging that. You were always the smartest of your siblings.' Charlotte nodded, seemed to accept Lydia's observation as commiseration. 'Of course, it's nothing like what you must be going through. Knowing that someone in your family did this.' Charlotte's zinger landed right in Lydia's bazooka, as Grandma would say, leaving her speechless.

At least she didn't visibly wince, but it took all of her energy to keep her expression neutral when she was able to reply. 'No one in my family did this, Charlotte.'

'Didn't your father have a bone to pick with Louie? Don't tell me you don't know about their falling out.'

'They had a falling out?' Lydia refused to react to Charlotte's animosity.

'Louie had to raise his prices this winter. Everyone thinks we had it made between my pension from the school district and Louie's job. But it takes more than my income to cover our heating bills, let me tell you. And we're still supporting Cindy and our dear grandchildren.'

'Did they stay in Georgia with their father?' She wasn't getting anywhere with Charlotte's tirade.

Cindy walked into the living room, her eyes the same shade

of beetle brown as her mother's. 'I won't expose my children to this tragedy. And my divorce and personal life are none of your business. I think it's time for you to leave, Lydia.' She spat her name out and Lydia didn't have to be told outright what Cindy thought. She believed that a Wienewski had killed her father.

'Yes, Cindy's right. We probably shouldn't have let you in in the first place.' Charlotte sniffed.

'Again, I'm sorry for your loss.' Lydia mustered every scrap of poise she'd ever possessed to keep her chin up as she let herself out the front door, which Cindy forcefully closed behind her.

Her fingers itched to grab one of the plastic pink flamingoes, or the whole flock of them, and smash them one by one. Instead she got into her Gremlin and made herself breathe in and out several times until her hands stopped shaking from muffling her anger. Anything to be rid of the negative energy that Louie's former home was full of. She pictured a white light surrounding the Gremlin, its video game character shape protecting her from all evil.

Oh, geez. Now she was thinking like Grandma.

'I'm telling you, Grandma, I think Charlotte McDaniel killed Louie. I mean, you should have seen her face! She hated him. And her every response seemed over-the-top. Calculated, you know?'

Lydia and Grandma were in the back office of the shop, the only place safe to discuss the case in private. Both Vi and Johnny had stepped out for lunch, as the lack of customers didn't require more than Lydia's presence. She called Grandma who'd still been at home, helping out with Pop, and asked her to come to the shop, right away.

Grandma nodded. 'I can see that. You're probably right. But I can't go to Harry with this yet. We're missing some important facts. Like why did she shoot him in the car, if that's what she did? After wearing or not wearing the too-tight underwear she says he bought her? Although, I have to admit, too-tight panties will put anyone in a bad mood. But in a mood bad enough to kill her husband? Then again, I'm sure she knew the lacy underthings weren't for her. She had to. And where's the gun? Whose gun was it?'

Lydia fought against gritting her teeth. 'I agree with you on all of this, Grandma, but you have to promise me you won't go to Nowicki with this, ever. Once we figure it all out we'll call it into Ned and let him take the credit.'

'Nonsense.' Grandma sniffed. 'We will take all and any credit coming our way. Women need to stand up more for themselves.'

'This isn't about ERA or Women's Lib, Grandma.' Lydia had no desire to taint a perfectly solved murder with any suspicions on Nowicki's part that she or Grandma had concocted any of this. 'It's about getting the real killer arrested and announcing it to the public so that we can clear our name. And get the store going again.' The fact that there hadn't been a single *ding* of the service bell over lunch hour spoke volumes.

'OK, honey child. I do think you may have cracked the case, but we'll keep it to ourselves until we get a little more evidence. In the meantime, may I suggest you take care of the business at hand?' Grandma motioned at the shelf where they kept the financial records in binders.

'You're right. I'll get to it early tomorrow. I'll make sure my suspicions are backed up with facts.' Lydia was certain something was off with the books, and even if they were perfect, she was still going to let Vi go. The payroll was too costly for her lackluster performance. 'She's been putting in an extra effort since last week.'

'Don't let her fool you. She sees the writing on the wall and is using this vulnerable time to play on your heartstrings. It worked with your father when she wanted the job because he's always been a sweet man at heart. Why, as a boy he used to slip his bologna sandwiches I made for his lunch to his classmates he knew weren't going home to a meal.'

'There's something to be said for compassion.' Maybe Lydia *was* jumping the gun, firing Vi right now.

'Helping out little kids during the Depression is one thing. Paying someone who's not pulling her share is insanity.' Grandma stood and took her coat off the door hook. 'I need to get back to the house and finish your parents' laundry. We'll talk more when you come home. Good luck with the rest of the day, honey.' Grandma gave her a quick peck on the cheek, and left.

Lydia stared at the binders marked bills, receipts, payroll, and promised herself she'd take care of the Vi issue. *Soon.*

The sound of the back door opening, followed by Vi's tinkling laughter and Johnny's baritone, reminded her that now wasn't the time to examine the books. Not with Vi back. The tone of their voices had turned intense and she paused before walking out of the office.

She peeked from the door and saw Johnny's hand on Vi's shoulder.

'It'll be OK, Vi.'

'Thanks, Johnny, you're a gem.'

Lydia waited until they got their coats off before she stepped out, making sure her footsteps were audible. She wanted to ask what the problem was, but the moment wasn't meant to be shared, not from the woebegone expression she'd seen on Vi's face.

But later, after Vi had left early – Lydia's insistence since Vi was hourly and Lydia was unwilling to pay for her to file her nails – she approached Johnny.

'Hey, is everything OK with Vi? I didn't realize you two were so chummy.'

Johnny tilted his head and a heavy lock of his wavy brown hair fell over one eye. No wonder Teri had fallen for the guy. He was handsome, yes, but also a good listener. Was he also a murderer?

'We're not, not really. At least, we never talked a lot before . . . before last Friday. It's just that no one ever thinks about Vi. You're always busy out here' – he motioned at the empty store – 'and so was your pop. Vi's job never ends. She's in the back office doing the numbers no matter how many customers there are.'

Lydia nodded to signal she had heard him. Her protectiveness over Teri was in overdrive. She didn't trust herself not to remark on Johnny's naiveté. Johnny had no clue that she suspected Vi of cooking, or at least parboiling, the books, either. No one but Grandma knew her concerns over the accounts. It wasn't fair to put any of this on Johnny.

Johnny must have misinterpreted her silence for disapproval as he held up a beseeching hand. As if she was the bad guy here.

'Vi just needs people to understand her, where she's coming from. It makes sense, you know, that she's going to be most affected by Louie's murder.'

'Oh? Why do you say that?'

'In practical terms, Vi was the one who dealt with Louie the most. She took delivery of the meat, kept the records, made sure he got paid. So she's the one who's missing his physical presence the most. You know, the everyday stuff.' He shrugged.

'Actually, Johnny, I've been the one paying Louie since I came home.' She'd explained to Vi that she'd needed to be involved in every aspect of the shop until Pop got well, so that she didn't miss anything. In truth, she'd been suspicious of Vi's accounting ever since she saw the decent size of weekend customers that didn't jive with the lower-than-expected profits for the same time period.

'You have? Huh. Well, all I'm trying to say is that you aren't the only one feeling the pain over Louie's death, Lydia. It's affecting everyone, you know? Especially with it being a murder and everything.'

She nodded. 'You're right, Johnny, and I'm sorry if I snapped. It's been a long few days, hasn't it?' Lydia studied him closely.

Louie's murder had galvanized her determination to get Wienewski's Wieners & Meats back in the black. Vi was one last roadblock she needed to clear.

Along with finding the killer.

EIGHTEEN

'We should have drove.' Lydia walked with Grandma to bingo, the last gasp of winter clinging to the night air. Since their creekside vigil her grandmother had been more sensitive to the cold. 'It'll be even chillier when we leave.' Buffalonians rarely uttered 'cold' as if by omitting the noun it wasn't really that cold.

'Nonsense. We'll need the fresh air after being in that smoker's pit.' Grandma referred to the excessive chain-smoking that was pervasive amongst ardent bingo players. Her springy gait effused anticipation. She'd taken no less than an hour to get ready and Lydia had to admit, the makeup and form-fitting outfit took a good decade off Grandma's already svelte figure. She'd never lost it, according to Pop.

'Remember, make sure that we find out if they've found the gun.' The murder weapon was the one piece of evidence Lydia was confident would clear their family name. And allow them to attempt a reputation repair. Today had been slow, no matter that a smattering of new customers from downtown had come in to check out the meat case. Five total pounds of cold cuts and sausage later, the shop was in the red.

'I know, honey, I get it. Don't worry.'

Lydia knew that Grandma 'got it,' but she also knew Grandma was cruising for love in what might be the wrong place. Her internal jury was still out on Nowicki.

'I'm not worried, Grandma.'

'As far as I'm concerned, after your visit with Charlotte, it's clear to me that she did it. She knew her husband was a cheating dog. Once Harry has the gun with her prints on it, case closed. In the meantime, keep the shop open, have it ready for your father because you're going to be busy with your café and bakery!' Grandma squeezed her in a half-hug around her shoulders.

'You're right.'

'Of course I am. You're still planning to get rid of Vi, right? That woman makes more work for you than she's worth. Did you see how she messed up all the phone-in orders on Good Friday?'

'I know. She said she'd recorded the orders but the cassette was blank. She even erased all previous orders, which I like to hang onto for our records.' It was why she had a half-dozen spare cassettes in the desk drawer under the tape recorder. 'I'm going to fire her this week.' After she had a chance to catch her breath. She had to make time to go over the books, in private and without Vi present, before she let her go. Louie's murder had taken over everything, of course.

'Don't forget to look at the books one more time. Before you fire her. Have your ducks in a row.' Grandma read Lydia's mind, again. 'Here we are.'

They'd arrived at the parochial grade school building, where its center doors were open, spilling bright yellow light into the spring evening. Bingo players were as sturdy as they came, braving all the varied elements living beside Lake Erie brought.

Lydia fell into the line behind Grandma, paying for both of their boards and 'specials' – single-use paper boards in an assortment of primary colors. They bypassed the separate table selling ink daubers for the specials, instead grabbing a few waxy red crayons from the freebie box.

'Ugh.' Lydia couldn't help her reaction to walking into a cloud of smoke, redolent with the stench of nicotine and smoker's breath. Long tables with fold-out chairs occupied this main room, which the school also used as a gymnasium, cafeteria, and theater. Tonight the stage featured a large light bingo board, an automated ball mixer, and a microphone.

'I know, honey. They need to get some circulation in here.' Grandma weaved between patrons as they shucked off their outwear and got down to the business of laying out their boards in whatever order their particular bingo ritual necessitated.

Because bingo was a big deal in Western New York. Lydia didn't remember a time that a woman in her family hadn't gone to play at least once a week. She'd enjoyed going along when she was young, before her interest in boys and sports and baking shoved being with Mom and Aunt Dot, or Grandma out of its top spot. As a little girl she'd been allowed to play one board at a time, not the four she currently held, and if she won, it was really the adult who won, New York State law preventing a minor from playing bingo. The church turned a blind eye to minors as long as they were accompanied by an adult. Lydia figured the kids at bingo made up for most of the refreshment sales, anyhow, with the endless bottles of ginger ale and grape soda, the slices of pizza dripping with mozzarella and grease, the vast assortment of bagged snacks in individual sizes. She'd been partial to the cheese popcorn that dyed her fingertips orange, but now preferred the sharp tang of vinegar potato chips, washed down with a diet cola.

'Speak of the devil.' Grandma nodded at a woman two tables away, her display of no less than a dozen boards impressive.

'I forgot that Vi likes to play, too.' A twinge of guilt tugged on her stomach. Vi wouldn't have the extra funds for that many boards after Lydia fired her. Nor for her professional manicures. Her dusky rose polish sparkled under the commercial lighting as she set up several troll dolls, naked save for their various shades of neon-dyed hair.

'Does she ever. She's here every night!' Grandma's judge-y tone made Lydia laugh.

'How do you know this?'

'I'm friends with Dick Dingler.' Grandma pointed to the stage, where a man wearing a dress shirt and slacks was preparing to call the numbers. 'It's never a bad idea to know a man who works the balls, Lydia.' Grandma waggled her eyebrows.

'Excuse me!' A patron pushed into Lydia's backside and she wondered if they were frustrated with the crowd or had overheard Grandma's risqué comment.

'We're doing the best we can.' Lydia turned and faced the aggressor, letting down her guard when she recognized Stanley's mother. 'Mrs Gorski! I'm sorry, I didn't know it was you.'

'Lydia.' She gave her a quick peck on the cheek, as both their hands were full of game paraphernalia. 'It's so crowded tonight. The kids are off from school.' She frowned at the long line of pre-teens at the snack bar. 'I'll never get my pop before they start.'

Lydia spied four empty seats and threw her boards down on the table. 'I'll get your drink. Here, let's all take a seat.'

'Don't forget I need one for Harry.' Grandma put her purse on one of the empty seats before unloading her boards.

'I'll find a seat elsewhere.' Mrs Gorski seemed more flustered than navigating a crowded bingo hall should cause.

'No, no, Annette, sit with us, please.' Grandma spoke up. 'Take that seat there and Lydia, you're there.' She pointed to the two seats across from the pair she'd claimed. 'I'm waiting on a friend, is all. No reason we can't all have fun together.'

They got situated and Lydia took food and drink orders. Grandma promised to watch her boards if the game started before she returned.

Standing behind a group of twittering girls wearing brand-new spring outfits despite the winter temperatures, she decided joining Grandma at bingo was the best decision she'd made since deciding to fire Vi. Not only might Harry show and give up some more details, Mrs Gorski was here. Stanley said his father had been in the doldrums over Louie's murder. A good investigator kept all suspects on the table until proven innocent, she figured.

Which meant that Mr Gorski, along with his son, was still a suspect. Had Grandma realized that, too, and that's why she'd encouraged Annette Gorski to join them?

'Order?' A teenager wearing a Journey T-shirt prompted.

Lydia listed her requests, all the while figuring out the best way to get information from Stanley's mother without being too obvious.

'Bingo!' Vi screamed out from her spot two tables away. As she held up her board, she must have felt Lydia's stare because she turned and met her gaze.

Lydia offered a quick wave and thumbs up. What else could she do, without tipping Vi off that she was planning her butcher shop demise?

'Look at that. She just won sixty-five dollars! That'll cover her until she finds another job.' Grandma leaned over her boards as she whispered, her eyes bright. 'You shouldn't worry about what happens after you do the right thing, Lydia.'

'You're letting Vi go?' Annette Gorski spoke with her usual voluminous candor, which wouldn't normally be a problem if everyone in the bingo hall was jabbering. But she'd uttered her query at the exact point the hush happened. The near silent reverence that occurred whenever a bingo official called out a winner's numbers and the caller – Dick tonight – gravely repeated each number as he compared it to his balls. The balls that he'd called, of course.

Most of the patrons paid little notice to Annette's blurt. Lydia hoped two rows away was far enough. She risked a peek at Vi to find the woman's steely gaze on her.

'Crap, Grandma, she heard.'

'Shhh. She heard her name, sure, but she didn't—'

Vi shoved back from her table, ignoring the unwritten sacred bingo code of silence, and made a beeline for their table. Her heels – who the hell wore heels to bingo? – clicked on the hardwood floor. To Lydia the footsteps sounded like a death knoll. Lydia held her breath. She'd faced down Charlotte McDaniel earlier today – what more was an altercation with Vi?

Vi kept coming, all eyes on her. When she got close to the head of their row, determination stamped on her face, Lydia braced herself.

Only for Vi to turn and head for the exit that led to the restrooms. Lydia exhaled. Vi hadn't even made eye contact when she passed their row.

'See, she didn't hear a thing.' Grandma nodded.

'I'm sorry, I know I can be loud at times.' Mrs Gorski attempted to whisper, which was in reality a slightly toned down version of her usual bellow.

'It's not a big deal,' Lydia lied. Now that the risk of being verbally pummeled by Vi had passed, she refocused on her task at hand. Vi's board had been verified a winner, and the crowd was chattering as they moved onto the specials game. 'I'm glad we ran into you. Stanley told me that Louie's death has been hard on your family, too.'

Annette Gorski visibly startled. 'He, he did? What did he tell you, Lydia?'

'Well, actually it was me who was complaining to him. You know, it's been really, really hard for my pop, and now this. Stanley mentioned that the police had been to your house, too, is all.' She quickly attempted to soothe Mrs Gorski. The woman's rapid blinking and the way she'd been shaking her foot under the table made Lydia think she'd lose her shot at getting more clues before she started. The last thing she wanted was for Stanley's mother to bolt out of here.

'Yes, it's been downright awful. It doesn't help that my husband keeps acting guilty about it.'

Lydia gulped. Did Mrs Gorski realize how her words could be interpreted?

'Why do you think that is? That Mr Gorski feels guilty?' She knew what Stanley had told her, but asking the same question over and over worked for Angie Dickinson, so it had to be worth a try.

'Oh, he thinks he's responsible for everything. Just ask him! The recession, the labor strikes in Poland. He forgets that we're just average people making a living the best way we know how. Why, just last week he felt guilty over the cost increases for eggs. Louie and Stanley's father, they don't see eye-to-eye on much. Didn't, that is.'

So far Annette Gorski hadn't revealed anything Lydia could consider significant, except that she'd corroborated Stanley's premise that his father took the responsibility of the world on his shoulders. This proved nothing new to Lydia as their parents' generation had lived through some serious world events including three wars, if you count Vietnam, which some folks around here still didn't.

'Ladies, may I join you?' Detective Nowicki spoke to all three of them but only had eyes for Grandma. Lydia couldn't stop from rolling her eyes, but not before she caught Mrs Gorski's reaction. The woman blanched more readily than the sliced almonds Lydia sprinkled on a Danish pastry.

'Please do, Detective Nowicki.' Lydia spoke but was certain he hadn't heard her, his mustache twitching over a shy smile. Man oh man, the guy really did have the hots for Grandma.

Lydia shoved aside her initial reaction of gagging – always, when confronted with Grandma's or her parents' sex lives – to make room for gratitude. She had two persons of interest sitting right here at the bingo table.

'Harry, here, I saved you a seat. I hope you don't mind that I bought two boards for you, with a book of specials. You missed the green game but there are still four more. And here's your drink.'

'My favorite, birch beer. Thank you, Maria.' He responded with Grandma's childhood moniker.

'Shhh!'

'Pipe down!'

'We can't hear Dick shake his balls!'

The admonishment from all four corners of the large hall elicited a round of laughter and Nowicki's cheeks reddened. He took his seat, Grandma helping him ease his large overcoat off. Lydia looked at Mrs Gorski but any chance of further interrogation, uh, inquiry, was impossible as the woman's face was buried in her boards, her narrow shoulders hunched over like Quasimodo.

Fortunately it was only two games and ten minutes until intermission, when maybe Nowicki would give them some crumbs from his investigation.

As soon as the caller announced the fifteen-minute break, Mrs Gorski sprang up, claiming, 'I need the ladies' room.'

Which left Lydia and Grandma alone with Nowicki.

'I'm sorry I was late, Maria. You know my job. Unpredictable hours. I must say I'm happy to be here with you. It's nice to have a break.'

'Isn't it, though, Harry?' Grandma obviously believed Harry's definition of 'break' was 'date' from the way she gushed over him.

'Have you ladies been enjoying yourself tonight?' He shot Lydia a courtesy glance.

'Sure. I mean, we're close to home, and all.'

'Don't mind her, Harry. She has a lot on her mind. One of the employees she has to let go is here.'

That put Nowicki's full attention on her. 'I didn't realize the butcher shop was struggling that much. You know, once this case is solved, you'll get your customers back.'

'You sound as though you've had news, Detective.' Lydia figured he already knew she wanted details, so no use pussyfooting around. A law enforcement type like Nowicki appreciated forthrightness.

Grandma shot her a warning glance, but Lydia wasn't certain if it conveyed 'be careful, you don't want to shut him down' or 'hey, he's mine to question.'

Nowicki glanced at the empty chairs around them, cleared his throat, and leaned in. 'I'm happy to tell you we've most likely found the murder weapon.'

Relief as she'd never experienced washed over Lydia, right down to her toes. Well, OK, she'd had a similar sense of elation, whenever she and Stanley had—

'Oh, Harry, that's absolutely wonderful. You are brilliant!' Grandma cooed. To her credit, she kept her voice low, her movements guarded. Maybe Grandma was hipper than even Lydia gave her credit.

'It's not rocket science, Maria.' He took a sip of the dark effervescent beverage. 'The entire department is working around the clock and they're turning up evidence.'

'Where did they find the gun, Harry?' Grandma was able to ask questions as a matter-of-fact while Lydia felt the need to hold back, tread a little more lightly. She had to admit that Grandma's way got quicker results.

'In Cazenovia Creek, not far from where we found Louie's car.'

'So do you have a prime suspect now?' Lydia asked. She wanted to hear him say 'Charlotte McDaniel' for herself.

He shook his head. 'No. But we will soon, once the weapon's registry is confirmed.'

'Unless it's stolen,' Grandma said.

'Right.' Nowicki got quiet. 'There weren't any prints on it, though.'

'That was a rough spot, where he left his car.' Grandma pulled out a tissue and blew her nose. Cigarette smoke always made it run. By the way her eyes suddenly bulged, Lydia knew she'd realized her mistake.

'What do you mean, "rough"?' he asked.

'We saw it on the news. They said a car had been found near the creek.'

He stared at her and Lydia willed herself to not break eye contact. Just as in the Wienewski kitchen, it was another battle of the wills with him. Finally he looked down, drummed his fingers atop his boards.

'Is there something you two need to fill me in on after we're done with bingo tonight?'

NINETEEN

'Harry was a pussycat about it; I told you he would be.' Grandma spoke from the sofa, while Lydia sat in their single easy chair. Each was ensconced in a hand-crocheted blanket, chamomile tea in hand as they waited for the late news to come on. Both had already seen the rerun that was showing. They'd taken a ride from Nowicki after bingo, much to Lydia's discomfort. It gave him free reign to question how they knew so much about Louie's car and the creek. She'd let Grandma fill him in. Thankfully Grandma hadn't mentioned how long they'd staked out the scene, nor that they'd seen the black lace underwear.

'At least he doesn't think we did anything but a drive-by of the car scene at the creek.' If Nowicki knew that they were on to Charlotte as the killer he'd probably put them in a cell until he wrapped up the case. 'I'm glad you didn't mention what I think after being with Charlotte. We're lucky he's on the trail to the real killer and doesn't think it's us anymore.'

'He never thought it was us. He just has to play his part.'

Lydia stayed silent. She was never going to convince Grandma that they'd been in the PD's crosshairs for murder only days earlier.

They watched the last scene of a *Hart to Hart* rerun. It wasn't either of their favorite show as far as detective procedure went, but Grandma liked to watch it for the fashion and Lydia liked the romantic banter. In this particular episode, the killer was a jilted ex-lover.

'What did I tell you, another murder motivated by passion. If Charlotte hated Louie as much as you say, that's enough motive for me.'

'But you're right about waiting to find out more facts, Grandma. We need to keep thinking about this. What if Louie's lover is the killer? We haven't looked at that.'

'Hmm. That's possible, but my money's on Charlotte. She wasted her good years on him and he goes chasing now? Maybe he's been chasing all along and she finally snapped? Who knows. We'll figure it out, though, honey child. And stop fretting about me blabbing to Harry. I promise, not a word to him.' Grandma shifted, pulling her legs up to her chest. 'But I still believe we can trust Harry with our lives. He's the best at what he does. Look how quickly he cleared us. Besides, I see the whole man when I look at him. Harry's a lover, not a liar.'

'Mmm.' Lydia watched the commercial end, listened to the dramatic opening music for the WKBW eleven o'clock news.

'Breaking news. Tonight WKBW news team has learned that not only has the murder weapon for a Cheektowaga slaying been found, but that there was reportedly a second victim who was shot at and lived. We go to our reporter on the scene for the latest.'

Grandma gasped while Lydia steamed. Nowicki mentioned the gun, all right, but not a second victim.

'I'm telling you, when I heard the gunshots, I looked out my window and saw a man running up the creek.' A woman wrapped in a quilted satin baby blue robe, her hair in rollers, spoke into the microphone. Her breath formed clouds and the glare of camera lights reflected off her thick lenses. Lydia made out the door behind her – part of a trailer. There was a trailer park up the hill from the creek, which she figured offered a good view of the Lovers' Lane area. 'He was tall and skinny, and he got into a car – it looked like a Jeep – and drove away.'

It hadn't been Louie driving away. Or Charlotte. While a man or woman could disguise themselves as either, neither one of the McDaniels would ever be described as 'tall and skinny.' So yes, a second person was involved.

'What do you think, Grandma? About this second gunshot victim?'

'It sounds like it was a man. Could be relevant, might not be. Except they are definitely another suspect, or at least a witness I'd like to get my hands on.'

'I agree.' But the chances of them finding out who the

second victim was were close to nil as far as Lydia was
concerned. She'd leave this to the police, too.

Let Nowicki find the witness he'd failed to tell them about.

Early the next morning, Lydia took her stalling by its pointy
horns and finally tackled the shop's financial records.

Two hours in, she'd drank half a pot of coffee and the sun
had risen, but she hadn't found the smoking gun. Not yet.
Every expenditure appeared to be accounted for as she first
skimmed, then carefully read the ledgers. There was a check
receipt for every bill paid, receipts for the quarterly taxes –
annual taxes were in boxes Pop kept in the basement at home
– and the payroll was without error. While Lydia balked at
the hours Vi had been paid for, she also knew that Vi had been
bodily present for same time. Vi hadn't cut a check for herself
for any more than what she'd done on the clock.

The phone rang and she answered it automatically, involuntarily
bracing for bad news. It seemed to be de rigueur these days.

'Wienewski's.' She abbreviated the greeting; no customer
called at seven a.m. the week after a major holiday.

'Honey, it's me.' Grandma's voice was the boost she needed.
'Have you found anything yet?'

'No. In fact, Vi appears to have kept very, very good records.
Nothing looks amiss.'

'Don't give up! Trust your gut. You think she's skimming,
so she probably is. Although you could be picking up on her
erratic energy, with the mess her auras are in.'

Lydia laughed, her first one of the day, maybe the week. It
hadn't even been a full week since Louie's murder but tell
that to her downtrodden spirit. They hadn't solved the murder,
her much anticipated Easter boon was a bust, and she hadn't
made any headway on a better motive to fire Vi other than her
own misgivings.

'Sorry, Grandma, but I can't fire her on how you're reading
her auras.'

'You can fire her for any reason you want. What's she
going to do?'

'A lot. I don't want her bugging Pop. When he comes back
to work, I want it to be smooth sailing. No stress.'

'Phooey. There's no such thing as a business without some stress. It's what kept your grandfather going, and your pop is no different.'

'OK, well, thanks.'

'I hate to hear you so upset, Lydia.'

'I'm fine, Grandma. But I have to hang up now. I need more time in here before Vi and Johnny come in.' Teri was going to take the afternoon shift since Johnny had a dentist appointment. He'd cracked a tooth on an errant piece of sponge candy.

'Well, at the least you can move Vi to only one or two days a week. It'll give her a clue to start shopping for another place to file her nails.' Grandma paused. 'Listen, when I worked for Woolworths years ago, my boss caught one of the managers cashing checks for themselves with the company account. Check all the numbers, do you know what I'm saying?'

'Will do. I'll call you if I find anything.'

She hung up and went back to the books. All of the check numbers she'd noted in the rows of expenses matched the numbers on the bank statements to date, so there was no need to go over that again.

Except . . . all Lydia had done was match the check numbers to their line item on the bank accounts. She hadn't made sure they were all in order.

Going back to earlier, before she'd returned from Ottawa, she pulled out all of the bank statements and the corresponding shop books. Lydia was no financial whiz but if she were going to steal from her employer she wouldn't try to do it when his bossy daughter showed up to run things.

It took only one look, but right there, printed on the bank OCR checking statement, was confirmation of what she'd suspected all along. And there was more. Vi had cut checks for ten dollars, twenty dollars, throughout the month, but the numbers didn't match the series of numbers the shop's bills had been paid with.

In the year that Lydia had been in Ottawa, Vi had taken enough money to keep Pop in dire straits.

The sound of a car door slamming reached through the walls and Lydia looked at the clock. It was either Vi or Johnny. She quickly sorted and refiled the paperwork, her thoughts racing through what she had to do next. First, she'd run back home and talk to Grandma.

'Thanks for understanding, Johnny. I can always count on you.' Vi patted Johnny on the shoulder as they entered the shop together. Vi normally arrived several minutes after Johnny. It was almost as if she knew what Lydia planned.

'Good morning. How's everyone doing?' Lydia forced a cheerful note in her voice.

Johnny shrugged. 'Fine. How are you, Lydia?'

'What a nice young man, asking his boss how she feels. Am I right, Lydia?' Vi shrugged out of her coat and Lydia took a good look at her outfit, another new one she'd never seen.

Lydia was still staring when Vi straightened and their eyes clashed. Vi's eyes narrowed and her face paled.

'What is it, Lydia?' Vi visibly held her breath for a moment.

Stay cool. You don't want her on to you.

Lydia shook her head. 'Nothing.'

'Oh, come on, you can tell me. Did I get coffee on my blouse again?' She made a show of brushing off her top.

'I'll, er, go get the meat in the case.' Johnny averted his gaze, his cheeks six shades of red as he left the backroom.

'Your blouse is fine, Vi.' Lydia looked at her watch, at the clock on the wall, as if comparing the two. 'Look, I have to run home. Mom just called. She needs help with Pop.'

'Oh no! Why, the last time you left to go home, well, you know what happened.'

She'd reminded Lydia of Louie's murder – as if she could forget! Vi had regained her composure after ensuring her blouse was intact of any stains.

Lydia turned away so that Vi wouldn't see her face. 'Let's hope that was a once-in-a-lifetime event. I'll be back in twenty.'

'Right.' Vi retreated to the office that only minutes earlier had been an explosion of all the financial records. Lydia escaped out the door before her face revealed any more of her ire to Vi. She wanted to talk to Grandma before she did anything stupid. Like they'd learned from the detective shows, patience beat impulsivity every time.

*   *   *

Once home she ran up the driveway and thudded up the garage apartment stairs, bursting into the apartment.

An empty apartment.

'Grrrr.' She whirled around and retraced her steps, veering off the driveway for the back door of the house. She opened the door as quietly as she could, not wanting to alert her parents of her presence if she didn't have to. She had to get to Grandma ASAP.

'Is that you, Lydia?' Mom yelled from the front room.

'Yes!' She stifled a groan as she walked into the kitchen. No sign of Grandma in here, either.

'Can you bring your father and me a warm-up on our coffee?'

She turned to the half-empty carafe and grabbed it. 'Sure.' Gritting her teeth, she wound into the parlor to find her parents glued to the TV, atop which sat their plaster statue of the Infant of Prague, dressed in its frilly robe that Mom had dry cleaned yearly. They were watching a local news report.

'What's going on?' Lydia eyed the television screen as she poured coffee into each of their ceramic mugs. Mom's was milk white with the Serenity prayer on it and Pop's was a dull brown with a chipped edge.

'Look, there's Harry!' Mom cried. She grasped Pop's arm.

'He's figured it out.' Pop nodded as he patted her hand.

'Figured what out?' Lydia couldn't believe it. Had Nowicki solved the case?

'Shhh.' Mom waved at the oversized ottoman, her way of saying 'shut up and sit down.' Lydia sat.

'I'm on the scene of the investigation into the murder of Louie McDaniel, a Cheektowaga businessman who was slaughtered last Good Friday . . .' Lydia groaned again at the reporter's choice of words. But she listened, wondering if Nowicki had figured out what she thought she had. The reporter continued. 'Besides finding the victim's abandoned vehicle, police have uncovered the murder weapon, which combined with the report by a witness who lives in a nearby trailer park of hearing two shots and seeing one lone figure running away, indicates there may be a second victim on the run. Nowicki wouldn't comment further but our investigative reporting team is standing by for any further discoveries.'

Lydia hadn't learned anything new, nothing she hadn't heard from previous news reports or Nowicki himself, last night at the bingo. Grandma had been smart, the way she'd got him to talk.

Grandma!

'Where's Grandma?'

Lydia found Grandma in the basement, doing the family laundry.

'Lydia, honey. I was just wondering how it was going at the store.' Grandma took in her flustered appearance and smiled. 'You've caught her, haven't you? How much has she stolen?'

'No, I don't know, but I want to find out exactly how much Vi has stolen from us.'

'Fair enough. We're going to have to break into her house. She's bound to have the missing checks. Tonight is perfect because it's bingo night at the VFW in West Seneca. Vi never misses a game, I told you last night. She'll be gone longer with it being so far.' Fifteen instead of three minutes away was considered 'far' in Grandma's world.

Lydia wasn't thrilled with sneaking into Vi's bungalow. She'd only ever been there a handful of times over the years, mostly when Uncle Ray was still alive. She definitely didn't want Grandma to go with her, either.

'Look, Grandma, I know you want to go with me—'

'We're a team, Granddaughter,' Grandma admonished, anticipating Lydia's request.

'But I need you to be clean of this. Harry won't date a woman who breaks the law, especially after he's told you to stay out of it.'

Grandma rested her hands on a stack of orange flower print towels. 'You know, maybe you're right. It might not be a bad idea for me to go to bingo tonight like I usually do. If she doesn't show, I'll go to a pay phone and leave a message for you here with your parents. You can stake out her place until you see her drive away. If you don't see her leave by seven-thirty – the games start at eight – then come home and get my message. Meanwhile, assuming she's at bingo, I can keep her there longer afterwards, give you more time. You'll have over two hours to find the missing checks.'

'How will you do that? Keep her there longer?'

'Talk about men, how else?' Grandma winked. 'Oh, sure, Vi can be shy about men, except to chat them up in the store. And I understand her desire to never remarry. We're the two widows in the family, after all. If only I'd made a similar vow, I wouldn't have been jilted right before you came back. But Vi's never turned away from hearing about single men in her age group. Trust me, honey, I'll keep her busy long enough to get your mission accomplished. And if you're concerned about our tiff at Easter, forget it. It's like that sometimes between mothers and daughters-in-laws.'

Later that day, Lydia hoped she didn't look too conspicuous dressed in all black as she left her apartment. Her plan was to walk to Vi's and make sure the woman left for bingo at the time Grandma predicted.

She breathed a sigh of relief that all of the news crews along with their vans had deserted their stakeout in front of the house. The sun hung low and a strong lake wind was whipping up, casting off the balmy breeze they'd enjoyed earlier.

A car's motor sounded behind her and she forced herself to keep walking, act normal. She was being paranoid, she was certain. Heading for the house you were going to break into did that to a person, she figured.

But this car didn't drive past. Instead, it slowed to a crawl, matching her pace. She turned to see who it was and stopped when she recognized Stanley's face in the driver's seat. He leaned over the seat and rolled down the passenger window.

'Need a ride?'

'Uh, no. I'm fine. Just out for a walk.'

'You don't look like you're going for "just a walk."' His grin remained but his eyes were sober, alert. 'You still playing *Police Woman*, Lyd?'

'No.' But her denial was too swift, too strong. Stanley's brow raised and tickled her funny bone. She couldn't help but laugh.

'I'm fine, Stanley. Honest. Where are you headed?' Deflection was a good tool for an investigator, she'd discovered.

'Heading to the library to study.'

'Isn't it closed?'

'The university library. Need the law books to get my answers these days. I have an exam tomorrow.'

'Oh. OK, well, good luck, then!' She stepped back and offered him a vigorous wave. Stanley looked at her for several heartbeats and she stayed strong, never breaking eye contact, never allowing her smile to slip.

'See ya around, Lyd.' Stanley smiled, rolled the window back up and drove away. Only when he was out of sight did she bite her lip and brush the burning tears away.

She'd never lied to Stanley before.

TWENTY

'I can't believe you talked me into this.' Jenny held her hand protectively over her belly. 'I can't do anything that would put the baby in jeopardy.' A distant rumble of thunder punctuated her concern. It had been unseasonably warm all day and the balmy break was about to end with the cold front rolling across Lake Erie.

'You're not going to do anything risky. You're the lookout, remember? You sit here, in the car, and be ready to help us get away.' Becky, always the pragmatic one of their group when it came to teenaged hijinks, soothed Jenny from her perch on the back shelf as Jenny's Camaro had no backseats and Becky was the smallest of them. Lydia stared at Vi's house through the passenger window of Jenny's black and white tuxedo Camaro. They'd picked the most nondescript vehicle between the three of them. Lydia's Gremlin was out, as was Becky's royal blue Charger. Jenny and Pat hadn't traded the car in for a station wagon yet.

Becky had joined them tonight, much to Lydia's relief. Becky, a high school gymnast, could maneuver – aka break into – any house or building that Lydia and Jenny needed extra help with.

'Lydia, you're positively certain that Vi's gone?' Becky asked.

'Yes. She left fifteen minutes ago, I saw her go myself.' After making sure Stanley was gone, she'd walked the several blocks here, then waited behind a huge old oak tree across the street from Vi's place until Jenny got off work and rolled up. 'Grandma will stall her at the bingo hall if I don't show up and give Grandma a signal sooner. She says Vi never misses a bingo night.' And now Lydia was pretty damn certain where Vi was getting the funds to buy all those boards. And her manicures, her latest fashion accessories . . .

Plus she could be a murderer. Lydia wanted to make Vi a

frontrunner on her suspect list, but truly couldn't figure out
why Vi would want to hurt, much less murder, Louie. There
had to be a motive.

'Stay with me, girl.' Jenny spoke up, breaking Lydia's cycle
of worry. 'You're not doing this alone. We're here.'

Jenny's reassurance quieted her mental chatter but not her
conscience. 'You're right, though, Jenny. You're going to be
a mother, for God's sake, and I have you on a stakeout!'

'It's a break-in, actually,' Becky said. 'I can climb up that
window there, behind that pricker bush.' She pointed to the
side of the house. 'Remember when we fell into the pricker
bushes on the other side of Mrs Kemp's fence?'

The entire car erupted into gut-busting laughter.

'How could we forget? We were so lucky we didn't need
stitches from those thorns!' Jenny giggled, but in what looked
like a Hollywood special effect under the pale streetlight, her
smile suddenly morphed into a deep frown as tears poured
down her cheeks.

'Jenny! What's wrong?' Lydia's stomach plummeted. 'This
was a bad idea. Let's drive away—'

'No, no.' Jenny waved her hand in front of her face. 'It's
the pregnancy hormones. My mother says she wept the entire
nine months with both me and my sister.'

'Good reminder of why I don't ever want a kid. No offense,
Jenny. I'll love yours, you know I will,' Becky said.

'No offense taken. I get it. I never thought I'd want a baby
but then I met Patrick.' Jenny wiped her face with the ends
of her jacket sleeve and looked out the windshield. 'Let's get
this party going, girls.'

'So we're all on the same page, let's go over our plan.'
Becky quickly listed their agreed-upon strategy, via several
phone calls back and forth earlier in the day. She began with
'get into the house' and ended with 'get the hell out of
there.' In between was to look around for evidence of Vi's
stealing, to include cashed and uncashed checks, and piles
of cash.

'Let the break-in commence!' Jenny held up her hand and
they high-fived each other.

'Wait! There's no need for window entry. Besides, it's not

a break-in if I have a key, is it?' Lydia held up a single key, grinning. 'I do believe this is for her back door.'

Jenny's eyes widened in awe. 'How did you get that?'

'The same way private investigators have gotten copies of keys through the centuries. Or maybe it's years, I dunno. You were the history person, Becky.' Lydia looked at Becky's annoyed expression. Time to get a move on. 'I pressed it into a block of soap.'

'And you got someone to make you a key from that? Isn't that illegal?' Jenny asked.

'Well, actually, after I did that' – and realized that no legitimate locksmith was going to make her a spare – 'I remembered that Vi had given Pop a copy of her house key years ago, when she first came to work for him. She said it was "in case something ever happens to me." But my grandma said it was Vi's way of flirting with Pop.'

'Ew.' Jenny grimaced.

'That's not flirting, that's straight-up making a pass at your pop. A gross-out either way.' Becky had had enough. 'Let's go, before I get too stiff back here.'

Jenny placed the binoculars around her neck and Lydia let herself out of the car, holding the door open. Becky slithered from the back onto the passenger seat and then did some kind of pike-somersault thingy that had her landing on her feet right next to Lydia.

'Ready, Freddie?' She looked at Lydia.

Lydia nodded. 'Ready.'

Entering Vi's small house through the back door turned out to be anticlimactic as far as Lydia was concerned. The key still fit the lock and unlike the Wienewskis' weathered back door, opened smoothly. Vi's place was in a stretch of homes that had been built when an old salt warehouse had collapsed and the owner sold the property. Uncle Ray had wanted only the best for his wife, after being a bachelor for forty-plus years.

'She's not big on cooking, is she?' Becky had her head in the refrigerator, its interior light bright. 'There's nothing in here except cold cream and nail polish.'

'Shut the door before someone sees us in here!' Lydia moved past her and headed down the hall that led to the two bedrooms. The couple had used the spare room as an office and Lydia was hoping Vi kept her important papers – i.e. swindled checks – there.

'Is it still her office?' Becky breathed behind her, making her jump with surprise.

'Argh! I never heard you. Geesh.'

'It's my new Nikes. No one will catch me if I'm running away in these puppies.'

Lydia's flashlight beam illuminated a small filing cabinet and desk set against the far wall of the spare room. 'Yes, still an office.'

'Good to know. You go to work here and I'll snoop around her bedroom.'

Lydia didn't reply as she was already opening drawers, quickly thumbing through stacks of paperwork. It didn't take long to find the envelopes marked with each year, going back to . . . the exact year Vi had started working for Pop. In addition to the year, another number was written in the lower right-hand corner of the ubiquitous white business envelopes.

Opening the first one, Lydia withdrew six checks that bore the familiar Wienewski's Wieners & Meats name, printed with the shop address and phone number in the upper left-hand corner. These checks weren't made out to a particular supplier or utility. They were all made out to Mrs Violet Wienewski.

The first year, Vi had cashed only six checks amounting to a relatively paltry sum. As if she'd been doing it for kicks. And the total value of the stolen funds matched the number on the front of the envelope. Lydia rapidly added up the rest of the checks, determining that Vi had doubled her take each year, to the point that last year's amount would have made the difference between the shop being solvent or not.

Lydia's hands started to shake as the validation of her suspicions stared back at her. This was enough evidence to get Vi arrested, wasn't it?

A stack of postcards caught her attention. Tied with a black lace ribbon, they were nestled in the same drawer as she'd found the checks. Curious, she undid the bow and quickly examined them. All were from Canada, with photos of Niagara Falls, Niagara-on-the-Lake, Crystal Beach, and more. On the back the cards were addressed to Vi, of course. Nothing notable until she read the personal messages, all signed with a cross between a doodle and a scrawl. Maybe a heart with an arrow through it?

> This will be our home. Love x
> Can't wait to build our cottage. Love x
> Thank you for last night. Love x
> I promise I'll leave with you soon xox

Vi had a lover! She wasn't as 'shy' as Grandma had observed, and Lydia believed. Although she was adamant she'd never remarry, apparently that didn't extend to never having a love life at all. Well, wait until she told Grandma. Not only had Vi cooked the books, she'd been cooking between the sheets, too.

Lydia scanned through the rest of the stack with shaking hands. There was no sign of a name, of any identification of Vi's lover.

She put the postcards back as she'd found them and made sure the office had no sign of her visit before she left, taking the envelopes with her.

She found Becky in Vi's bedroom, staring at a magazine.

'What are you doing?'

Becky slammed the periodical shut and jumped up. Lydia spied the cover. It was a Frederick's of Hollywood catalogue. She'd looked at one before but the prices were beyond her as long as she worked in the butcher shop, and then she'd been saving for pastry school. Maybe once she had her bakery café going she'd be able to think about buying something a little sexier than her cotton print bikini undies. In case she and Stanley ever got back together, that is.

'This broad's got a lot of shopping going on. Look at her closet.' Becky strode the two steps to a sliding door closet. What Lydia would do to have something so fancy! 'Look.'

'OK, she's got a lot of clothes. I already knew that.' She shone her light on the hanging rod and noted that many of the tops and bottoms still had price tags on them. Looking more closely at one, she gasped at the numbers. 'This pair of pants cost more than my weekly paycheck.'

'Did you find proof that she's been on the take?'

'Yes.' She held up the stack of envelopes. 'Caught her red-handed, actually.'

'Good job. What more are we looking for?'

Lydia shrugged. 'Nothing, really.' She ran her flashlight over the room, taking in the new furniture, stacks of gift boxes on the fancy dresser, the standalone jewelry box. 'We should get out of here.'

'OK. Jenny didn't have to wait as long as we thought she would.' Becky sounded almost disappointed.

Lydia turned to exit the room but then pulled herself up short. 'Wait a minute.' She blinked in the darkness, her stomach flipping as her heart rammed against her ribcage. 'Give me a minute.'

'What is it? Lydia?' Becky followed her back to the dresser, where Lydia inspected the pile of gift boxes. With shaking hands she laid them side-by-side, so that she could see the department store logos. Two of the seven were from Sample, three from Frederick's of Hollywood, and two . . . had AM&A's in gold lettering.

'If this is what I think it is . . .'

'What, Lydia? Tell me!'

'Hang on.' Lydia took the cover off of each and every box. And found in each one, nestled amidst tissue paper, varied styles of lingerie. Black lace lingerie.

She sat down on Vi's bed, hard. Only to have it wave underneath her. 'What the hell?' Maybe this was all a bad dream.

'It's a waterbed.' Becky nodded. 'Talk to me, girl. You OK?'

Lydia shook her head. 'No.' She stood back up and grabbed Becky's shoulders. 'You trust me, right?'

'Damn right!'

'I can't explain right now, but we have to get to the VFW bingo hall.'

'What's at the bingo place, besides Vi?'

'My grandma. And her life's in danger.'

*   *   *

Lydia squirmed in the front seat as Jenny raced through the pouring rain. She looked at her watch – bingo had another hour to go, they'd make it in time, wouldn't they?

'Can you go any faster?' She tried to distract herself from her chaotic thoughts.

'Can't talk.' Jenny's hands gripped the wheel.

'It's OK, we'll get there. Don't take any extra risks, Jenny. Better to arrive where Lydia needs us than in the morgue.' Becky's calm reply anchored Lydia, saved her from totally freaking out. Never before had she needed to talk to Grandma, to go over what she'd come up with.

'Passion's a number one killer.'

Black lace panties in Louie's car.

Charlotte McDaniel's stack of lingerie boxes, meant for Louie's lover.

Vi's boxes of lingerie.

The postcards signed by an ardent lover, indicating that they'd run off together soon. But the 'soon' comments had been dated as far back as ten years and as recently as last month. Lydia knew she'd be angry at a lover who promised to take her away but never did.

The snippets of memories, conversations and mental images snapped into place like the one-thousand-piece jigsaw puzzle of Niagara Falls her family completed on the dining room table last Christmas while Pop convalesced. They should have seen it sooner. She should have put it together before now. Before Grandma was spending time with a cold-blooded killer.

Although, if it was a crime of passion, would the murderer still be considered 'cold-blooded'? Yes. Because this particular killer had gone to the trouble to get Louie's body into their family smoker, to blame the Wienewskis. To cover their tracks. If the killer so much as suspected Grandma was on to them, Grandma would be their next victim.

Jenny took the right into the VFW parking lot too sharply and both she and Lydia screamed through the fishtail.

'Ladies! Chill out.' Becky spoke up after the car regained traction.

Jenny pulled into a spot furthest from the last full row of

parked cars. 'Need I remind anybody here that I'm the one who taught all of you how to drive my car?'

Lydia spotted Grandma's car and let out a short breath. *Phew.* At least Grandma was still here. 'Both of you stay in the car until I come out with my grandmother, and we drive off. Just in case her car doesn't start or something.'

Before any of the Misfits could argue, she grabbed her purse, threw the long strap over her head, and slipped out of the car.

Lydia ran toward the bright entrance lights.

Please let Grandma be OK. Please.

TWENTY-ONE

The cloud of nicotine-scented smoke hit Lydia square in the lungs when she walked into the bingo hall. The VFW's space was smaller than St Ursula's but it didn't mean less people. Men, and mostly women, were packed in like sardines in a can, the kind you need the key to peel open. The *whir* of bingo balls tumbling in a large glass receptacle reached through the speaker system and Lydia heard the *woosh* of another ball being selected.

'O-sixty-nine,' the caller intoned. A soft titter of laughter waved over the crowd, as it always did at the sexually suggestive number.

'You're too late to play tonight, sweetheart. We're already on the cover-all.' A woman seated on a chair just inside the entrance spoke from her spot, her blonde curls stiff and unyielding in her up-do. Her gaze swept over Lydia, noted her closed purse. Lydia wasn't here to play. 'You lookin' for someone? I can have the caller announce it.'

'Yes, I am, but no, thank you, I don't need it announced.' Lydia started scanning the hall the second she entered. There, at the far end of the room in the corner nearest the restrooms – Grandma's favorite spot, actually – she spied Grandma's bright purple tam atop her flowing hair. Across from her sat Vi, with what looked like twice as many boards as she'd had last night.

'I see her. I need to go in. Family emergency.' She didn't wait for the sentry to comment but instead plowed into the room.

'Excuse me, thank you, squeezing by.' She murmured her apologies as she sidled down the longest line of folding chairs and players she ever recalled. And Lydia had been playing bingo a long while, on and off, with her family.

'O-seventy-five.' The caller continued. Several gasps arose, as players were on the edge of the most uncomfortable steel-bottom seats, hoping to take home the two-hundred-dollar winnings for this last, and longest game.

'Shake those balls up!' The cry came from a patron obviously close to claiming the prize. The person was immediately urged to 'shut up and play' by more than one other player.

Sweat ran down her back, making it itch, but Lydia wasn't wasting any time to take her jacket off. Finally she reached Grandma, and tapped her on the shoulder.

'Lydia!' Vi exclaimed. 'Oh my God! Who died this time?'

Lydia ignored Vi, not trusting herself to look at her. Her revelation had to be stamped on her face so she kept her head turned away from Vi, too.

'What is it? Victor?' Grandma's face paled. A loved one's stroke, like Pop's, did this to you. Made you think every bit of news would be dire.

'No, everyone's fine. I'm the one that needs you, Grandma.' She spoke low, just above a whisper, and made certain she had Grandma's attention before winking.

Grandma blinked. 'Oh, honey child, I'm right here for you.' Standing up as if for an ovation, Grandma grabbed her clear plastic tote, shoved her bingo accouterments inside, and turned to Lydia. 'I'm here for you. Did that bastard run off on you again?'

Grandma's declaration reverberated through the room. The crowd grew more restless than with the bad ball calls.

'You can do better, girl!'

'Dump him first next time!'

'Take it outside, for cripe's sake!'

'Please remain seated and quiet. The board checkers need to hear when you call a win.' The caller's grave tone cut through the uproar. Lydia grabbed Grandma's hand and dragged her from the main room. She didn't stop until they were in the dark, narrow hallway that hosted the restrooms.

'I – six—'

'Bingo!'

'Bingo!'

The caller's announcement was drowned out before he finished.

Lydia didn't have time to count how many winners there

were, but she did wait to make sure Vi hadn't won and was packing up to leave.

'Didn't I handle that well, honey?' Grandma beamed.

'Yes, perfectly.' She sucked in air, not realizing how breathless all of the investigating had made her. The smoke didn't help.

'So, why are you here? Tell me, quick,' Grandma implored.

'I know who killed Louie!' She blurted her discovery out. Her thoughts had been so succinct in her mind, but her tongue hadn't caught up. 'I don't know why we didn't see it before now! I'll tell you the rest outside. Let's get out of here.'

'Hold on, honey. Take it easy.' Grandma placed her hands on Lydia's upper arms for several seconds. 'We're fine right here. Besides, we'll never get through that crowd now. They're all like rats, shoving out that door. Calm down and take it from the top.'

'There's a back exit through here, somewhere.' She really had no desire to be anywhere near Vi when she told Grandma the deal. And she wanted Grandma far, far away from the killer. From Vi. She looked past Grandma one more time to make sure Vi wasn't nearby. By now her seat was empty. *Phew.* The crowd had cleared the back half of the room as it pressed into a single mass of cigarette-puffing humanity at the exit.

Satisfied they were safe, Lydia faced Grandma.

'Remember when I told you about the stack of AM&A's lingerie boxes Charlotte had, with the lace black undies in them?'

'The ones she said she couldn't wear? Yes, I remember.' Grandma tilted her head, in full listening mode.

'Charlotte said she'd found them in Louie's garage, under his bench. Hidden. She said she thought he was planning a surprise for their big anniversary, but we figured he was having an affair, and that Charlotte in all probability knew about it.'

'Right. Because the undies Charlotte found could have matched the black lace panties that the police took out of Louie's car. Go on.'

'So that would leave either Charlotte, if she knew about the affair, as our top suspect. Or, Louie's lover.'

'But we don't know who Louie was slipping his salami to,

honey bunny.' Grandma's expectant expression grew somber. 'We're still missing that piece.'

'No, no we're not. I found postcards from Louie to Vi – well, I think they were from Louie. He didn't sign his name, but they all tell a story. He'd been leading her on about going away to begin a new life together for at least the last three or four years! Add in that Vi had the same exact kind of underwear in her house as those panties. Remember when you said passion is the biggest motivator in murder? If it was Louie who wrote the postcards that promised her they'd run away together, it makes sense that it was Vi. Do you see it, Grandma? Vi was Louie's lover! That makes her at least tied with Charlotte as the number one suspect.'

'You're right!' Grandma crowed, snapping her fingers. 'She must have been with him in the car. She could have killed him in the middle of a lover's spat. And she placed the body—'

'In our yard, with our sausage pricker in his neck, to frame us. She's never gotten over Ray dying and her not being left what she thought was his share of the shop.'

'You're giving her too much credit, Lydia. Vi probably got sick of Louie making promises he couldn't keep. Getting our family in hot water was an extra bonus for her.'

The hallway grew cold as they huddled and Lydia shivered. She nodded toward the front door and the handful of remaining people straggling out. 'We should leave now, before we're stuck in here.'

'Let me be the one to tell Harry that we've figured it out. Although it is your scoop, so you can if you really want to. Don't worry about any holes or lack of hard evidence. We both feel it in our guts that it's Vi.'

'Grandma, the more I go over everything, the more I know it had to be Vi who killed Louie.'

'We have to tell Harry right away so that he can get that witch behind bars.' Grandma was on the Harry frequency again. For once, Lydia agreed with her. It was time to let the officials handle the justice part.

'Right. We'll talk more on the way to the police station. We can drive together.' She just wanted Grandma safe and sound.

'Hold up a second.' Grandma patted her hips, held up her

bingo tote and peered inside, even though it was made of clear plastic. 'Damn. With all of the excitement I left my purse at the table. Let me go get it and we're off.'

'I have your purse for you right here, Mary.' Vi spoke from a dark recess in the hallway, Grandma's macrame purse dangling from her arm. But Lydia wasn't focused on the handbag. The cold glint of the pistol in Vi's perfectly manicured hand held her attention.

Stay strong.

'Now Vi, before you do something you'll regret, let's lay our facts out on the table.' Grandma spoke as if they were chit-chatting in the backroom of the butcher shop.

'Regret getting rid of you two and your loose lips?' Vi's lip curled in a cruel sneer. 'Never. Both of you shut up and head out the back door. Try anything and I shoot, no questions. If you think I won't do it, guess again. I've got a clear get-away.' She motioned with her free hand toward where Lydia had felt the cold draft from earlier. 'After you.'

'Get in.' Vi motioned with the pistol. True to her word, Vi's car was parked only steps outside the back entrance. There were no other cars in sight. Not even the VFW volunteers parked back here, where the only light came from the single bulb light fixture set in the tiny overhang. Faint laughter and conversation reached her ears and Lydia desperately tried to think of how to alert the crowd on the other side of the large building to their plight.

But a shout or yell for help would result in a bullet being fired. She or Grandma would be dead before they hit the cold, graveled ground.

Grandma was in front of Lydia and tried the rear passenger door. 'It's locked.' She took a step backward and clutched at her chest. 'Oh, no, my heart! I can't take the stress!'

'Son of a . . .' Vi shoved Grandma aside, keeping the gun pointed at both of them. 'To hell with your heart, Mary. Get over there. Both of you.'

Grandma shot Lydia a quick wink. Lydia held her breath. If Vi figured out the car hadn't been locked, and that Grandma was faking a heart attack, would she kill them right here?

Grandma had her wits about her, that was certain. Lydia had watched enough TV detective shows to know that she and Grandma were goners if they got into Vi's car. Before Vi wrestled her keys from her pocket, Lydia spoke up.

'Listen, Vi. Leave my grandmother here. She's not involved in this. I'm the one who found Louie.'

Vi straightened and faced Lydia head-on as if challenged to a brawl. 'Yes, you did, you stupid girl. If you'd just left him there like I'd planned, no one would have found him until I was long gone. Then you could have blamed me, but it wouldn't matter.' Her hand shook but she kept the barrel aimed straight. Both Lydia and Grandma were easy targets.

'Leave a body like you did?'

Vi sighed theatrically and rolled her eyes. 'Yes, I killed Louie. Is that what you wanted to hear? But I didn't plan on killing him. I was upset.'

'Of course you were. There's more than one lover in my life who's angered me enough to want to kill him,' Grandma said. 'Look, Vi, your secret's safe with us. Why don't you go home and sleep on it?'

Vi paused and actually appeared to think about Grandma's proposal. 'Too late. You know too much. I heard what you said, about the lingerie.' Her hard stare was back on Lydia. 'What the hell you thought you were doing in my house? How dare you!' She took a step forward, gun aimed at Lydia's heart.

She's going to blow me away, just like she did Louie.

No. Lydia was not going to let Vi gun her or Grandma down as if they were tin ducks on a conveyor belt at the Erie County Fair.

'I saw the postcards. From Niagara Falls, and Niagara-on-the-Lake. Louie told you that you'd go there and build a life together. Is that why you killed him, because he never made good on his promises?'

'Yes, if you have to know. Though I don't see why you care. You're going to die no matter what. Stop that!' Vi screamed at Grandma, who'd begun jumping up and down, to one side and then another, her tote bag dangling from her wrist.

'Just keeping warm out here, keeping my blood pumping.

Oooh.' She bent over, hand over her heart. 'Not. Sure. It's. Working.' Her gasps were filled with pain. Lydia risked taking her gaze off the gun and glanced at Grandma. What if she really was having a heart attack?

Grandma winked. No, no heart attack. *Yet.*

'I'm not telling you again, Mary. Stop moving and shut your trap.' Vi's attention was solely on Grandma.

Lydia experienced a calm she'd never had in her life before this moment. As if she'd been preparing for this exact juncture when a killer's weapon was trained on her and her beloved grandmother, threatening all she held dear.

With a quick motion Lydia grasped the long strap of her leather saddle bag and swung it over her head, gaucho-style like she'd done with a rope in ninth-grade Spanish class during the unit on Argentina. Vi turned the gun on Lydia – away from Grandma – and fired, but not before the heavy bag hit her squarely on the side of her head.

Grandma went from feigning pain to slugging Vi with her tote bag in one fast move. But Grandma was shorter than Lydia or Vi, and her bag hit Vi square between the legs.

It didn't matter where Vi had been hit at this point, as she dropped to the ground, unconscious, her limp form prone, gun falling from her hand.

'You got her!' Grandma crowed.

'We did.' The words were whispers, though. Lydia wondered if Grandma noticed that the back drive behind the VFW post was undulating like Lake Erie during a storm. She reached out for the edge of the car, anything to keep her upright.

Pounding steps, crunching gravel, shouts of 'Freeze! Hold your fire, I repeat, hold your fire!' combined with walkie-talkie static.

Two uniformed police officers pounced on Vi, one removing the gun from her hand and the other feeling her jugular for a pulse. A small pool of blood formed next to Vi's left ear.

Did I kill her?

'Step away, ladies.'

'Oh, Harry. I thought you'd never get here.' Grandma went from murder-solving partner to flirting woman as quick as one of her winks.

'We were here for the last several minutes but we couldn't risk either of you getting shot.' Nowicki motioned to the small crowd forming several yards away.

'All clear, Mr Gorski.' He turned to Lydia, who was clasping the rear door handle of Vi's car with all her might. 'If not for your friend, we might have been too late. Here, why don't you sit down.' Nowicki grasped her elbow. Still, Lydia resisted sinking to the ground as she longed to do, afraid she'd never get back up.

A footfall sounded that Lydia knew. So well.

'I've got her, Detective.' Concern coated Stanley's baritone. He took Lydia in his arms and pressed her to him. Lydia allowed herself to let go and let Stanley's embrace carry all that had weighed on her shoulders.

'Yes, I'd say you do.' Nowicki smiled.

TWENTY-TWO

'Harry, you did an excellent job with the press brief. I didn't realize you were such a good public speaker!' Grandma leaned over the kitchen table and poured hot coffee into Harry's mug. Nowicki had asked to meet with the family on Saturday morning, a full week and one day since Lydia discovered Louie's body. Alongside the Chief of Police, he'd given a briefing to the press announcing that they'd caught Louie's killer, and that Vi – indicted by the Erie County District Attorney – would be facing the maximum weight of the law. She'd been held in the hospital overnight with a concussion, but was going to be fit for trial.

'More cookies, Harry? Help yourself. My mother makes the best butter cookies in Buffalo.' Pop pointed to the plate heaping with the Italian treats. Grandma pulled out her mother's recipe at Easter and Christmas. Recent events had prevented her from baking this past weekend, but she'd made up for it all day on Thursday, claiming that the entire family had cause to celebrate. Mom and Pop, Grandma and Nowicki, and Lydia and Stanley sat at the table. Teri and Johnny were minding the shop until Lydia came in at noon. She'd been checked out by their family doctor and told to take it easy for the next few days, so she'd agreed to half days. Stashu stood sentinel on the back-door stair landing, watching for backyard interlopers through the storm door. The weather had turned gentler overnight, and there was no doubt spring had come to stay.

'You're going to put all the weight I lost last year back on me, Mary.' Nowicki took three cookies and winked at Grandma. Lydia noticed that she didn't experience the nausea she first had when the possibility Nowicki and Grandma having a relationship arose. Maybe being off the hook for a murder none of them had committed had something to do with her wellbeing, too.

Or it could be the man sitting next to her, holding her hand under the Formica table. Stanley had been at her side for all of the past forty-eight hours except for when he had to study and take his law school exam. He'd been granted a reprieve for missing it the day after Vi had been arrested and took it late, yesterday.

'There aren't any calories in Easter treats.' Mom placed yet another loaf of her placek on the table, already sliced to serve. 'This is the last loaf, so I'm going to need you to do some baking, Lydia. We're having a party to celebrate Pop going back to work in two weeks.'

'You've been cleared by your doctor?' Lydia asked.

'I have. Two more weeks and you're out of a job, dear daughter.' He grinned and while it was still a little lopsided, it was a far cry from when he'd first been struck with the paralysis to his right side. 'I will still need your help with the knife, though.'

'No problem, Pop.' Elation made her heart beat hard and fast inside her chest.

Nowicki cleared his throat. 'I want to thank you, Stanley, for calling Officer Bukowski on Wednesday night. You saved your girl here and Mary.'

'I've already told Lydia I'm sorry that I butted into her investigation, but not sorry.' Stanley squeezed her hand, his gaze intent. 'I followed you, you know. All the way to Vi's house, and then the VFW. Then I used the pay phone across the street to call Ned. I got worried by the way you raced into the bingo hall after Jenny drove up.'

Lydia laughed. 'You mean fishtailed into the parking lot?'

'What are you talking about? I didn't realize Stanley was involved in this. What do you mean by Lydia's investigation?' Mom asked.

'I guess it's time to come clean, honey.' Grandma patted Lydia's shoulder. 'Tell them.'

'OK. You know how Grandma and I like to watch detective shows?'

Pop groaned and Mom gasped.

'It's not that bad,' Lydia defended.

'I beg to differ.' Nowicki reached for a slice of placek. 'But all's well that ends well, in this case.'

Lydia proceeded to summarize all that she and Grandma had uncovered, from staking out Louie's car creekside, to searching Vi's house.

'When I saw the postcards from Louie, it took me a second to connect all the dots. Apparently Louie and Vi planned to run away to Canada together,' Lydia said.

'The suspect told us during her confession that she'd acted in a fit of anger when Louie put off their elopement, which would have been bigotry, by the way. He'd promised for years to leave his wife for her. She said that she'd only planned to take the money he had in his glove compartment, and combined with the money she stole from your butcher shop, purchase her own cottage on Crystal Beach, Canada. Thieves always think they'll get away with it if they go across the border, as if we don't talk regularly to our law enforcement counterparts. But the suspect didn't plan on the other man who showed up also wanting Louie's cash. She fired twice, only meaning to hit the thief. The thing is the bullet wound in Louie's heart was meant for him. The man she claimed was the thief? He was a man Louie owed money to, and he'd followed Louie's car into the woods to exact his due. He witnessed the murder.'

'Dirty rotten jerk,' Grandma said. Lydia wasn't sure if she meant Louie, Vi, or both of them.

'Vi wasn't so smart. Why didn't she take off with the money that night? She could have crossed the border and disappeared,' Lydia asked.

'Too risky. That would have made her look guilty, if anyone saw her leave. She'd rather watch the Wienewskis take the wrap, am I right, Harry?' Grandma looked at Nowicki, who nodded.

'You're absolutely correct,' Nowicki continued. 'We knew Vi was guilty before she confessed. The second man on the scene that she shot at wasn't hurt.'

'We saw that on the news,' Lydia said.

'Right.' Nowicki nodded. 'He was trying to steal money

from Louie but ran off when she fired. She missed him but
not Louie. We finally brought him in, thanks to a neighbor's
tip. Vi's biggest mistake, though, was calling on an old
boyfriend to help her move Louie's body. He confessed after
we traced his muddy footprints to him. Turns out he wears
custom-made shoes only available by order, from a single store
in Western New York.' Nowicki mentioned the family-run
shoe store that had been servicing Buffalo for generations. 'We
found the prints near the scene of the murder, and again in
your backyard. When we arrested him, he confessed his part
as a body mover.' Nowicki turned to Lydia. 'And I thank you
for your earlier concern, but as you now know, the footprints
matched the suspect's cohort.'

Lydia wanted to kiss Nowicki's cheek. The man hadn't
mentioned Johnny, thank Jesus, Mary and Joseph. She wouldn't
have to endure Teri's censure.

'Did Vi say why she stuck my grandfather's pricker into
Louie's neck?' Pop asked.

Nowicki frowned. 'Yes. She blames everything on you.
She's convinced herself that you took the business from your
brother.'

'That's a lie,' Lydia said.

'We know,' Nowicki replied. 'And what she's delusional
about is irrelevant. If you ask me, she was clear-headed by
the time she stabbed his corpse. Tell me something, will you?
Did any of you ever get the sense that she resented your
family?'

The entire table erupted in laughter.

Lydia reveled in the heartwarming sound, at her family's
joy. Grandma flashed her broad smile and motioned with her
brows at Stanley, then winked. She turned to the man she'd
missed so much, whom she'd not allowed herself to
appreciate.

'Thank you for saving me.'

'Aw, Lyd, you saved yourself. And your grandmother.' He
kissed her, briefly, full on the lips. 'Just don't go scaring me
like that again, OK? Next time, maybe trust me more?'

She would. Trust Stanley more. And ask for help. Except . . .

'Why did you go and get engaged so fast after I left?' she

whispered into his ear, not wanting anyone else to hear. It was cowardly to ask him right here, on the spot, but timing had never been her thing except in the kitchen.

'Stupidity. I thought the distraction from my broken heart would make a difference.' His reply was heartfelt, and Stanley didn't whisper.

'Your heart was broken?'

He grasped her hand, pulled it to his mouth and kissed her fingers, all while maintaining eye contact with her. The heat in his gaze curled her toes inside her fuzzy slippers. 'It isn't anymore.'

'Hear, hear. You two work this out on your own. For now, let's celebrate that the family's back together.' Pop beamed with his entire mouth.

'Sweetheart, your smile is the same on both sides! First time since the stroke.' Mom leaned over and gave Dad a smackaroo on his cheek.

'Good going, Pop!' Teri smiled and her gaze met Lydia's.

'I'm proud of you, son. And you, too, Lydia. You did save us both, you know,' Grandma said. 'I tried to help, but faking angina only allowed me to hit her in the vagina.' She giggled. 'Did you hear that? How I rhymed "angina" with "va—"'

'Stop, Mary. Please,' Amelia begged. Hearing her mother-in-law talk about specific female body parts was apparently worse than listening to how Louie had been brutally murdered.

Lydia remained silent. Helping a murder victim find justice after they couldn't do it for themselves was surprisingly satisfying. Almost as good as the feeling when her prized lemon meringue pie turned out well, or her placek melted on the tongue. Maybe if she hadn't always considered herself a baker, she'd have found her way into law enforcement or private investigation. *Naw.* Cooking and baking were more her speed.

Lydia knew this had to have been a once-in-a-lifetime event, however. Solving Louie's murder would fast become a memory. Pop was healed from his stroke, too, and could return to the butcher block soon. Lydia's Lakeside Café and Bakery was all she had to worry about. And how she and Stanley were

going to do things this time around. She had enough on her
plate with no room for solving crimes other than on TV, with
Grandma as her show-watching sidekick.

What were the odds she would ever find a dead body again,
anyway?

TRADITIONAL POLISH PLACEK (YEAST COFFEE CAKE)

Author Note: this recipe is a handwritten recipe I found in my Polish-American grandmother's recipe box. I transcribed it exactly as written from 3 x 5 inch notecards. Grandma sliced it like pound or banana cake and served with hot coffee.

Ingredients

2 ½ sticks butter
2 ¼ cups milk
1 ¾ cups sugar
12 egg yolks
1 teaspoon salt
2 ½ packets of yeast (powdered)
1 ½ cups golden raisins (soak in brandy if you like, optional)
6 cups flour

Method

1. Heat butter and 2 cups of the milk almost to a boil.
2. Beat egg yolks until thick, add sugar and beat well, then add the hot butter and milk. Beat until lukewarm. Add salt.
3. Dissolve the yeast with 2 tablespoons of sugar and ¼ cup of lukewarm milk. Add to the egg mixture. Add the sifted flour and beat until smooth. Then stir in the raisins.
4. Let rise for 1 hour then punch down and let rise again for an hour or less. Grease loaf pans and pour in the batter, top with crumbs.
5. To make crumbs combine 2 cups of sifted flour,

1 ¼ cup of sugar, 1 ½ stick of butter. This makes enough crumbs for 3 pans (9 x 5 x 3 inches). Bake at 340 degrees (F) for 35 or 45 minutes or until done. This makes 3 small loaves.

AUNT DOT'S CHEESECAKE

Ingredients

For the filling:
4 eggs
3 8 oz pkgs cream cheese, softened (my mother used
to leave out overnight but updated food safety
knowledge says just leave out for a few hours)
1 cup sour cream
1 cup sugar
1 teaspoon vanilla (if you make your own with vodka
and vanilla beans like Aunt Dot, all the better)

For the topping:
1 cup sour cream
2 tablespoons sugar
1 teaspoon vanilla
Crust:
4 tablespoons (½ stick) butter
2 sleeves of graham crackers, crumbled (I use a food
processor but you can place in a plastic bag and
crush with a rolling pin)
Butter to grease the 9 x 13 inch baking pan (you can
use a springform pan if you prefer)

Method

Preheat oven to 350 F. Prepare the crust: Grease the 9 x 13
inch baking pan (I prefer glass). Pour crumbs in, mix in sugar
with a fork. Add melted butter, stirring with fork and begin
to press on bottom of pan, all the way to each side. Place in
refrigerator to chill while you make the filling.
  Make the filling: Using a stand or portable electric mixer,
beat cream cheese until smooth. Add in eggs, one at a time,

continuously beating. Add sugar, gradually, until combined. Add vanilla.

Pour filling onto crust, spread evenly. Bake for 45-55 minutes or longer, until knife/toothpick/cake tester comes out clean when stuck in the center. Allow to briefly cool while you make the topping.

Topping: Combine the sour cream and sugar until smooth, add vanilla. Pour and smooth over cheesecake. Bake for five minutes at 350 F or until set.

Allow cheesecake to cool, then immediately refrigerate for several hours or overnight. Cut into squares and serve cold.